EDEN'S BLUFF ACADEMY BOOK ONE

POISONED GARDEN

TRACY KORN

Chapter 1

I didn't need the walking stick—at least not for walking. It was dumb I guess, but carrying it just made me feel better.

I called this part of the woods the eye because everything seemed to stop down this stretch. No birds, no breeze, just the sound of my own breathing and footsteps.

Mercy Creek flanked the right side of the path, though it was more like white water rapids than a creek, and a steep, banded rock wall rose up on the left. I'd have gone any other way to get to school, but given the rather inconvenient landscape on either side of the eye, it was the only way to get from my house to Portland Prep.

Like I always did at the beginning of this path, I tried to focus on the sound of the birds and the breeze blowing through the leaves. I wanted to hear the exact moment everything stopped, but no matter how hard I focused, I could never pinpoint when it happened. It weirded me out to think about it, so I pushed the whole thing out of my mind and concentrated on the worn, dirt path before me.

The air almost immediately felt different after just a few steps—heavier somehow like an invisible weighted blanket was sliding over me. It even felt like I was walking more slowly, though my pace was never quicker in any other part of these woods.

"You want to live forever?" a man's voice said, which stopped me in my tracks. In the years I'd been walking this path to and from school, there was never another soul on it coming or going. The man stepped into the shadows several yards ahead. "Time is money these days..." he added, and I nearly fell backward in shock before extending my walking stick out like a spear.

"Leave me alone!" My voice was shaky thanks to the adrenaline hitting my bloodstream. He took a few steps toward me, into the light, and to my surprise, he didn't seem much older than I was. His new-looking hoodie paired with the significant lack of grease and patches on his jeans made it pretty clear he wasn't from The Grind, as we referred to everything here outside The Citadel wall.

"They say legacy debt *isn't* population control, but do you see the politicians with any?" the man said, pushing the hood off his head to reveal a mass of black, wavy hair. His eyes were dark and his skin was unnaturally pale, but it was his smile that was the most disturbing. It was too polished, like he'd somehow taken it straight off the face of one of those politicians he was just talking about.

"Get out of my way."

He eyed my backpack. "Going to school? Trying to get Authorized?" he asked, his grin widening. "The Citadel will cost you twenty years," he said, then raised an inky eyebrow at me. "Unless you've got the cash for tuition. You got the cash, sweetheart?"

"I have to go," I answered. "Get *out* of my way." I brandished the walking stick as I took a few steps forward.

"Red, blue, yellow… They'll all make you immortal. You could go through The Citadel a hundred times," he said, pulling three small vials out of his hoodie pocket and shaking them gently at his side. "All your legacy debt, gone—poof, just like if you were a politician. Don't even have to shoot these anymore. Just pick a color and drink."

"I said leave me alone. Back up." I took a few more steps toward him, keeping him at the end of my stick, but I pictured him grabbing it. If he did, I'd let go and run. I could tell he was stronger than I was, and I wouldn't win a tug of war.

That was the plan, then. Just let go and run.

But he didn't grab the end of the walking stick. He just pushed his smile to the corner of his mouth and held up his hands in mock surrender, folding his fingers over the three vials.

"Run along to school then," he said, his unblinking, dark eyes staring straight into mine. I didn't want to turn my back on him, so I walked backward the rest of the way down the path until I made it across the threshold of the woods.

I almost stumbled as my feet turned over on the sloping hill that led down to the street. There was no sign of the man following me, but I was still hesitant to turn my back to the woods. Where had he even come from, especially this early in the morning? My heart drummed in my chest and my skin began to prickle—physiological responses, I told myself. Just like they said in psychology class. Fight or flight, then fear…

I turned to face forward slowly, checking over my shoulder every few seconds just to be sure I wasn't being followed. After confirming three or four times that I wasn't, I started to relax.

It was several more minutes before the rest of the adrenaline finally cleared out of my system, and I took a few deep breaths to settle my nerves once and for all. It was still too early for most people in The Grind to be on the streets, so I didn't worry about slowing down as I made my way to the prison on earth that was Portland Prep. I'd never dream of doing that on the walk home, or I might not make it home, even carrying a big stick.

There had been six *Feral* attacks in the last few months—people just becoming randomly violent and then disappearing without a trace, so it took weeks to connect the dots between the missing persons reports and the crime scenes. The Citadel Pathology Center kept telling everyone the Feral attacks were caused by a virus called Red Fever, and The Citadel promptly posted extra security around their precious walled city. They also kept saying the pathologists were close to a cure, but close didn't mean anything in the meantime, and some people, like my Uncle Ray, didn't even believe it was a real disease. He thought it was just the pent-up hostility from the oppressed people in The Grind finally coming to a boiling point. With any luck, next semester I'd be at The Citadel where there were no Feral attacks, regardless of the cause.

The man in the woods had been right about one thing, though. I didn't have the cash to go even if I did get in. It would cost me twenty years of my life in legacy credits. According to the census, my natural expiration date would be at eighty-seven years, four months, seventeen days…blah blah blah. How did I feel about dying at sixty-seven years instead if I didn't manage to land a career with social percentage? It would be worth it to live behind The Citadel wall until then.

There was a hard pull on my backpack, but as I turned, I was pushed against one of the crumbling building walls. I started to maneuver my walking stick to hit the person in the head, but then stopped myself when I heard familiar, idiotic laughing.

"Max! You scud! I almost bashed your head in!" I said, pushing him off me. He could barely catch his breath because he was laughing so hard. "You think it's funny you almost got your brains splattered all over the sidewalk?" I tried to keep my stern expression in place, but it was hard not to laugh when he actually lay flat on the sidewalk with his arms over his eyes, still laughing.

"Your face…" he sputtered.

"Yeah, *hilarious*."

"OK, sorry…sorry…" He regained his composure just long enough to lose it again when he looked at me. I rolled my eyes and started walking the rest of the way to school. "Wait! OK, wait…" Max said, scrambling to his feet.

He was just over six feet tall and a sprinter on the track team, so it wasn't long before he caught up to me.

"Don't ever do that again. I thought you were some *Feral*," I chided, watching him struggle to keep a straight face.

"Sorry, you were just off in space or something," he said, his blue eyes extra bright after laughing so much they'd become glassy. He scrubbed his hands over his face, then pushed them quickly through his blond, shaggy hair like he'd just come out of the water. "Gotta pay attention out here, you know? I was just keeping you on your toes," he added.

I glared at him and gestured to my walking stick. "Why do you think I carry this?"

Max narrowed his eyes at me and pressed his lips into a hard line. "All right, what's really wrong?" He crossed in front of me and walked backward at a snail's pace.

"Move, Max." I tried to dart around him, but he was too fast. We'd been best friends since elementary school, and I could never hide anything from him.

"Tell me what happened?" he asked, all traces of levity gone now. "Was it Alice? Did she tell you you're the *salad antichrist* or whatever again?"

"No." I pressed my lips together to keep back the imminent smile. My aunt Alice had, in fact, and not too long ago, accused me of being an *actual*-from-Hell demon when her garden was raided by animals a few days after I'd weeded it.

"You don't have to live way up on that hill with them, Halsey," Max said, moving back to my side. "My parents said the offer still stands to stay with us."

"As much as I wish I could, you know I can't." I glanced at him.

"You really believe putting your aunt and uncle on your application to The Citadel is going to help anything?"

"Better than putting *orphan who lives with her best friend's parents because her next of kin are superstitious nutwhacks*," I answered.

"I'm sure even The Citadel would understand about your parents getting sick. *The wasting* hit a lot of people."

"Oh, I'm sure they would too, so long as I'm living with my aunt and uncle," I nodded at him. "The last thing I want to do is to have to answer questions about why I live with a guy my age and his family instead of my perfectly alive relatives. You know the system. The Citadel doesn't want people who can't fit their mold."

Max shook his head in resignation. "Which is exactly why it baffles me that you're so hell-bent on going there."

The street was starting to get busier with people rolling up the gates to their shops. Mr. Burke, the supermarket owner, opened the doors and let his two new, enormous dogs come through to the sidewalk.

"Heel, Draco—Heel Fate," he said, tying his red apron. Both huge, black dogs stopped in place and sat like statues.

"Are they on duty yet?" Max called to Mr. Burke, who smiled.

"Not yet, go ahead. Relax!" Mr. Burke said to the dogs, who immediately started wagging their tails and leaning into Max when he approached, which nearly knocked him over. I took a few steps forward, and both dogs dropped to their bellies, putting their heads on their front paws.

"Whoa…" I said, surprised.

"Wow, they like you I guess. Come on, they're big babies." Max motioned me over. "Aren't you a big baby, Fate? Yes, you are…" he cooed to the dog in front of him, which earned him a tongue bath.

"Ewww…" I laughed, kneeling to pet Draco's thick scruff. He moved to a sitting position and buried his head under my chin. "Aww," I said, resting my cheek on the top of his furry head.

"They're good pups—brother and sister," Mr. Burke said with a nod to me. "They know what you're all about before you even get through the door—*Feral* or otherwise," he added. "Had some hooligans come in yesterday afternoon and these two turned them right around."

"You keep the trouble out," Max said. "Don't you keep the trouble out, you smart girl?" he cooed again, this time fishing a few treats he'd brought from his pocket and slipping one to each dog. "I'll see you after school then," he said to Fate with a final head rub.

"We've got a truck today, so don't be late." Mr. Burke winked at Max.

"No, sir. See you then."

Mr. Burke nodded, then turned to the dogs. "On guard!" he said, and both of them dutifully leapt inside, posting themselves again like statues on the cushions flanking the register.

"Wow," I said, marveling at how well they listened. "When did those guys arrive?"

"Beginning of the week," Max answered. "They've neutralized a lot of the tension in the place already, believe it or not. Everyone loves them. That is, except for people who have intentions other than picking up their grocery order."

"I bet."

"Weird how they dropped to the ground like that. I haven't seen them do that before with anyone, not even Mrs. Burke, who slips each of them pieces of steak when the old man takes one of them out back to go to the bathroom." He laughed as we walked.

I shrugged. "Well, they're definitely well behaved. You save up enough credits yet to fix your car?"

"Almost," Max answered. "This summer should do it."

"You're really not going to apply to The Citadel?"

Max sighed. "Halls…come on."

"You could get in if you tried. I know you could. You have the grades, you run track, you're their model student—more than me even because you have both parents."

"I don't know. Ask me later. We have other problems right now," he said as we approached the front steps of Portland Prep, which were mostly obscured by the swarm of flies known as Brian Dunwin and his band of degenerates. One by one, each of them lifted their eyes to us, stupid grins peeled across their faces as they started walking toward us.

Chapter 2

"Since when do they show up before third period?" I asked Max under my breath.

"Internship fair today, remember?" he answered. I swore under my breath, totally having forgotten about internship selections with my focus being on my Citadel application.

"Oh, right..." I groaned.

"Did you forget? Halls, not to be an ass, but you can't count on the Citadel." Max's voice had an edge in it now, but I wasn't sure if that was because of his impatience with me, or the imminent harassment we were about to endure from Brian and his band of merry idiots.

Brian got to his feet as we approached while his minions spread out on either side of him, blocking the doors.

We stopped at the bottom of the steps. "Get out of the way, Brian," Max said, trying to sound intimidating.

Brian laughed and pushed a dirty hand over his buzzed hair as he took another step toward us. "Or you'll do what, Barrett?"

Max sighed, apparently not having prepared a rebuttal.

"Come on, let's just go," I said, pulling Max's elbow.

"Yeah, go on, Max. *Balls* here can't be late for her before school quickie with Warren." Brian's gaggle of delinquents squawked and laughed, and when I turned back to them, they acted out their ignorant sound effects with obscene pantomimes.

Max took a few purposeful steps toward Brian, but I gripped his arm. They wouldn't hesitate to beat him half to death if he tried to stand up for me. I, on the other hand, had an idea.

"It's OK," I said to Max, taking a few steps toward Brian, forcing myself to paste a sweet smile on my face and maintain eye contact with him, which was about impossible. "Brian, if only you wouldn't make it so hard to get close to you…surrounding yourself with all these guys," I said, slow and wide-eyed, then took a few more steps toward him. "It's a little intimidating for a girl to let you know how she really feels."

"*Halsey*," Max said. I ignored him, hoping he would just trust me.

Brian's mouth twitched as he came down another step. "Is that so…"

I nodded. "What could I possibly want with Mr. Warren when *you're* right here?"

He took one more step, his legs just far enough apart for me to whip the end of my walking stick into his crotch as hard as I could. He dropped like an invisible piano had landed on him, and his fledglings all groaned and doubled over in various degrees of sympathy pain. Max's eyes were wide when I turned back to him, his mouth frozen in a reaction that was equal parts ghost pain, shock, and uncontrollable laughter. We walked past Brian, who was writhing on the ground, and made our way up the steps into the school.

"Halls!" Max finally said, not sure which expression to wear—shock, hilarity, or pain. "OK, you know they're going to come after you. That's bad."

"I'll get a Sweeper droid to escort me home," I said casually, but in reality, my heart was pounding so hard I was surprised Max couldn't hear it.

"I don't even know if they'll wait that long." Max pulled me toward a janitor's closet since people were starting to raise eyebrows at my walking stick. "Just put that in here for now," he said, opening the door. "I'll make sure Marvin doesn't get rid of it." Marvin was the day custodian, and fortunately, he had no great love for Brian or his buddies. "We need to go to Mr. Glenn."

I shook my head. "He's not going to do anything."

"No, not if we don't tell him."

"Max, I can't deal with this right now. I didn't prepare anything for the internship selections. I don't even know who's here."

He rolled his eyes, then scanned the hall in both directions. "All right, look, just don't go anywhere alone today, OK? Not to the bathroom or anything. Somehow that bag of dicks has friends who are girls too, you know? He'll try to set you up when he thinks no one will be watching."

"You're giving him too much credit, Max." I tried to laugh, but I hadn't actually thought of that, so the casualness I was going for fell flat. "He's not that smart, remember?"

"He doesn't have to be smart. He just has to find some people who don't like you, and that's not going to be too hard."

"Gee, thanks, best friend."

"Halsey, come on. You know these paint sniffers are half a braincell from being confused about how to eat their own lunch," Max said as we stopped by my locker and grabbed my planner for the internship selections. I laughed. "I'm serious," he added. "They think you walk around like you're better than they are."

"Why? Because I applied to The Citadel?" I asked, hearing the edge in my own voice now.

"Uh, yeah," Max looked at me dumbfounded. "That's exactly why, Halls."

"They could apply too if they'd stop wasting their time sitting around huffing primer from the body shop, or whatever else they do when they're not making every second of being at this school a hell on earth."

"Yeah, well that's not going to happen," Max added as the first bell rang. "Just watch out today—

don't go anywhere alone. I'll catch up with you in the gym for the internship selections."

I nodded to him and closed my locker, then headed to my homeroom where we'd all soon be sent down to pick out the career paths we qualified for based on our grades. If only they'd have the results of The Citadel applications too, I could finally get out of the limbo I'd been in for months now.

****

I walked into Mr. Warren's class and immediately felt a stab of embarrassment as I remembered Brian's stupid comment earlier about a quickie before school.

Sure, Mr. Warren was attractive in that new, young professor kind of way with the tweed jacket and open collar Oxford, but it honestly hadn't occurred to me to be attracted to him. He just kind of blended in with everyone else, even though he'd gone to The Citadel. Everyone in The Grind was just getting through each day doing the same thing over and over. Seeing the same people and having the same conversations. I felt like there was something more to the world though… at least, that there could be. The only way I was going to find out was by getting into The Citadel and training for a career that could *take* me somewhere else.

"Halsey?" Mr. Warren said, startling me out of my thoughts.

"Uh, sorry, yes?"

"The rest of the class is leaving for the Internship fair," he said, though it sounded more like a question —an, *are you going to join them or what*, question.

"Oh, sorry."

"Anything happen this morning you want to discuss?" Mr. Warren asked, taking a seat on the corner of his desk and putting his clipboard under his arm.

"No, everything is fine," I answered, trying to inch my way toward the door.

"Nothing involving Brian Dunwin?" he pressed, giving me a knowing look. I froze for a second wondering how the news had reached him already, but then again, this *was* a high school.

"Oh, that was nothing. I handled it," I said, giving him a quick grin and rushing through the door. "See you later, Mr. Warren!"

I darted down the hall and caught up to the others in my homeroom before he could reply. The last thing I wanted to discuss with him was what Brian could have said that provoked me to aim for the bleachers with my walking stick.

We shuffled into the gym, which was already about ten degrees warmer than it had been in the hallways thanks to the sheer number of people, not to mention the sanitation stations pushing out negative ion mist every five feet. As the droves of humanity made their way to the tables and kiosks set up around the perimeter, I must have counted at least ten different machines puffing out a little virus assassin heat mirage before it dissipated in the air. Representatives from all the businesses in The Grind were there, everything from Mr. Burke's supermarket —his kiosk manned by his son—to the health clinic and local veterinarians.

Depending on our grades, we could get apprenticeships at the clinic or in a vet office, but that's as far as we could ever go without going through The Citadel for an Authorized license to actually practice as a doctor at either place. In my lifetime, I'd never known anyone actually from The Grind who ever got into The Citadel. Everyone in a position that required an Authorization had been born and raised behind that wall already.

I pushed the thought to the back of my head as I made my way through the crowd. There was a first time for everything, right? I could become a psychologist and help people solve their problems. I could help them hold on and fight through them. Problems were just puzzles, that was all, and I could *still* get into The Citadel.

But if I didn't...

I had no idea what I wanted to do if I didn't, and I had approximately one hour to not only figure it out, but to make a good enough impression on the business owners to get them to consider picking me over someone else. Someone who probably had brought them a résumé and cover letter, and who had worn their best outfit today instead of a ratty pair of jeans and a faded T-shirt. This was a disaster.

I scanned the gym for Max but didn't see him in the sea of faces. I did see Brian Dunwin and his flea infested entourage, however, so I quickly maneuvered into the current of people streaming around the perimeter on the opposite side of the gym. Brian stopped at Mr. Burke's supermarket kiosk, and I chuckled to myself. Let Draco and Fate get one whiff of him, and we'd see just how long that internship would last.

"We currently service the entire Eastern Seaboard, as well as selected overseas markets," a familiar voice said, and I looked around for the source. It was coming from the direction of a large, red kiosk tent with Chinese characters on either side of a golden dragon. In the middle, the words Wu Fong Pharmaceuticals were printed in block letters. *Who were Wu Fong Pharmaceuticals?*

The voice I heard belonged to a young man with slicked back, dark hair. He was familiar, but I didn't know why as I studied his expensive looking suit.

"So it's just, like, selling drugs, but legally?" Lauren Stover, one of the brainwashed girls in Brian's group of friends giggled at her own question. It was the kind of condescending giggle that only mean, usually stupid girls employed when they wanted to make it seem like they were just passing judgement on an answer they already knew, rather than reveal they actually just had the IQ of a gum wrapper. I rolled my eyes.

"Well, sales *is* a position within Wu Fong Pharma, if that's something you'd be interested in. Do you like to travel?" the man asked, then casually met my eyes. For the briefest second, his seemed to widen in recognition of me, and the ghost of a grin passed over his lips.

A gasp caught in my throat when it dawned on me that he was the guy from the woods, somehow cleaned up…and *here*.

Chapter 3

I looked away abruptly and lost myself in the crowd again, ducking behind a wall of shuffling students. My heart started pounding in my ears, and I was sucking in gulps of air. *Fight or flight...* I thought, and this was definitely flight. *What was a guy from Wu Fong Pharmaceuticals doing in the woods trying to sell me those little, colored vials?*

Out of nowhere, the thought was knocked out of my head when I crashed full force into someone and nearly fell backward. The person grabbed my arms and pulled me in.

"Whoa! *Halls...*" Max chuckled, his arms tight around me. He glanced down at my hands, which were pressed flat against his chest, then cleared his throat and let me go.

"Uh, sorry about that. I was...um, can we go?" I said, feeling like my mind was already several steps ahead of me.

"Go where? Did you already turn in all your internship requests?" he asked.

"*Shit.* No. OK, then let's go this way," I said, pulling his forearm in the opposite direction of the Wu Fong forest guy.

"Halls, what's wrong with you?" Max looked back toward where we'd come from. "Was it Lauren? Did Brian send her after you?"

"No," I said. "She didn't see me. Just come this way."

"Stop! Halsey, the body shop is over there and—*hey*, will you wait?"

"*Just come on!*" I shouted back to him, letting go of his arm eventually to weave through the people coming into the gym. It felt like trying to swim upstream as I bumped into one person after another until I finally got through the doors and into the open foyer. Flight accomplished. Now, it was time for fear.

My whole body started shaking and my knees felt weak. In fact, my muscles felt rubbery and my head was spinning.

"Halsey!" My name sounded muffled as the room turned upside-down, and the next thing I knew I was sitting on a bench with my face pressed against the side of the water fountain. "Here, drink this," Max said, handing me a cold soda. He held it to my mouth, and I took a sip, which actually helped a lot. He held the frigid can to my cheek, and that brought me the rest of the way back. I took the can from him and moved it over my face.

"What just happened?" I asked, then took another long drink, not even minding the burn it caused going down my throat.

Max looked at me skeptically. "You almost face-planted. Did Brian try something?"

"No, it wasn't him."

"What then? You look like you saw a ghost."

"I kind of did."

Max narrowed his eyes at me, then sighed impatiently. "I'm going to shake it out of you in a second if you don't spill it already," he said, but then his hardline expression softened as he rose to drop some coins in the vending machine a few feet away. "Here, eat these—the salt will help," he said, returning with the bag of pretzels that he'd just opened. "How did you bonk just running out of the gym?" He grinned.

I pushed a few pretzels into my mouth and chewed. Max was right, the salt did help everything inside me feel a little less like it was floating around in zero gravity. After another drink of the soda, I took a deep breath and finally felt back to normal again.

"OK, so this morning on my way to school, there was this strange guy in the woods," I started.

"*What*? Where?" Max's expression hardened again.

"In the eye—by the stream there, you know? Anyway, he was trying to give me some kind of drug."

"And you're just now telling me this?"

"I didn't have a chance, anyway, I just—"

Max pushed his hands over his face. "No wonder you were so bitchy about me scaring you..."

"What? I wasn't bitchy." He dropped his hands and gave me a deadpan look. I shook my head. "OK, that was legitimate self-defense mode, and it was your own fault."

"Whatever," he grinned again. "So what happened to weird you out in the gym then?"

"That's what I'm trying to tell you. That guy is in there. The one from the *woods*. He's working the Wu Fong Pharmaceuticals kiosk, and he recognized me!"

Max sobered and sat up a little straighter. "The drug pusher was pushing drugs on you in the woods? *That's* what you're telling me? And he recognized you?"

"Yes!"

"Did he say anything? How do you know he recognized you?"

"Because he gave me the same grin he did in the woods when I shoved him off with my walking stick."

"*You shoved him with your walking stick*?" Max gaped at me. "Halsey, shit! Anything else life threatening you forget to mention today?"

"I think that covers it..."

Max got to his feet and peered back through the gym doors. "We need to tell someone. That guy can't be here," he said, then took a few steps toward the crowd.

"Where are you going?" I asked.

"You said the kiosk was called Wu-what?"

"Wu Fong Pharmaceuticals. It's red with the dragon right under the name."

"OK, but I don't see him."

I got up and looked into the gym, but of course I couldn't see through the crowd, and I wasn't tall enough to see over it. I grabbed the bench and dragged it over, then climbed on top of it. To my complete amazement, the man from the woods was gone.

*But...*Brian Dunwin and the brain-donors were not. They spotted me almost immediately, and started pushing through the crowd.

"We gotta go!" I jumped down from the bench and grabbed Max's wrist, pulling him along toward the double doors that led back to Mr. Warren's room.

We had enough of a head start to make it back before Brian and his cronies ever so much as made it out of the gym, but we still stumbled over the threshold of Mr. Warren's class like they were right on our heels. We closed the door behind us and leaned against it.

"Halsey? Max, what's going on?" Mr. Warren asked, pushing his glasses to the top of his head.

"Brian Dunwin," Max answered before I had the chance. "And there's a drug dealer in the gym. Or, I mean, there was."

"What?" Mr. Warren's dark brows crashed together.

"It's true," I said. "A guy stopped me this morning trying to give me a vial of something, and he was just at the Wu Fong Pharmaceuticals kiosk."

"Wu Fong..." Mr. Warren picked up a clipboard and flipped through a few pages. "Ah, here they are.

Yes, they've sent Emily Runyon as their representative for the internship fair."

I felt the blood drain from my face as a chill ran down my spine.

"No, there was a man," I said. "Ask Lauren Stover. She was talking to him! She asked if they just sold drugs, only legally."

Mr. Warren wrote something down on the clipboard, then tapped his temple. A 3-D hologram of the office secretary appeared in his field of vision.

"Hi, Mae. Could you please page Lauren Stover to my room, and could you send one of the Sweeper droid units too?"

"Is everything all right?" Mrs. Poole, the secretary asked.

"I think so; just a precaution. I'll keep you posted," Mr. Warren smiled.

A few seconds later, Lauren's name came over the announcement speaker with instructions to report to Mr. Warren's room. A few seconds after that, a Sweeper droid let itself in the room, its cylindrical, brushed chrome body, for lack of something better to call it, hovering in the air.

"That was fast," Max whispered to me.

"How may I help you?" The droid voice was a warm, male voice that actually helped dissipate some of the tension building in my chest.

"Go ahead and tell it the name of the business you saw, and about what you saw this morning." Mr. Warren nodded to me.

I told the Sweeper droid about the man at the Wu Fong kiosk being the same one from the woods this morning, having just enough time to finish when Lauren Stover came into the room.

"I heard my name?" she said in her normal, pinched tone. She gave me a weak side glare. "I didn't do anything to her," she said to Mr Warren, who seemed momentarily confused.

"No, Lauren, you're not in any trouble." Mr. Warren shook his head. "I just needed to know, did you happen to talk with someone from Wu Fong Pharmaceuticals in the gym just now?"

"A man," I emphasized.

"Wu-*what*?" Lauren laughed nervously.

"The guy in the black suit with the slicked hair." I shoved the words at her. "I saw you talking to him under the big dragon banner. You told him, *so it's just like selling drugs*." It took everything in me not to reenact her prissy, demeaning tone.

"Are you stupid?" Lauren looked at me like, in fact, I was, as she pushed her stringy blonde hair behind her ear. "Why would I talk to anyone about drugs *here on school grounds*?" She huffed a laugh in my direction and rolled her eyes. "I don't know what she's talking about, Mr. Warren."

"Liar!" I took a few steps toward her with every intent to throttle her, but Max stopped me.

"Whatever," Lauren rolled her eyes again and returned her attention to Mr. Warren. "Can I go back now? I still have three more internships to apply for."

Shit! I thought again, remembering I hadn't even done *one* yet.

"Yes, that's fine, Lauren. Thank you for your time."

She left, glaring at me until the last few seconds before she walked out the door, and I was a hundred percent positive she'd have half the gym after me by lunch. Great. Like I didn't have enough problems today.

"Mr. Warren, I swear there was a man here at the Wu Fong kiosk, and that he was the same guy from the woods," I insisted.

"She went running out of the gym pretty spooked," Max spoke up.

"All right, I'll head down there myself and have a look around," Warren said. "Have you both finished your internship applications?" Max and I exchanged glances. "That's what I thought," Mr. Warren smiled. "Get back at it then before you run out of time. Lunch is in an hour, and the businesses will be gone this afternoon."

We followed Mr. Warren out of his room and back to the gym, passing Brian Dunwin and his paint sniffer parade in the hallway. His eyes locked on mine, and I forgot all about Lauren.

Chapter 4

I couldn't believe I'd messed up the most important day of my high school career by not preparing for any internship submissions. Fortunately, I was able to transmit about half-a-dozen copies of the academic résumé Ms. Pike had made us do in business class a few weeks ago. They were general rather than tailored for the actual places I was interested in, but they were better than not having anything to give the prospective employers at all.

I'd tucked in my T-shirt and pushed my hands through the long bangs of my otherwise short hair and managed to have six halfway respectable meet-and-greets with the City Engineer's Department, the Department of Natural Resources, Raphael's Tea Shop —which wasn't on my radar, but it sounded kind of exotic—and a few landscaping companies. If I couldn't get into The Citadel to study psychology, at least maybe I'd get to see something new each day.

"You're decided on eventually taking over Mr. Burke's store?" I asked Max as we made our way to the cafeteria, our mission accomplished for the day.

"His son already said I'd be the ideal manager," Max answered as he passed me a tray. "He's happy just doing the accounting and all that from home."

"I guess it sounds perfect then. People will always need groceries." I smiled at Max, but inside I was struggling to be happy for him. He was easily one of the smartest, most well-rounded kids in the school, and he didn't even take a chance on The Citadel. It made me feel like maybe I was a little delusional for applying.

I barely had a chance to wallow in the existential dread I was creating before someone shoved me hard into the pillar to my right, which smashed the tray of pasta I was carrying all over me and two other people sitting at a nearby table. I lost my footing with the impact and crashed to the ground, along with my tray. Lauren Stover walked by with Brian Dunwin and about four of his Cro-Magnon brethren, all of them laughing.

"Are you OK?" Max helped me to my feet, but something in me snapped, and he suddenly seemed a layer away. Lauren's laughter and Brian's disgusting snorts were crystal clear, though, and I bolted straight into Lauren's back, shoving her hard to the ground. When she turned back, her face and neck were covered in spaghetti.

"What the shit, Balls!?" Brian gaped, and I saw red again, kicking him as hard as I could right in the beans. He dropped to the ground, and I vaguely heard his cronies laughing about his impending sterility.

"My name is Halsey. *Those* are balls—see if you can remember the difference next time!" I managed to say just before Lauren jumped on top of me, making both of us fall to the ground. "Ow!" I yelled when burning flooded my forearm. *Was she biting me*!? Whatever was left of the pent-up rage that made me shove her in the first place concentrated in one final, glorious burst as I closed my fist and punched her in the ear. When she stopped biting, I closed it again and this time, hit her directly in the nose.

Blood splattered all over her shirt and onto the floor, and the sight of it shocked me enough to break the trance I'd fallen into.

"Halsey! Holy shit!" Max yelled, close to my ear now as his arms wrapped around me from behind and pulled me off of Lauren. "Calm down. Calm down—it's OK," he repeated.

Sweeper droids hovered over to the scene, their cylindrical, brushed metal casings reflecting each other's blue and red flashing lights. Everything was in slow motion as one of the floating units moved quickly to me and flashed a scanning beam over my face, temporarily blinding me.

"Halsey Rhodes, Maxwell Barrett, proceed to the Ice Box or you will be escorted by force," the robotic droid voice commanded. Two other Sweeper units were hovering over Lauren and Brian, and I tried to stretch to see if they were going to take *them* by force. A second later, two robotic arms emerged from the hovering cylindrical Sweeper unit's body next to us, both of the hand-like grips crackling with electricity.

"No, we're going! We're going! Halsey, come on," Max said, moving me bodily to walk in front of him in the opposite direction. The Sweeper unit followed us a few feet back. "Stop looking back at it or it's going to get jumpy and nuke us," Max added, and something about the way he said that made me laugh. Once I started laughing, though, it was like a dam inside me had broken. I laughed harder and harder until I couldn't control myself. It was the funniest, saddest, most enraging thing I'd ever heard. "Halsey, what's wrong with you? *Hey...*" Max pulled me in again with one arm, then wrapped the other around me in a side hug, but the tightness of his hold made it clear it was more to keep me in place than for comfort. "You have to stop that shit, Halls, or they're going to lock you down. Take a deep breath," Max coached as we arrived at the Ice Box, which was what everyone called the holding room just outside the office. The Sweeper droid flashed a light combination that made the door slide open, and we all went inside.

"Remain to the right," the droid said, directing us to the far side of the room. Once we were there, a metal divider slid from the wall, closing off the left side of the room. Max and I sat at the metal table, which was bolted to the ground, along with the chairs. Everything was made out of molded chrome, even the walls, and it was freezing in here.

"That looks bad," Max said, eyeing my forearm, which was bleeding and swollen. "Is that...a bite mark? She *bit* you?" Max squinted, recoiling.

"I don't know what happened to me out there," I said absently. "I just reacted. I didn't even think, Max. Something just snapped."

"Yeah, that was pretty clear," he chuckled. "What is that?" he asked, leaning closer and glancing at my forearm again, which had started dripping a black fluid that faded to white as soon as it hit the air.

"I don't know." I winced, horrified.

The Ice Box door opened, and for a fraction of a second, I saw Lauren ushered in by another Sweeper droid, a bloody towel held to her face. Brian wasn't with her, so I wondered if that meant he was in the infirmary, or still crumpled into a wad on the cafeteria floor. The nurse came in after Lauren, along with Mr. Warren. He came through the opening left by the divider wall and pushed his now crooked glasses to the top of his head, his eyes wide in shock.

"There's a veritable riot in the cafeteria right now, so all the administrators are a little busy," he said, crossing his arms over his chest. "What just happ—? Oh…" Mr. Warren stopped himself when he saw my arm. "Jan! Can you bring your kit?" he called to the nurse, who was still on the other side of the divider. She came over with a small string backpack and a lunchbox-sized medical case.

"Bite wound. Wonderful. Hold your arm out please," she said with a sigh. "*What is this*?" she said to herself as she got a little closer. I did as she asked, and tried not to make any noises when she sprayed what was clearly either *battery acid* or maybe just plain liquid nitrogen on the broken skin.

Because it hurt.

A lot.

I gulped a breath and pushed it down my throat to keep the imminent screams from coming out.

"The droid replay shows Lauren shoving you into the pillar, so no need to go into what provoked you there," Mr. Warren said, leaning against the wall. "Did that have something to do with what happened this morning, Halsey?"

I squirmed in my seat trying to figure out how not to tell him what Brian said about a morning quickie, but still say enough to justify my attempts to make him the newest—*and hairiest*—soprano in our school.

"No," I answered simply.

Max cleared his throat. "Actually, I would bet Brian had Lauren attack her just now. They were right there in line together," he said, raising his eyebrows at me.

I didn't have a chance to reply before a loud crash hit the wall next to us, then another, like Lauren was trying to break through the divider. But that was impossible since all the furniture in both spaces was bolted to the floor.

"What the—?" Mr. Warren darted to the gap in the door, but ducked just in time to avoid being crushed by one of the Sweeper droids hitting the wall near his head.

"Emergency-police!" the nurse screamed.

"Blue unit respond. PP743 droid is disabled. Standby for live feed," the Sweeper droid with us said just before snarls from the next room made it seem like we'd just been transported to a lion's den. The Sweeper droid moved into the space between the rooms left by the divider gap. Max moved like lightning just behind it, his expression immediately blanching.

"*What...*" he said through a gasp, then backpedalled into Mr. Warren. "Hey...hey, we need to get out of here!"

"What's happening?" I shouted.

"How do you close the door? Close the door!" he said, his voice raised in panic as he hit random buttons on the wall panel. He stopped abruptly and shouted in pain as he pulled his hand back, a gash across his palm already starting to bleed. The Sweeper droid with us zipped through the opening just before Mr. Warren keyed in a combination that sealed the wall the rest of the way. More crashing, more growling and snarling, but this time, the sound of scraping also came through the wall.

"Are you OK? *What's happening*!?" I shouted to Max.

"I don't know! Lauren's just—I don't know. She's... *broken.*"

"What the hell does that mean?" I shook my head at him as the burning sensation on my arm intensified.

"She's crouching on the table in there!" Max said, all the blood having drained from his face. "And her arms and legs—I don't know, her neck—it's all just… bent the wrong way," he continued, shaking his head seemingly in disbelief of what he, himself, had just seen.

"What?" I said quietly, moving closer to him as another loud crash hit the wall, and we all jumped.

"Get under the table and don't make a sound," Mr. Warren said. "Help is coming."

Chapter 5

It was at least another thirty minutes before live patrols arrived—we could hear their voices coming through the metal divider, which was dented inward at us in various places from whatever Lauren had apparently launched against it. My guess was it was the other Sweeper droid unit that had been in here with us not too long before. The nurse had dressed Max's gash, but he held his hand tightly to his chest, obviously in a lot of pain.

"All clear!" a male officer's voice said. "All clear on that side?"

"We're good in here! "Mr. Warren answered. "It's safe."

The divider wall opened, but stopped about two-thirds of the way into the wall since it was too damaged to slide back in. There was black fluid all over the room next to us, but it didn't seem to be blood.

"Is that oil?" Max and I exchanged glances.

"Must be." I nodded, holding my bandaged arm, which had started to throb now as well as burn where Lauren had bitten me. I would be lying if I said I wasn't just a little worried about what kind of germs were coursing through my veins after seeing the damage in the little room—the metal table and chairs all dented and broken—and after Max's visceral description of Lauren crouching on the table and bending in weird ways.

"Any injuries?" the live patrol asked.

"We have a bite wound and a gash, but they're patched up," Mr. Warren told the officer, who was looking a little out of sorts himself. "Where's Lauren? There was another student on that side of the divider."

"We had to put her in a net restraint," the officer said, shaking his head a little before he blinked purposefully a few times and refocused on Mr. Warren's question. "She's heading to St. Agnes's," he finished, referring to the hospital just a few miles from the school.

The officer looked around the room again shaking his head at the splatters of oil and debris from the smashed Sweeper droids.

"That's where we need to take you," the nurse said with a nod to me. "If Lauren is the girl who bit you, you'll need some tests. Don't you watch the feeds? People are—" she stopped herself, but I knew what she was going to say. *People are going Feral out there.*

"I—no, I'm OK," I said, knowing full well there was no way my aunt and uncle could afford a hospital visit, even with the discounted rates we got since I was a student and they were gainfully employed. It would still wind up costing years of life in legacy debt that they'd either have to slowly pay back with actual money or...*not,* and I didn't want that on my conscience. "I really have to go finish my internship applications." I lied. "I'll be sure to tell my aunt and uncle when I get home. They'll take me for a follow-up." The nurse narrowed her eyes at me. "It already stopped hurting..." I lied again. "Whatever you did fixed me right up. Thank you so much."

Her dubious expression finally started to lift, and I quietly exhaled in relief that it didn't seem like she was going to keep insisting that I go to St. Agnes's.

"If you start feeling the slightest bit off, I want to know about it. Let me know what the doctor says after you're seen," she said with a slight nod, which I interpreted to mean she was going to trust me. I made a mental note to stop by her office—on her way to lunch so she wouldn't ask too many questions—to tell her everything was fine.

And I really hoped it would be fine. The burning was getting worse, and it was all I could do to keep the pain from registering on my face.

"I'll stop in, for sure," I replied, then grabbed Max's arm and maneuvered around the wreckage to get to the outer door.

"Halsey!" Mr. Warren called after me, but I pretended not to hear. I just needed to get outside before I actually started screaming and crying like a baby with the pain in my arm now spreading up into my shoulder and down into my hand.

Max and I were halfway down the hall before I just couldn't keep up the façade anymore, and hot tears flooded my eyes. I held my arm tightly to my chest and turned to Max.

"Do you know a Grind medic?" I asked. "I can't go to St. Agnes's. How's your hand?"

"It's fine. Your arm is *not* fine? You said it didn't hurt." Max looked confused.

"I told the nurse that so she didn't haul me off to the emergency room," I said impatiently. "That would cost like, six years minimum."

"Halsey…" Max rolled his eyes. "You *can* pay that off with actual money."

"Look, can we argue about this later? This really hurts, and it's spreading," I said, looking around to make sure no one was listening. With both our internship applications turned in, I didn't feel one bit obligated to try and figure out how I would make it through the rest of the day like this. "Just come on," I said, hitching my backpack over one shoulder as I pushed through one of the outer doors.

Chapter 6

Max and I made our way to town without issue, which was a welcome relief. The spreading pain in my arm was about all I could handle.

"We could ask Mr. Warren if the school would pay for treatment since it happened there?" Max suggested, but I shook my head.

"I don't even want to bring it up again there, OK?" I insisted." I'm lucky the nurse believed I would go to an Authorized doctor on my own. How much farther is it?" I asked, my head starting to hurt now since I'd been clenching my teeth.

"Up the street," Max answered. "The medic's place is behind Raphael's Tea shop."

I exhaled slow, controlled breaths to try and keep my composure in check. I'd made it this far, I could go another block without a full-on pain-inspired panic attack.

*Twenty steps to the giant pots...ten steps to the front door...*I thought as we made our way as inconspicuously as possible to the entrance. I could smell the citrus blooms from the potted trees and different flowering shrubs a good six feet before reaching the door. Inside, the smell of spices and florals seemed to weave in and out of each other with every step we took toward the front counter, which was almost completely hidden by large, round baskets of loose teas. Greenery and giant paintings of mountains and sunbursts covered nearly every square inch of the walls, and to the side were about a half-dozen sets of small tables and chairs.

"Do we just ask at the counter?" I said, losing any patience I had left.

Max shook his head quickly and abruptly. "*Ni hao!*" he called over the counter.

"You speak Chinese?" I managed.

"That's all I know." He smirked, and after a few more seconds, a young Chinese woman peeked at us from behind the beaded curtain doorway. She took a look at Max, then looked me up and down before waiving us back through the curtain with her. I briefly wondered how Max knew about the Unauthorized medic here, the illegal practice punishable by nearly a few decades of legacy fines if any of us were caught. That would be doubly bad for me since they'd also tack on an additional cost to undo whatever illegal procedures this medic would perform. But, that's if we were caught. Taking the risk right now was the only option.

We moved quickly through a winding corridor, and then through a few rooms before we finally reached what looked like a basement, though we hadn't gone down any stairs that I could recall. The floors were concrete and the walls were painted, white cinderblock, interrupted only by the hanging metal cabinets and metal countertops along the perimeter of the room. In the middle were two metal gurneys without padding, a huge lamp contraption that mounted to a rolling cart, and a tray that extended from the long lamp stand.

"You lay," an older Chinese woman said in a thick accent as she gestured to the gurney table. I climbed up, but didn't lie back. The younger Chinese woman who had waved us through the curtain earlier came into the room and looked me up and down, then met my eyes.

"What happened to you two?" she said with no accent whatsoever as she studied us.

"I'm fine," Max gestured to his bandaged hand. "She's not, though. Tell her, Halls."

"My arm feels like it's—on fire," I started, but the words were nearly cut off by a fresh wave of pain.

"Someone bit her," Max finished for me. "There was a weird black fluid from the bite mark, but then it turned white."

The woman's face contorted in confusion, and she moved to unwrap the bandage. "Here?" she asked, then started cutting the gauze when I nodded.

The bite was clearly marked by an angry red outline, the skin broken in places and oozing more of the black fluid Max had mentioned. Once it hit the air, it turned a milky white again like it had back in the Ice Box.

"*Huh,*" the woman said, raising a feathery eyebrow.

"It really burns." I pushed the words through my teeth. "Can you make it stop hurting?"

"I'll try," she said, opening a cabinet behind her and pulling out a white can without a label. "This will be really cold." She nodded and sprayed the bite wound. The shift in sensation—from seething to freezing—in my arm was almost immediate, and I nearly cried in relief. "That should have helped," she asked, but I was too choked up to answer with actual words. I nodded again and felt a hot tear spill down my cheek.

"*Halsey*?" Max looked hard at me.

I shook my head. "It's OK. It stopped for a second —that spray stopped it."

"The pain is coming back already?" the woman asked, and I nodded again. She sprayed the wound again, but this time, also injected something into my arm just an inch or so from the bite mark. I didn't feel a thing.

"What's that?" I asked, trying to resist the compulsion to pull my arm back.

"It's like an antibiotic, but not," the woman said. "A human bite is worse than an animal bite, so this will kick up your immune system," she added, scrunching up her face.

"What's the black stuff?" Max asked. "And why is it turning white?"

"I don't really know," she answered. "The only other thing I can do is swab a sample to run some tests. My guess would be maybe it's just your body's way of pushing out the infection that's trying to take hold? Blood mixed with white blood cells—puss, you know? When did this happen?"

"Maybe an hour ago," Max answered.

The woman's face blanched, and she quickly masked the expression with a neutral one.

"Well, that's a little fast for an infection to have taken hold. Maybe it was something whoever bit you had in their mouth at the time, and your body is expelling it."

I could tell that not even she thought that was remotely probable, so she clearly was out of guesses about the fluid. I needed to stop thinking about it because there was literally nothing else that could be done to fix it other than what I was currently doing: sitting here in this illegal medical office getting illegal medical treatment from an unauthorized, illegal doctor. Now that the pain had subsided, the fear was starting to set in.

"Jen, the person who bit her was—" Max started. "This is going to sound crazy, but she turned into this... I don't even know how to describe it." He looked at the floor and shook his head. "Like she was halfway to becoming a grasshopper or something. She just crouched down on the table with her arms and legs bent in the wrong direction." He shook his head and closed his eyes, apparently to dismiss the image.

"Sorry?" Jen tilted her head to the side. "Her legs and arms were hyperextended on *purpose*?" She turned to me. "Is that when she bit you?"

"No, it was before she…changed," I answered, trying to be careful with my words so I didn't sound deranged. "I didn't see her, but Max turned ghost white when he did."

Jen gave us both a dubious, but curious look and grabbed an empty syringe and what looked like a fat rubber band. She turned back to me and took my wrist so my inner forearm was exposed.

"I'm going to take a blood sample and run some tests for pathogens. Then, I'm going to re-bandage that bite wound. Come back tomorrow and I'll know more," she said, tying the band around my upper arm, then drawing the blood from the bend in my elbow. I winced, surprised I even felt anything with the pain I had been feeling,

"Thanks, Jen," Max said, pulling out his wallet.

"No, I'll—" I started to protest.

"Don't worry about it yet," Jen said, waving away the cash he pulled out." We'll settle up when we find out what's wrong."

***

Max insisted on walking me all the way back to my aunt and uncle's house just in case the guy with the little vials reappeared. My arm had started to hurt a little again, but it wasn't nearly as bad as before.

"What do you think happened to Lauren?" I asked once we were far enough away from the people in town. "How did her arms and legs do what you said without her screaming in pain?"

Max shook his head. "I don't know. That's what I was wondering. She didn't walk in like that," he added. "She got up on the table though, and—I just don't know…" He trailed off, still seeming to be in a state of disbelief about what he saw. We stopped at my front gate, and Max darted a glance at my arm. "Do you know how you're going to explain that?" he asked.

"Nope. Not to mention where I've been all afternoon if someone from the school has already called."

"Tell them you decided to hand out extra résumés to the businesses that hadn't come to the school today," Max suggested, which wasn't a bad idea, but if it were up to my aunt or uncle, I'd just apprentice at the water treatment plant where they both worked. Let's see, fielding customer requests all day like my Aunt Alice, or adding sludge-eating microbes to the waste water like my Uncle Ray? Neither, thanks.

I shrugged, suddenly too exhausted to care what either of them had to say. I pulled my sleeve down over the bandage and half-heartedly counted on them not even noticing.

"Thanks for walking me home," I said through an unexpected yawn. "But now you have to walk all the way back to work."

Max shrugged. "I like walking. You look like you're about to fall asleep on your feet."

"I don't know why I'm so tired," I said with another yawn. "Maybe it's the antibiotics."

"Maybe." Max looked me up and down, his brows darting together. "I'm off tomorrow, so I'll go with you back to Jen's."

I nodded. "Thanks for all your help today," I said, fighting another yawn. It was almost getting too hard to keep my eyes open.

"Halsey!" My aunt's disembodied voice hit my ears so sharply I felt it in my teeth. She came bounding into the front room from the kitchen, wiping her hands on her apron. "Care to explain why your name came over the Sweeper reports today?" she asked, her wiry, gray hair sticking out of her braid. I would have rolled my eyes at the knowledge that she was listening to the police radio chatter again, but I didn't have the energy.

"Why do you even listen in on that thing?" I managed, too tired and dizzy to worry about how I must have sounded after the incensed look she gave me.

Her voice got quiet and menacing. "One of these days people in The Grind will get fed up enough with those pompous asses behind the wall and start rioting. Do you think the politicians who control the newsfeeds are just going to allow reports about what's really happening on the streets then?" she said defensively.

Normally, I would have at least attempted a few rounds of arguing about her paranoia that everything would fall into anarchy sooner rather than later, and that only the people like us who could live off the grid, independent of the Citadel-controlled water pipelines, grocery stores, and electrical services in The Grind, would have a chance of surviving. But not this time.

This time, things just started going black, slowly at first, then quickly. I barely had time to glance at Max before I nearly fell through my bedroom door, promptly passing out three seconds after it abruptly closed behind me.

Chapter 7

The fermented smell of cabbage and what could only be hot garbage filled my lungs even before I opened my eyes, and I coughed at the shock of it. What actual demon was my aunt trying to summon in the kitchen?

I hopped out of bed, thoroughly motivated by the idea of opening my window, and was a little surprised at how much energy I had. My arm didn't hurt at all anymore, and when I checked the bandage with a wince at what I was sure would be the gruesome state of the bite Lauren gave me, I had to sit back down. The bite mark was totally gone. There wasn't even an outline.

I double checked the bandage, which was still stained with blood and other discolorations I didn't even want to know about, but my skin was perfectly smooth. It didn't make sense. What kind of antibiotics had Jen given me yesterday?

I took a quick shower and got dressed, hiding the bandage in my jeans pocket since I figured it would be better to throw it away somewhere else rather than risk my aunt discovering it in the trash. I touched my temple to queue Max.

"Hey, I'm on my way," he said, the 3-D image of him appearing a few feet from my face. He was walking, but he didn't have his surround vision connected, so I could only see a white background behind him.

"I dreamed I was being swallowed by a garbage monster," I said, leaning on my window sill. "Then I woke up and realized my aunt was just making her cabbage stew. Or she's trying to reanimate corpses because I promise you, Max, not even dead people could be around this smell. I'm about to throw myself out the window."

Max laughed. "Well, it sounds like you're feeling better at least."

I nodded. "About that..." I said, holding up my arm to the 3-D screen projection in front of me. "The bite is totally gone."

Max's brows crashed together. "Gone?"

"I don't understand it either," I added. "It's like nothing ever happened. And I feel like I slept for a week. What kind of antibiotics did Jen give me?"

"Standard issue, I guess?" Max shrugged.

"How's your gash?"

"It's fine. Barely know it's there," he smiled. "I'm about to knock on your door. Just come down so I don't have to come inside—I can smell the zombie juice from here, *ugh*."

I tapped my temple again to close the comm queue and took one last, deep breath of fresh air before shutting my window and heading into the foyer.

"I'm going to check up on my internship applications from yesterday, Aunt Alice!" I lied so I wouldn't have to answer a thousand questions as I was trying not to breathe. Max knocked on the door in the time it took me to walk to it, and I'd never been so grateful for his fantastic timing. I swung the door open and took in another deep breath.

"*Oh my god…*" Max said, his expression crumpling. "It's the smell of actual death," he added, pulling the front of his shirt over his nose and mouth.

"I told you. Come on." I took a step out the door, but stopped in my tracks when my Uncle Ray bellowed my name.

"Halsey! Come in here!"

"Please no." Max shook his head. "No, Halsey."

I rolled my eyes and grabbed his shirt, dragging him into the house with me, despite his pleading and whimpering.

"Alice is digging up some potatoes for the stew out back. Gonna need to double down on the immunity this winter against that wasting sickness that's on the rise again, and now they're saying those Ferals in the valley have an actual disease. Calling it *Red Fever*." My uncle rolled his eyes. "Just people fed up with oppression is all that is. Just people starting to lose their minds and take to violence. This whole place is going to hell, but do you think they care behind that wall?" he added, his already narrow eyes nearly disappearing under his bushy, gray brows as he glared at me. "You lost your mind now too, did you?"

"What? No!" I answered, not sure what he was talking about until I remembered that my aunt had been listening to the police scanner yesterday.

"So you *weren't* put in custody by Sweeper droids at the school?" My uncle's jowls wrinkled back like a hound dog's when he pressed his lips together into a tight line, waiting for my answer.

I shook my head and made a concerted effort to keep my voice steady. "That was nothing. Lauren Stover tried to start a fight with me in the cafeteria," I said, which wasn't a lie. "They just wanted to get both our sides of the story." I nodded casually, hoping my uncle wouldn't be able to see the holes I was leaving in that explanation.

He gave me a hard look for several seconds. "Alice!" he shouted toward the back door. "You said that girl went to the hospital?"

"Uncle Ray," I said quickly, my heart jumping into my throat. "We really have to go. Like, right now. Internship follow-ups," I stammered.

Ray narrowed his eyes at Max. "Mr. Barrett… You still working for that cog in the machine, Burke?"

Max swallowed hard. "Uh, yes, sir."

"You know he's just part of the problem, conditioning everyone to be dependent sheep instead of growing their own goods. Selling that cheap, cloned produce. Probably what's giving everyone The

Wasting sickness around here. No damn nutrients. *That's* why nobody gets it from being sneezed on."

I felt compelled to roll my eyes and call out the lunacy of this logic, but that would mean we'd have to stand here under threat of my aunt coming back at any second, not to mention breathing in more of the radioactive sewage she was simmering in the kitchen.

"I think I have some internship leads you'll approve of, Uncle Ray, but we have to go *right now* before they're inundated with the other people who applied," I babbled.

"Nothing in the valley, I hope," Ray mumbled. "Nothing by the—"

"OK, bye!" I added before he could say anything else, then grabbed Max's arm and rushed out the door. Both Max and I sucked in a huge breath and jogged out of the noxious cloud surrounding the house.

"*What* does she put in that stew?" Max scrubbed his hands over his face as if to wash the smell away.

"It's never smelled that bad," I answered. "They've been getting creative with food now that my uncle has decided Mr. Burke is part of some big government conspiracy to further oppress the people in The Grind. I tried to tell him prices just go up sometimes."

Max sighed. "So, what's with your arm?" he asked, dismissing the other conversation. I rolled up my sleeve to show him as we made our way through the woods back to town.

"It had to be whatever Jen did I guess," I added. "I just woke up today and the bite mark was gone."

"That doesn't make sense. Antibiotics don't just do that overnight," Max said, darting glances from left to right as we approached the eye of the forest. "You haven't seen that guy who tried to sell you the vials again, right?"

"Not since yesterday." I shook my head. "And you've been with me every time I've passed through here since then. Lauren had been talking to him just before everything went sideways, though," I added.

"Are you thinking she took one of the vials?"

"I don't know. But people don't just change like that—her arms and legs bent like you said. They'd know what was wrong with her at the hospital, right?"

"If anyone would…" Max nodded, and we made our way to St. Agnes's before following up with Jen. Whatever we'd maybe learn after talking with Lauren might be something Jen could use to figure out how the bite wound healed so quickly.

It was early enough on a Saturday morning that most of the shops hadn't opened yet, which meant that most of the people who would otherwise harass us weren't loitering outside the doorways begging for cash from people walking in and out. I paid more attention now that I knew there had been more Feral attacks within the last few weeks. I tried to stay away from the newsfeeds because they never had anything good to say, and the fact that The Citadel wasn't even really acknowledging that anything was happening just made it all worse. I sighed and pushed the thought out of my head. We had other things to deal with right now.

We made it to St. Agnes's in record time and walked right up to the reception desk. An older woman with a tight, gray bun flashed a big smile as we approached.

"We're here to see Lauren Stover," I said, smiling back at the woman. She nodded and tapped the holographic display in front of her. After several scrolling swipes, her brows started to pinch together.

"Stover, you said?"

"Yes," Max answered. "She was brought in yesterday after a fight at Portland Prep."

I shot Max a quick side eye, a twinge of guilt pulling across my chest. But Lauren had started the fight by shoving me into the pillar in the cafeteria.

The woman suddenly covered her mouth with her hand, then cleared her throat and looked up at us.

"What's wrong?" I asked, noticing the sudden chill in the air between us.

"I'm afraid Lauren Stover is no longer here," she said. "But I'm sorry, that's all I can tell you if you're not immediate family members."

"She went home?" Max asked, sounding as confused as I felt about why that would be a confidential kind of thing.

"I'm sorry," she continued. "That's really all I can say."

We thanked her after another few seconds and went out the way we'd come in.

"Should we go to her house?" I asked Max, since we weren't far from the school, and if she lived in the same house she'd been in since we were in elementary school, it wasn't far.

Max narrowed his eyes at me. "And walk up to the door to say what? *Hi, I'm Halsey, the one who kicked Lauren's ass so hard she turned into a grasshopper?*"

I laughed and rolled my eyes, but instantly felt guilty about it. I didn't see Lauren in that state the way Max did, but I imagine it wasn't painless. "Who do we know who hangs out with her? Is there anyone we can get on the queue?"

Max shook his head. "I guess let's just walk by her house. Maybe a little sister or a neighbor will be outside and we can just ask as we pass by."

"Good idea."

We were in her neighborhood about ten minutes later, and I was momentarily grateful that I lived up on the hill on the other side of the woods. The street was full of trash, and loud, bratty kids were throwing pieces of broken pipes or rocks at each other while screaming at the tops of their lungs. If this was a game, I'd hate to see what fights looked like. No wonder Lauren was the way she was.

"Does she still live in that yellow house?" Max asked as we turned a corner. Several junky cars were parked in front of the house, and a fairly large group of people were going in an out. "Oh shit, is that Brian?" he said, quickly darting behind a tree in the next door neighbor's yard so we wouldn't be seen.

"Yeah, and Mr. Warren! Look on the porch," I said. "I think he's talking to her mom…"

"She's crying?" Max asked more than stated, but it was obvious she was crying when she turned to greet someone coming up the porch steps.

"I have a bad feeling about this," I said as a chill ran through me.

"Who are you?" an abrupt voice said behind us, which made me nearly jump out of my skin. Max and I both turned around to find a little girl standing indignantly with her hands on her hips, her messy ponytail full of leaves and twigs like she'd just fallen out of a tree or something.

"Do you know Lauren Stover?" Max asked, not missing a beat. The little girl wiped her dirty face with the back of her dirty hand.

"She caught on fire," she said casually, and all the blood in my veins turned to ice.

"What did you say?" I whispered, only because my voice had completely left me.

"She caught on fire at the hospital yesterday."

I blinked at the girl. "*How*? How does that happen?"

The little girl shrugged. "Dunno. Her mama said the para-somebodies didn't check her right before they took her out of the ambulance."

"What does that mean?" Max asked. "How would she catch on fire?"

The girl shrugged again, this time, annoyed. "Do I look like a para-somebody to you? The oxygen blowing all over from her mask maybe. Like maybe they were smoking or something and blew everything up. *Duh.*" She rolled her eyes at us like we were the stupidest people she'd ever met, then wiped her nose again with the back of her other dirty hand and yelled at the top of her lungs to the people in Lauren's front yard. "Hey! Lauren blew up because the para-somebodies were smoking, right?"

"*Oh my god,*" I gasped as Max and I both took off in the other direction, running like the whole world was about to start chasing us.

Chapter 8

Max and I were only a few blocks from Jen's practice before we finally slowed down to catch our breath. Only when we stopped, I wasn't out of breath.

Max was a sprinter on the school track team, and while running what had to be a quarter of a mile may have been pushing his limits, I couldn't understand why he was bent over his knees heaving and sucking in air while I wasn't. From the incredulous look he gave me, neither could he.

"*How…?*" he gasped, shaking his head at me. "How are you good?"

"I don't know," I said, not even remotely winded. "I was just wondering the same thing."

"You were…ahead of me," he panted. "Most of the way."

"I don't know how," I said again, confused because not only was I not winded, but I felt like I was just getting started—like that run was about as hard as stretching after first getting out of bed. "We need to talk to Jen and find out what she really gave me."

Max straightened and gave me a quick nod as we started walking the rest of the way to Raphael's Tea Shop.

"Caught on *fire*… I guess that's why the lady at St. Agnes's wouldn't tell us anything," he said.

"How does that even happen?" I asked. "We need to talk to Mr. Warren and find out what went down."

"Maybe it's on the feeds," he added, and I tapped my temple until I heard the news playing in my ear.

"Filter for Portland Prep," I said, hoping this would weed out all the regular horror stories that happen in The Grind on a daily basis, including, but not limited to those Feral attacks and Red Fever.

"Well?" Max said impatiently.

"There's nothing." I shook my head, then looked at him. "How could there be nothing?"

"Maybe that kid didn't have everything straight," he said, clearly scrambling for an explanation. "Let's just follow up with Jen, and then we can worry about this."

We walked for another five minutes or so before coming upon Raphael's Tea Shop again. The front counter was abandoned when we first walked in, but Jen almost immediately poked her head through the curtain and motioned for us to follow her.

"How do you feel today?" she asked, eyeing my arm as we walked down the corridor to her examining room.

"Better than I probably should," I answered after a beat. We walked through the beaded curtain into the chrome-covered examining room a few seconds later, and Jen motioned for me to sit on the metal gurney. I did, and she reached for my arm, her eyes darting to mine the instant she saw the bite was gone. Her dark, feathery brows knotted as she quickly looked at my other arm, then at me.

"What happened?" she asked.

"We were going to ask you the same thing," Max said with a sigh. "What kind of antibiotics did you give her yesterday?"

"Some jicambi bark enzyme." Jen shook her head. "It's just a boost to the immune system for a week or so, but it wouldn't have completely healed the wound like this."

"Would it boost her speed, too?" Max raised an eyebrow at me. "And her lung capacity?"

"Uh, no," Jen said, now looking even more confused. "OK, *what* happened?"

"Just what Max said," I answered. "I woke up this morning, and the bite mark was gone. We had to run from a messed up situation just before we came here, and I was really fast, also, not even a little out of breath. That has to be from the hiccup bark enzyme or whatever, right?"

"Jicambi bark," Jen corrected, but then shook her head again. "And no, that doesn't sound related. But, I don't have another theory other than it's because your test results are off the charts. Have you been feeling particularly aggressive lately?"

"What?" I said abruptly. "I mean, I've felt a little edgy, but there's been a lot of stuff going on."

Jen crossed to the counter and brought back a handheld tablet. She entered a button combination, and a hologram of scrolling data started populating.

"This is your resting oxygen level," Jen said, pointing to a bar on the graph chart. "And this is a normal resting oxygen level," she added, pointing to a blue, horizontal line that ran a good inch below the top of the bar.

"Damn, Halls…" Max's eyes widened. "Your levels are like somebody who's about to be attacked by a tiger."

"Or like a tiger who's about to attack someone." Jen glanced quickly from Max to me. "Halsey, you've heard about Red Fever on the feeds?"

I narrowed my eyes at her because the air in the room suddenly started to feel thick and heavy.

I nodded. "It's what's causing the violence outbreaks—the people going Feral," I finished, stopping just before launching into how my uncle thought it was all just a media overreaction so no one had to talk about the pent up hostility and oppression of people in The Grind.

"Right." Jen gave me a flat smile. "Well, since The Citadel doesn't seem to think it's a major concern if the R nought number behind the wall is *zero*, which of course it is since they don't have anyone infect—"

"Sorry, the R-*what*?" I asked.

"R nought—the number of people an infected person can also infect. One person infects three people, etc., and the R nought would be three," Jen explained. "Anyway, since Red Fever doesn't seem to present behind the Citadel wall, the Citadel pathologists have concluded it's not airborne."

"Well that's good, right?" Max asked.

"For them, sure. As long as they have their wall it doesn't affect them. If it did, there would be a cure by now." Jen pressed her lips into a tight line and cleared her throat. "Anyway, since they don't seem to be working too hard on it, some of my colleagues and I have been trying to isolate the cause, but we haven't been able to find anyone with active symptoms who wasn't already Feral, and then subsequently MIA." Jen nodded slowly this time, a resigned conciliatory nod as if to say, you understand, don't you? In the same moment, two vacant-eyed, very tan men came into the room, and all the hairs on the back of my neck stood on end.

I got to my feet, but two men shut the door behind them.

"Max, let's go." I started walking toward the door, my heart pounding like a hammer in my chest. Jen turned away from me and took a long syringe off the table at our side just as one of the men grabbed Max and the other grabbed me.

"Hey!" Max struggled.

"I only need to run a few more tests, Halsey," Jen said as the man wrestled me back to the gurney. "I won't even charge you for the treatment of the bite. You could be part of the cure! Don't you want that?"

"Stay away from me!" I shouted. Max kicked a rolling metal table at the man holding onto me, but it just ricocheted off his leg and clattered to the ground.

"Jen, what are you doing!?" he shouted, but Jen didn't acknowledge him.

"If you struggle, this is going to hurt," she said, reaching for my sleeve.

"Jennifer Kwan?" a tall woman loudly announced, her dark hair cut in a razor line at her chin. Everyone stopped moving.

"You can't just come in here and—" Jen started to protest, but two cylindrical Sweeper droids hovered behind the woman and immediately drew laser tracks on Jen and both of the men restraining Max and me.

"Miss Kwan," the tall woman started. "You're under arrest for illegally dispensing medical services. Sam here will read you your rights, won't you, Sam?" She tilted her head toward the Sweeper droid that was currently centering a red guiding laser on Jen's forehead. A second later, the light pulsed, and Jen fell to the ground.

"Miranda rights uploaded," the metallic droid next to the woman said, its male voice surprisingly calm. It moved toward Jen and lifted her off the floor in a suspension field, which looked like a blue cocoon of light. She'd be out cold for the time it took them to put her in a cell. I'd seen this go down too may times in The Grind.

"You two go jump in the bay," the woman said to the men, narrowing fiery green eyes at them. To my surprise, both men let go of Max and me immediately to follow Jen and the droid floating her out of the room. The other droid stayed with us, but it turned off its laser.

The tension in the room got thicker in new the silence, and I was terrified she was going to arrest us, too, for receiving unauthorized medical treatment.

"Look, nothing happened here," Max spoke up. "Jen was just getting started. We didn't break any laws," he continued. And he was right, as long as he meant we hadn't broken any *today*.

"It would make my life much easier if I could just haul you in, but—"

"Run!" I gave Max a quick look, and we both darted out of the room.

"Halsey, stop! You're on the radar now!" the woman called after us.

A wave of panic ran through me at her words. I didn't know what she was talking about, but she had Sweeper droids listening to her, and she just put Jen in a custody bubble, which meant she was with the police, and there was no way in hell I was going to pay a twenty-year legacy fine, plus whatever else they would charge for the treatment Jen gave me. I'd take my chances in The Grind.

"Go! Go!" Max shouted as we made our way up the winding corridor, through the curtain, and finally, out to the street.

We ran as far as we could in the opposite direction of Raphael's Tea Shop, but it soon became clear we had no idea where we were running to until we found ourselves in the southern parking lot of Portland Prep. Several cars were parked outside the baseball diamond, and it looked like the coach was hitting fly balls to the outfielders. Max and I leaned against the brick wall of the school. Again, he was winded, but I felt like I had only walked a few steps.

He shook his head at me. "What the hell just happened?" he asked, though the question seemed rhetorical. A million non-rhetorical questions flooded into my mind. *What did she mean by saying I was on the radar now? Did they know who I was? And then there was the matter of what crazy biology was currently playing out in my body.*

"I don't feel sick," I said out loud, as if trying to take inventory of myself." I don't feel violent—*Feral*—whatever they want to call what's happening out there."

"You're *not* Feral," Max said, still trying to catch his breath. "They don't even know if it's really an actual disease, Halls."

"I'm a little more impatient and edgy, but that's just because of graduation and trying to get into The

Citadel, and then I forgot these internship applications until—"

"*Halsey...*" Max gripped my upper arms. "Take a breath. Stop trying to rationalize everything. You're not Feral. Jen never said you had Red Fever. She just wanted to...experiment or something." He shook his head.

"Why did she have those men try to keep us there then?" I protested. "She said my oxygen levels were crazy. Maybe that's why I'm not out of breath when we sprint halfway across town. What if I turn into whatever happened to Lauren, Max? What if—"

Max cut me off. "OK, look..." He let go of my arms and held up his hands for emphasis, one of them still bandaged from yesterday. "Jen gave you that supershot after Lauren bit you, so if she was contaminated with Red Fever, it looks like you're fine. Being fast and healing is probably just an unexpected result of the shot."

"Jen would have guessed that," I reminded him. "She said the shot wouldn't have healed the bite mark so fast."

"She could have been wrong, Halls." Max shrugged. "She's a Grind medic—all her equipment and medicines are scavenged. There's a big margin for error, and again, nobody even knows if it's an actual disease or just some kind of psychotic break or whatever," Max assured. "Jen's all we've got, I know, but you have to take everything with a grain of salt."

He smiled a little at me, and for the first time, I took a deep breath and actually felt myself relaxing until I remembered the officer.

"OK, but that officer knew my name, Max. What if she comes after me?"

He looked at me without an answer for several seconds, but finally took a quick, deep breath and shook his head. "If she wanted to arrest you, she'd have had that droid chase us down."

"No, that doesn't make any sense," I argued. "Why *wouldn't* she arrest me too? It's just as illegal for me to get Unauthorized treatment as it is for Jen to dispense it."

"Technically, she didn't catch you getting any treatment in there, Halls," Max lowered his chin and nodded. "We were trying to get out of there when that Sweeper patrol arrived."

And that made enough sense for me to relax the rest of the way. I blew out a breath. "OK..." I said, nodding.

"Good. All right, Jen said that injection would super-charge you for a week, right? So just ride it out. If you feel anything weird, we'll figure it out then."

I agreed, nodding again several times to cement the idea in my mind. "But one last thing...that lady said I was on their radar now—does that mean they'll be watching me?"

Chapter 9

Max had to work both Sunday shifts at Mr. Burke's grocery, and I used the time to clean every square inch of my house to avoid going outside.

What the officer at Jen's had said about being on the radar, whatever that meant, was still haunting me. In fact, if today weren't the day I found out if my Citadel and internship applications were accepted, I probably would have found a way to stay home.

I maneuvered to Mr. Warren's room hoping to find Max on the way. Everyone in the hall was buzzing with chatter in groups of twos and threes, but Max wasn't anywhere to be found. I was afraid I would crawl out of my skin—maybe literally—if I didn't find him soon to tell him what had just happened.

Mr. Warren came into our homeroom a few seconds after I did, so I took a deep breath and made my way over to ask about Lauren. If any of what was happening to me had something to do with her, I needed to know.

"Mr. Warren!" I said, making sure my sleeve was pulled down over where the bite wound on my forearm used to be.

"Halsey, how are you feeling?" he asked once I got closer, but then raised his voice over the noise in the class. "Everyone, please take your seats so I can distribute your codes!"

"I'm OK, thank you, but how's Lauren?" I asked, and though I know he heard me, he didn't answer for several seconds. Finally, he nodded at me slowly. "She's no longer with us," he said hesitantly.

"*What*?" I whispered, in disbelief that maybe the little girl outside her house on Saturday was right. Mr. Warren nodded again. "It seems she was exposed to a neurotoxin of some kind, but there were complications at the hospital."

"Is it true that she caught on fire?" I asked too abruptly and instantly regretted how callous I sounded. Mr. Warren's eyebrows flinched in surprise. "Sorry, I'd just heard…" I trailed off, unsure how to recover from the outburst.

He cleared his throat. "They're still gathering details," he said neutrally and gave me a nod, which was the clear teacher signal that the conversation was over and I should take a seat. I gave him a sheepish smile and turned into the sound of my name being called from across the room. Max started waving me over as Mr. Warren announced for the class to find a seat again.

"Could I have everyone's attention, please? I have some unfortunate news," Mr. Warren said over all the conversation. He went on to tell us that Lauren Stover had passed away over the weekend due to complications from a sudden illness, and that the counselors would be available all day for grief support.

Another round of buzzing conversation filled the air, and he quieted everyone down again. There was also no good way to transition into the rest of the announcements for the day—specifically about the report on internship and Citadel acceptances—so Mr. Warren just gave everyone a few minutes to process what he'd just told us.

And just like that, life went on. There should have been more. I was no fan of Lauren's, but still, there should have been more. There should have been more regarding the Feral attacks, even if they *were* just in The Grind. About Red Fever and how it caused The Wasting sickness. Why didn't we know for sure how it was caused? Why wasn't everything quarantined until we did know? *Why did nothing matter unless it happened behind that stupid Citadel wall?*

I forced myself to calm down as Mr. Warren started handing out our college and career login codes, then sent us to the gym to enter them into the reader booths they'd set up since not everyone in The Grind had an ocular communication lens. The only reason I had one was because my uncle had a friend who used to work for the Department of Communications…*before* he was caught handing out free OCLs to his friends.

I heard snippets of conversations about Lauren as I was about to message Max *again* on the way to the gym, but he caught up with me before I could.

"Halls! It's true," Max blurted, barely waiting for me to acknowledge him. "Brian told the Neanderthals the same thing that little girl said. Lauren just caught on fire as they were taking her out of the ambulance to go into St. Agnes's."

"But how?" I asked, as he led us out of traffic to the side of the hallway. "People don't just spontaneously combust like that," I said in a lowered voice.

Max shook his head. "They don't know how. Her family is blaming the paramedics just like that kid said. They're talking about suing the hospital," he added, rolling his eyes. No one in The Grind had the cash for a lawyer, and no one would risk using legacy credits to pay for one, so threatening to sue was about as far as that would go.

Max and I took a right turn to avoid one of the puffing sanitizer machines and headed straight out the side door. We already had the codes to access our reports on our OCLs, and finals, even the graduation ceremony, had been at the beginning of this past week, so there was nothing else to do at school anymore now that we had our application results. These last few days were all about what we were supposed to do with the rest of our lives, but right now, after confirming what happened to Lauren, I didn't know how much longer that would be for any of us, and no one was even talking about it.

I rubbed the spot on my arm where the bite used to be, suddenly more worried than ever. I looked up at Max.

"What if Lauren infected me with something and it's only held at bay temporarily until the stuff Jen gave me wears off?" I asked, not that I thought Max had the answer, but because I had to get the question out of my head before it took over all my thoughts.

He met my eyes as we walked. "Maybe we can find another Grind medic. I'll ask around," Max said. "And by the way, somehow, Jen paid her fines. I saw her going into the tea shop this morning."

I gaped at him. "How could she possibly have that kind of money?"

"Maybe she paid with legacy credit," Max said, shrugging one shoulder.

"No way. That would be like, twenty years minimum."

"I don't know, but she's out. The woman who arrested her dropped her off."

"Why would she do that?" I asked. "She had Jen red-handed administering Unauthorized medical services."

Max shook his head, and I stared down the dirt path in front of us as it wound around to the front of the school. Jen had tried to get me to stay in that examining room by force if necessary. She wanted to run tests, or so she said. Why would the same officer bring her *back* the next day? It didn't make sense.

"OK, Are you ready to do this?" Max held out the little card with his code on it as we made our way to the curb and took a seat. All we needed to do was look down at it, and our reports would load in our field of vision, so I nodded and pulled my card out of my pocket.

"We go at the same time—double blink for external projection," I said, and once he agreed, I started counting. "One…two…three…"

I glanced at the square, blotched design on my card, then double blinked to project everything in the file into my external view. I quickly scanned through the internship application results without even reading them, needing to find the decision from The Citadel. Finally, I saw the crest with the Old English letter C in the center at the top of their announcement form.

Dear Ms. Rhodes:
Thank you for your application to The Citadel. We have reviewed your many promising potential contributions to the academy, but unfortunately, we are unable to offer you admittance at this time…

Everything else the letter said just blended together, the words falling into each other and blurring beyond recognition. I blinked and felt the hot tears stream down my cheeks, which momentarily cleared the letters, but they quickly blurred again as I suddenly felt the need to sit down.

I found my way to the curb and sat motionless, my mind somehow racing, but without any thoughts beyond an awareness of feeling cold.

"Halsey…" Max said, sitting next to me. I felt his arm move around me, and saw the abrupt disappearance of his file display. That snapped me out of my trance, and I blinked my file closed.

"Why did you kill your display?" I asked, though it sounded like an accusation.

"It's nothing. Let's look back at your other responses, OK? The Citadel is stupid."

"Max, pull your display back up," I ordered.

"Halsey, it's really—"

"*Max.*"

He sighed and after another few seconds, the file flashed in his external field of view, and the Old English C was at the very top of the first response letter in his queue. *We are pleased to inform you that you have been selected*...was all I needed to read. All the breath left my lungs.

"I wasn't going to apply, but you were so adamant… I thought *maybe*, you know? But I'm not going to go. Mr. Burke told me he accepted my application at the grocery, so I'll—"

"Max, you *have* to go," I gaped at him. "Are you kidding me? You have to. You *have to*, Max." I felt the tears streaming down my cheeks again as the reality set in. Not only had I lost my chance to get out of The Grind, but now I was losing my best friend too. He would live behind The Citadel wall, and I would probably never be allowed there even as a guest. It hit me then that had I been accepted to The Citadel and he didn't, the situation would have been the same. I'd been so busy focusing on my own plans I hadn't considered that.

"Whatever, we're not talking about my Citadel letter now, OK?" Max said, raising his hand to my cheek and wiping the tears away. "Blink your file back open and let's see what else is in there."

I took a deep breath and did as he asked, the file projection loading a few feet in front of us. I'd been accepted to all of the other internship positions I'd applied for…the landscaping companies, the City Engineer's department, the Department of Natural Resources, and I almost choked when I saw the acceptance from Raphael's Tea Shop. How could I have forgotten that I applied there? I almost closed the file, thinking that was the end of the feedback, but it looked like there was another letter after the one from Raphael's.

"What's Eden's Bluff?" Max asked as my eyes took in the elaborate logo—the scripted name against a backdrop of vine covered, arching gates.

"I don't know," I said, dumbfounded. "I didn't apply anywhere called Eden's Bluff. I've never even heard of it."

"Halsey…" Max said, his voice low and serious. I pulled myself away from the trance of the logo and tried to make my eyes focus on the words.

Dear Miss Rhodes:
We are pleased to offer you admission to Eden's Bluff Academy. You may not be aware of your application to our institution, but rest assured. We do not accept applications, rather, our students are selected each year from judicious reviews of potential candidates at trusted institutions all over the nation.

In addition to the prestigious honor of admittance to Eden's Bluff Academy, please be advised that you have also been selected by one of our generous benefactors to receive a financial package which includes full tuition, room, and board for the duration of your studies.

Please review the courier materials that were dispatched to your residence, and kindly reply with either your acceptance or your decline of this offer within the next few days. Should you choose to accept our offer, all transportation to Eden's Bluff will also be provided.

Congratulations again, Miss Rhodes. We look forward to welcoming you to campus.

I read the words, but they wouldn't process in my mind until Max started shaking my shoulders.

"Halls!" he said through a rolling laugh. "That's a full ride! I didn't even know that place existed!"

I shook my head at him. "How can it exist? Only The Citadel campuses are sanctioned for Authorized careers," I added, feeling strangely excited, but also a little numb. "Something isn't right. I don't feel right," I said, noticing the swimming feeling starting in my head.

"It's probably just shock." Max chuckled. "Let's go to your place. They sent you a package!"

We only got about twenty steps when a van pulled up next to us and slammed on its brakes. Before I could even process what was happening, a small group of men poured out and began trying to haul me into the van.

"Let her go!" Max yelled and started pulling one of them off me, but the man turned and punched him in the stomach. He dropped to the ground, and the man started kicking him.

"Don't worry about him!" I heard Jen yell from inside the van somewhere.

"Stop!" I screamed as loudly as I could, but it wasn't the word I heard. It was a screech…the highest pitched, longest, most inhuman screech ever. The men let me go to cover their ears, and in the same moment, from nowhere, dozens of birds started dive bombing them, forcing them back into their van. They pulled away with the birds following, and Max's eyes were wide as he stared at me in shock. I took a step toward him to help him get up, but he stumbled as he took a step backward, avoiding my hand. Alternating waves of fear and embarrassment crashed into me.

"Halls? What the hell was that?" he asked, his blanched expression unchanged as he dropped his arm from his stomach. I opened my mouth only to realize I had no idea what to say. I didn't know what had just happened either, and I couldn't stand the fear in his eyes as he stared at me.

Without thinking, I ran. I ran as fast as I could, and in what seemed like just a minute, I was already back to the eye of the forest. I stopped at the end of the rock wall, again, not even a little winded until I looked down at my shaking hands, and all the breath escaped my lungs at once.

Feathers were slowly changing back into my fingers. "*What...*" I gasped, then blinked as hard as I could to clear whatever crazy illusion I'd just seen.

I looked again at my hands just to be sure they were still hands and blew out a breath in relief to see that they were. *It was just a trick of the light or something,* I told myself as I took a few more steps, but then stopped and looked at my hands again, wondering if maybe it wasn't a trick—if maybe I could *make* them change into feathers.

I tried to remember how they'd looked a few minutes ago and concentrated, but only my same uneven nails and spindly fingers remained. I immediately felt stupid and started walking again, telling myself I needed to focus. Jen had just tried to pull me into a van. She had been released, and the woman who arrested her even *dropped her off*!

My head started spinning with everything that had just happened, and I needed to go inside and lock myself in my room before something *else* happened that I couldn't control. But of course, one look at my porch told me it already had.

Chapter 10

My mouth went dry as I saw the woman who arrested Jen at my door talking with my Aunt Alice. I darted behind a tree and waited to see if she was coming or going. My aunt's face was hard to read because it was usually always crumpled in the same dissatisfied way it was now, but there were also flashes of shock. What was this lady telling her?

Finally, the woman turned and walked toward a black car that was parked on the side of my house. My aunt closed the door, and the woman checked over her shoulder, then made her way to my bedroom window. She cupped her hands around her eyes and peered in for a few seconds, then got in her car and finally started driving down the hill.

I moved completely behind the tree I'd been peeking around and waited for the car to drive out of sight. In what seemed like just five strides, though it couldn't have been, I was outside the front door of my house.

I couldn't stay here. I had to get out of The Grind before either Jen's goons tried to kidnap me again, or that officer arrested me and brought me back to Jen anyway.

My mind was racing again. I opened the door as silently as I could and made a B-line for my bedroom —the fermented, sweat sock smell of my aunt's cabbage concoction still hanging in the air. My stomach dropped when I heard the deep bellow of my uncle's voice not three steps after I came into the house.

"Halsey!" he called, stopping me in my tracks. His voice was stern, but it didn't seem angry so much as impatient.

"What have you been doing?" My aunt Alice asked as she darted into the room. "I want to know why we had the Director of Crisis Management here looking for you not five minutes ago, and why she was asking questions about how you've been feeling lately." She gave me a hard glare.

"Uhh…" is all I said, scrambling for words because I realized I couldn't tell her about the men who just tried to grab me. I couldn't think of a logical way to explain about Jen and why we were with her in the first place. But then I realized what my aunt had said.

"Director of Crisis Management?" I asked. That didn't sound like a job title for someone who arrests people for Unauthorized medical care, but she *had* arrested Jen.

"Did you hear your aunt?" my uncle asked, this time, his voice a little louder. "Why was the Director of Crisis Management here for you?"

I cleared my throat. "Because Lauren Stover died?" I answered, though it sounded like a question. "Complications or something at the hospital for a disease she had. Lauren attacked me, remember?" I blurted, then kicked myself because I no longer had the injury that was bandaged just yesterday. I quickly tried to change the subject. "The director was probably just making sure I didn't feel guilty or something, but I know it wasn't my fault." I was starting to babble and knew I needed to find a way to shut my mouth so I could get to my room already.

My uncle studied me, then turned to Alice. "She did say the girl died," he nodded, then seemed to resolve something. "Negligence by that blood-money hospital from the sounds of it." He pressed his lips into a line, nodding again for emphasis, and I breathed a sigh of relief since he seemed to be on track to drop his inquisition. I needed to get out of here before that director woman decided to come back.

"Well, she left her card for you," Alice said, taking it from her apron pocket and handing it to me. It read *Eve Adams, Crisis Management Director* in bold, black letters, with her contact number and queue code embossed in the lower left corner. "She said to call her the minute you got home. But see what's in that box first," Alice added, pointing me to a shoebox-sized package still wrapped in brown paper on the table. "A nice young man dropped this off for you. He said he was from a prestigious school—a direct competitor to The Citadel monopoly," she continued, impressed.

I took a few steps toward the box, but a knock at the door jolted me back.

"Why are you so jumpy?" my uncle asked with a chuckle. A few seconds later, the ping of my communications chip sounded in my ear, and I blinked to see what it said.

Max:

Sorry about back there. I was just surprised. I'm outside, and we have some trouble.

He was surprised? How did he think I felt?

I crossed to the door and opened it, half expecting Max to run the other way when he saw me. But instead, he visibly exhaled.

"I'm sorry," I said to him. "I got embarrassed and just started running and—"

"No, me too, it's OK," he said quickly, catching his breath. Bird caws filled the air from somewhere in the distance, and a chill ran down my spine. "Halls, I just passed that police lady's car," Max said quietly. "I hid so she wouldn't see me, but I could tell it was her. She might know where you live."

"She *does* know where I live," I said too quickly and handed him the card she'd left me. "She was just here wanting to talk to me."

"Are you plotting a revolt? Let the boy in!" my uncle bellowed from behind me. I stepped aside to let Max in and watched his expression crinkle as the lingering smell of the cabbage stew obviously settled over him. I held back a smile.

"Open the package," my aunt said impatiently. Max and I exchanged knowing glances, and I made my way back to the box.

Inside was a T-shirt and another box, this one covered in a thin, white, crepe material. I lifted the lid and a 3-D projection began hovering over the box, which I nearly dropped. I set it on the table and watched the large, gold letters *E* and *B* become animated and dance around each other until they settled over the gate of a huge, rod iron fence. A few seconds later, a multitiered, white building with pillars materialized behind it.

As the scene panned out, a wide expanse of blue stretched out to the horizon in the background, and in the foreground, palm trees came into view over the top of the iron gate. A few seconds later, an impossibly perfect looking man with white-blond hair pushed the gates open and stepped through.

"Hello, Halsey. My name is Uri," the man said, startling me at the personalization. "We at Eden's Bluff would like to welcome you to paradise," he continued, spreading his arms out and glancing over his shoulder. "You were chosen from thousands of students across the nation to be a member of our academy—among the first, might I add, in hundreds of years to receive an education that rivals that of The Citadel Network of higher learning. Rest assured, all our career paths guarantee Authorized credentials upon completion. Care to take a look around?"

The man gave a quick nod, then turned to go back through the gates. A second later, he was walking through the door of a huge estate house. Inside, two hallways spread out in opposite directions, and a winding staircase disappeared into the top of the screen.

"Wow," Max said under his breath. "I've only seen places like that in old movies."

"This is our welcome wing, as we like to call it," Uri continued. "All the administrative offices are in this building, but if you'll follow me…" he added, curling a finger at the screen as he walked toward the huge bay window at the back of the room. "This is the pride and joy of campus. Six student dorm buildings, an archery field, not to mention two hundred acres of rolling forest, fields, and curated gardens, all nestled by the sea in the Caribbean. Quite a view, no?" Uri turned back to face us and smiled. "Please feel free to upload the included school information to your cloud so you can take your own virtual tour, and if you have any questions, my personal queue code is also included. If you decide to join us at Eden's Bluff, Halsey, please RSVP by midnight tomorrow, and we'll arrange for your complimentary transportation. I apologize for the narrow window, but given the timing of your school year's end, this was the soonest we could approach you with our offer. If you agree to join us at Eden's Bluff, we'd like to have all travel completed while the weather is ideal so you have a chance to acclimate before classes begin. Please take the virtual tour for details on what to pack, travel, and more. Welcome to paradise, Halsey. We hope to see you soon."

With another perfect smile, the transmission faded, and a small drive chip lay at the bottom of the box.

"I'll take the virtual tour first," my aunt said, immediately picking up the chip and pressing it to her temple as she crossed to the nearest chair.

"Looks promising." My Uncle Ray met my eyes. "Must cost a fortune, though."

"Actually, they gave me a full scholarship, room and board too," I added, still not quite sure why I wasn't jumping up and down in elation.

"It's completely *free*?" Ray asked, blinking a few times as if to clear his vision.

"That's what the letter I got said. Here…" I blinked to pull up the file, then blinked again to send it to his inbox. "I just sent it to your queue."

He blinked twice, and I waited while he read the 3-D projection of the letter I'd sent him. His gray brows gathered, then raised as he shook his head.

"I guess I don't have to worry about you working for some idiot in the valley," he said through a weak laugh.

"Ray, look at this place…" my aunt Alice crossed to us and handed the chip to my uncle so he could apparently take the virtual tour, then turned to me. "If you let these people know you're coming by midnight tomorrow, they'll have you there in twenty-four hours. *Twenty-four hours.* Now that's efficiency."

"But we just ended high school *today*," I said, surprised.

I thought I'd have more time, but I already knew I couldn't stay here anymore. Not with Jen sending thugs after me, and Eve *whoever* from Crisis Management either wanting to arrest me or deliver me to Jen herself.

"What's the problem?" my aunt asked. "It's just as fancy as The Citadel you insisted on applying to...even though it's just an oppressive governmental tool, designed to pigeonhole everyone on the wrong side of the wall, but I digress."

I didn't want to defend The Citadel so much as I wanted to defend my choice to apply there, but it didn't matter now. I couldn't argue that Eden's Bluff looked just as prestigious and legitimate as The Citadel, and from what I could tell, there was no reason not to be excited about the opportunity.

But I met Max's eyes and confirmed my stomach was turning for a reason. There were some things we needed to settle before I could make any promises to Eden's Bluff.

***

Max sat in the chair in my room, still not saying a word, and I couldn't take it anymore.

"I don't know what happened," I said abruptly, not meeting his eyes. "I don't know how I made that sound back at the school when those guys jumped out of the van." Max took the chip from Eden's Bluff off his temple, apparently having finished the virtual tour. I narrowed my eyes at him. "Were you just watching that Eden's Bluff thing?"

He sighed. "Vetting. I was vetting that Eden's Bluff thing," he answered with a weak smile, then pushed a hand through his shaggy blond hair when I raised an eyebrow at him. "OK, Halls, look, I figured if you knew what happened, you'd tell me, and if you didn't, then me asking a bunch of questions about it wasn't going to help anything."

I collapsed on my bed. "It had to be whatever Jen gave me, right? The hiccup enzyme or whatever she called it?" I asked the ceiling.

"I looked it up—*jicambi* is only supposed to do what she said, give your immune system a boost. It didn't say anything about making you sound like a velociraptor," Max said, and I could hear the laugh in his voice.

I debated telling him about what I'd seen happen to my hands—how my fingers looked like feathers for a second—but decided not to. It had to be some kind of stress-induced illusion because nothing had happened since. I didn't feel any different besides, and I didn't need him thinking I was seeing things now, too, because he'd just worry.

"Maybe it's a side effect, like it strengthens your voice or something along with everything else." I smiled, feeling much better about the rationalization the more I talked about it.

"Those guys Jen sent after you..." Max said, his voice full of warning. "I heard her yelling at them as they drove away. They'll be back, Halls."

"I don't think it's a coincidence that the officer who arrested her was just at my house either," I added. Max shook his head and flopped down next to me on my bed, both of us staring at the ceiling now.

He handed me the chip from Eden's Bluff. "At least this place puts The Citadel to shame. I mean, it's on its own island in The Caribbean. *Its own island.*"

I didn't know what to say, although my throat was still tight and my muscles tensed like I wanted to throttle someone. I sat up quickly and got to my feet, then moved to peek through my blinds.

"It seems too good to be true," I said, mostly to myself.

"Hey..." Max crossed to me and turned my shoulders toward him, lowering his eyes to mine. "You want to know what I think?"

"Do I have a choice?"

"No." Max chuckled. "I think you're trying to find something wrong because it's not The Citadel. That's been the only legitimate place in your opinion for so long, anything else seems, well, either not good enough or too good to be true. But Halls, this is what you've always wanted."

Again, he was right, but I still couldn't shake the feeling that this wasn't really happening.

"Something just doesn't seem right, Max. It's all too fast. How can they want an answer by tomorrow?"

"It's not exactly down the street, you know? And you heard that Uri guy. They want everyone to get there while the weather is nice so they can get acclimated. Though I think that was actually code for *please arrive before the hurricanes knock your plane out of the sky.*"

I laughed a little at that. He made sense, as always, and for a few minutes at least, I felt better.

"I guess I just don't like feeling forced down a path," I said, somewhat to myself. "I think you're right about Jen. She's not going to stop. And if she has some corrupt officer on her side now too…"

Max glanced up and nodded. "I didn't want to say it because I didn't want you to worry if you decided to stay here and take one of the internships, but…" he trailed off. We both knew there was only one option that made sense, as abrupt as it all seemed.

"Then this is it I guess." I blew out a breath as tears filled my eyes. "You're going to The Citadel, and I'm going to The Caribbean."

Chapter 11

It was 11:45, and the car was supposed to come at noon to take me to the airport. From there, it was only supposed to be a two-hour flight to Eden's Bluff, which seemed a little short to me for flying all the way to The Caribbean from Portland, Maine.

My aunt and uncle said their goodbyes before they went to work earlier this morning, and to their credit, they were sorry they couldn't wait with me for the car to arrive. Neither of them could afford to take a day off at this time of year with so many internship applicants just waiting to take their place. Anyone who didn't find a job would just become another scavenger south of The Valley where the Sweeper droids tended to be less prominent. I rolled my eyes at the thought since that was the very place they should have been the *most* prominent, but there was really no way to control that part of the city. The Citadel had forgotten about us for the most part, but especially them, and after so many years in the failed system, they were just as happy to be forgotten.

I shook loose from the tangled thoughts and glanced at Max, who was waiting for the car on the front porch with me. Neither one of us had said a word since he arrived, but I knew it wasn't because we didn't have anything to say. It was because we both had too much.

"We can always queue," Max finally said in a voice so quiet, I wasn't sure I'd heard him. "I don't start classes for a month, so I'll be around. I mean, I'd be around anyway, but I'm just saying..."

My throat felt tight, so I swallowed hard, refusing to turn into a teary mess right before I had to leave.

"For sure. You'll be the first one I queue," I said. Max pressed his lips into a closed smile and leaned forward in his chair, nodding at the ground. "I probably won't even be able to make it to the airport without pinging you." I tried to laugh.

He got to his feet and leaned over the railing. I crossed to him and leaned on my forearms st his side. The front yard was wild forest, save the dirt path that wound over the hill toward us. Any minute, a car would roll up, and that would be the end of everything so far. It would be the beginning of something new. Somewhere I've never been. And for the first time in as long as I could remember, Max wouldn't be there with me.

Tears came so fast they almost choked me. I sniffed reflexively, but it was too late to push them down.

"Hey..." Max said, his hand moving over my back. "Come here." I straightened, and he pulled me into a hug. His arms closed around me as I let the tears fall, though, it wasn't as if I had much of a choice. He took a deep breath and held it as his heart pounded against my cheek, and this broke the dam. He cleared his throat. "It's not forever. OK? Oh, and I have something for you."

I nodded against his chest, then pulled back to see the mess I'd made of his shirt with all my crying.

I gasped. "Sorry...geez." I swallowed hard and wiped my face, but he just laughed it off.

"I'll be right back." He trotted down my porch steps and around to the side of my house, returning with my walking stick a few minutes later. "I got Marvin to let me back in the school over the weekend. Not sure you can take this with you or anything, but I figured you'd want it..." he added, then pushed a smile to the side of his mouth.

"Yeah, I doubt they'll let me on the plane with that," I smiled. "Keep it for me? And thank you, Max." I crossed to him and fit myself under his arm in a side hug, and before either of us could say anything else, a long, black car with tinted windows rolled over the hill.

"Whoa," Max said as the car came to a stop and the driver got out to greet us. He was about our age and tall, even taller than Max by what seemed at least a few inches. His dark hair was pulled into a short ponytail, and his black t-shirt and jeans were form fitting. I caught myself staring at his form, in fact, and blinked a few times to snap myself out of the momentary trance.

"You must be Halsey?" he said in a semi-deep voice as he extended a hand to me. He flashed a shockingly white smile, the contrast all the more apparent against his tanned skin. His dark eyes twinkled as he approached. "And you're the boyfriend?" he asked with the same brilliant smile and a nod to Max.

"Um…" Max said around an abrupt chuckle. "No, just good friends," he added with a squeeze to my shoulder.

"All right, well, a friend of Halsey's is a friend of mine. I'm Leo Red-Cloud. It's my third year at Eden's Bluff," he said as he shook Max's hand, then turned to me. "Sorry if you were expecting Uri. He thought it would be more comfortable for you to have someone close to your age pick you up. Did you have a chance to watch the welcome message? Sorry, I know I just dropped it off yesterday."

"I did," I said, trying not to stare at him." It doesn't seem like that place could be real."

He flashed another wide, perfect smile. "Wait until you see it in person. Anyway, Sylvie is getting everything ready with the flight, so we can take you to her if you're ready." Leo gave me a nod, then reached for my bag. "Let me just put this in the trunk."

"*We?*" Max said, looking over at the car.

"Oh, Tia. She's driving," Leo said. "Tia, come out and say *hi.*"

A few seconds later, a strangely familiar woman, tan, like Leo, stepped out of the driver's side of the car and gave me a silent nod.

"Hello," I said, but Tia only smiled.

Leo gave me a wink and grinned. "She's a little shy. I'll just put your bag in the trunk, and we'll be off," he added, reaching again for my bag.

I thanked him, then turned to Max. His eyes were narrowed and his brows drawn together.

"What's wrong?" I asked, which seemed to break the consternation spell he was under.

His expression relaxed as he met my eyes. "Nothing," he shook his head and smiled. "You sure you got everything?"

"I think so. I found a welcome guide in the files that said not to pack too much since they had most things there already," I said, still feeling a little wary. It must have shown on my face because Max raised an eyebrow and leaned closer.

"You sure you're all right? You can always change your mind, you know? It's not too late."

I shook my head. "I'm OK. I think it just won't seem real until I'm there."

"All set?" Leo called, opening the back door for me.

"All right, then. Queue me when you get there. Or before. Just…whenever," Max said with a slow smile.

"I will. Same goes for you. I want to know everything about your Citadel orientation." He gave me one last bear hug, picking me up off my feet and squeezing me tightly before setting me back down.

"OK, go," he added, and I made my way to the car. Leo gave me another quick smile as I ducked in, and he closed the door behind me. I rolled down the window to wave at Max, his arms crossed over his chest as he gave me a wide, closed-lip smile. With a final nod, we pulled away from my house, down the dirt road, and finally, out of The Grind.

***

"Have you ever been to the islands, Halsey?" Leo asked as we boarded the plane. It was a private jet, so Tia just drove right up to the stairs of it, then gave the car keys to an attendant who got in and drove it back in the direction we'd just come from.

"No," I said, watching the car over my shoulder until it disappeared back into the shadows of the airport roads. "I've never been out of The Grind—*er*, Portland. Whoa…" I whispered as I reached the top of the last boarding step. Inside the plane, white recliners lined either side of the wide, open seating area, separated by an aisle down the center. Windows that were easily the size of the one in my bedroom back home ran the length of each wall.

"Choose any seat you like, Halsey," Leo said, holding a hand out for me to walk ahead of him. I got about three steps when a woman in a colorful floral dress stepped into the seating area. She seemed about ten years older than Leo and I were, maybe more, and I wondered if she were a teacher from Eden's Bluff. Her dark hair fell over her bronzed shoulders in several braids with beads at the ends, which made a chorus of pleasant clicking sounds as she walked toward me.

"It's lovely to meet ya, girl," the woman said, her accent thick and melodic. "My name is Sylvie, and back on da beach, dey gettin' yer room fixed as we speak." She smiled, the brightness every bit the wattage of Leo's. "De trip will take about tree hours. Tell me what questions ya have."

I'd had so many questions, but in that moment, I drew a blank on all but one. "Are we the only ones on the plane?" I asked, glancing out the window for what would surely be several other cars approaching.

"Jes' us, Tia, and her co-pilot." Sylvie beamed another broad smile at me, and I felt my expression shift to surprise that Tia wasn't just our driver, but the pilot too. "Yer de only one Eden's Bluff selected from dis area," Sylvie added.

"Wow…" I said, genuinely surprised. "I mean, why? I didn't get into The Citadel, and everything I saw said you're on the same level as they are."

Sylvie exchanged glances with Leo and laughed, a heavy, full sound.

"De Citadel is a fine institution, but der a little less so wit-out ya now, Miss Halsey Rhodes," she said, sobering. "We look for a little extra in prospective students. A little some-ting showin' yer wantin' to be more dan what everybody's tellin' ya is possible." Sylvie's dark eyes seemed to flash gold for a fraction of a second as we started to taxi. Sun shone through the large windows and streaked down her face and shoulders as she gave me a knowing smile.

"So you just looked at my records? My activities?" I asked, still not quite sure how, out of everyone in the Portland area, I was the only one they'd selected.

"A little of all those things," Leo said, typing something into a tablet he must have taken out of the bag in the seat next to him. "Eden's Bluff is a fairly new school, just four years old this fall, but they've developed an algorithm that identifies the traits they're looking for in prospective students." He turned the tablet to face the front of the plane, and a 3-D projection of the world map appeared. On it, white dots lit up in several countries, too many to quickly count, but I couldn't help but notice there was only one in Maine.

"Are all those *students*?" I hesitated to ask.

Leo nodded. "The ones they've selected so far, yes. The school is small, just about three thousand students so far, but it's growing," he added with a quick, knowing glance at Sylvie.

"Plenty of room to grow wit no dirty streets and shops clutterin' up da place," she said, which sent a chill through me.

"Wait, there's no town?" I asked. "It's just the school?" I tried to remember if they'd said anything about this in the virtual tour, but if they had, I *know* I would've remembered.

"I wasn't sure about that prospect at first either," Leo said with a laugh. "But honestly, at Eden's Bluff, there's no need for a town, Halsey," he said with another slow, brilliant smile. "It's paradise."

Chapter 12

We took a helicopter to the island, which wasn't even in sight of the mainland airport where we'd just landed. I'd never been in a helicopter, or a plane for that matter, so I was glued to the window this entire trip.

After about an hour more of blue sea and fog, which finally dissipated, the island appeared in the distance. As we flew closer, white beaches stretched out from dense, green forests and clearings until in the center of it all stood the multitiered structure from the virtual tour. It was even bigger than I imagined, with flocks of brilliantly colored birds soaring in the skies above it. I could actually smell all the flowers in the air before we even got out of the helicopter.

"Welcome to Eden's Bluff," Leo said, his voice loud and clear through the headset I was wearing. The ground grew closer as the helicopter set down in a clearing, and three men who looked like natives rushed to the perimeter. "When they recruited me a few years ago, I spent the whole time looking out the window too," he added. "I came from Reno, *The Ridge* —kind of like what you call The Grind—in Nevada. I couldn't believe the mountains could look so small." He chuckled.

"You have a Citadel wall there too?" I asked, a little embarrassed about the one we had in Portland until he all but choked on a laugh.

Leo raised his dark eyebrows. "I was surprised to see you only had Hover droids guarding it."

"Hover? We call them Sweeper droids," I said, which provoked another chuckle from him.

"What do they sweep?"

"Nothing," I answered, now chuckling too. "I mean, I guess because they scan everything. A person, a building, anything they're trying to read for information. They *sweep* for it, you know?" It was the first time I'd ever had to explain anything about a Sweeper droid to another person, so I didn't know when to stop talking.

"Makes sense," Leo finally said with a neutral smile. As soon as he turned back around, I rolled my eyes at myself, feeling the heat rush into my cheeks. Fortunately, the pilot turned off the engine a few seconds later, and I removed my headset after watching Sylvie and Leo do the same.

"Let's get ya settled," Sylvie said, extending a long arm full of bracelets as we made our way down the steps. One of the men darted in and came back out with my bag while the other two escorted us up to the enormous house, which looked a lot like an old southern plantation. In the distance, several more houses were scattered near the water, though they were smaller and simpler.

On the other side of an enormous, swirling iron gate, I counted at least eight columns supporting the roof of the wrap-around porch, raised several feet off the ground. Once through the gate, we followed the men escorting us up the driveway, then the steps. They opened the huge doors to reveal an elaborate staircase in the center of the room, and directly in front of it was a table with the biggest, most exotic collection of flowers I'd ever seen.

"Take her bag to Griffin Hall, room seven," a man said as he came into the room. His nearly white blond hair was startling until I recognized him as Uri from the virtual tour. He wasn't wearing the fancy suit he had on before, not even one like it. Instead, he wore a pastel blue polo shirt, which made his eyes of the same color seem to glow, and flowing white pants over sandals. The whole ensemble made him look more like someone from a vacation advertisement than the director of a prestigious school. But he turned to me and smiled, folding his hands in front of him. "Halsey, we are so happy to have you here," he said, beaming. "You must be hungry after your trip. Please, follow me."

We walked further into the foyer, winding around the back of the enormous white staircase to the dining room, which was full of even more exotic flowers and trays of colorful fruit, various greens, cheeses, and soups. A handful of attendants stood at the back of the room, all of them wearing the same light gray and white uniform shirts and shorts—all of them with the same tanned, but hollow-eyed expressions as Tia and the men who greeted us at the helicopter.

"I'll take you on a tour of the grounds later," Leo said as we washed our hands in an antique bowl. "Though some of the buildings won't open until classes start in a few days."

"A *few days*?" I blurted, surprised classes started so soon. I thought there would be time to get acclimated like the 3-D tour said. Not to mention, I hadn't even seen what official programs they offered here.

Uri chuckled. "Don't worry, Halsey. These aren't the program classes you might be expecting—you'll still need to decide that path," he said, and I sighed in relief. "The classes Leo is referring to are the honing classes, designed to help you acclimate. Some say it's the best part of the year." I must have given him a strange look because Uri chuckled again, but this time, so did everyone else. "Now, shall we eat?" He held out an arm, gesturing for everyone to have a seat at the table. "The soups are getting cold."

***

I barely knew where to start with the array of choices from the buffet.

"Try these," Leo said, spooning some dark, heart-shaped berries onto my plate. I also opted for a bowl of stew that smelled *nothing* like cabbage. He sat next to me while Sylvie and Uri sat across from us at the table. The number of attendants had nearly doubled in the time it had taken to get our food, but I wasn't sure why if it were just the four of us who were eating.

One of the attendants poured water into our glasses, and I immediately took a drink, not realizing how thirsty I was until I saw it sparkling in the glass. I was astonished at how unreal it tasted, which is to say, it tasted like nothing at all—and that was what made all the difference. In The Grind, the water always had a metallic taste that I'd apparently become accustomed to. This water made me look intently through the glass...the *perfectly* translucent glass.

"Comes from a spring right here on the island," Uri said, apparently noticing my fascination. I put down the glass quickly, a little embarrassed.

"I can tell," I said sheepishly. "The water in The Grind doesn't taste anything like this. What are these called?" I asked about the berries Leo put on my plate in the hopes of changing the subject.

"Hurricane berries," he answered with a small grin. "They're native to the island as well. Try one."

I did as he suggested and was shocked by the explosive flavor. It was tart, but also sweet, and nothing like I'd ever tasted.

"Why do they call these hurricane berries?" I asked, barely willing to stop chewing long enough to form the words.

"Because dey ripen at de beginnin' of hurricane season," Sylvie answered, and it took me a second to process what she said. *This, then, must have been the beginning of hurricane season, just like Max had mentioned.*

"Then storms are coming soon?" I asked, swallowing.

"We have a little time yet, and plenty of experience under our belts." Uri nodded, then seemed to study me again. *Why was everyone watching me?*

In the same second I registered their odd attention, my fingers and lips started to tingle, and my throat felt like it was starting to swell.

"I think…I'm allergic," I said, dropping the next berry I was about to put into my mouth. "My fingers are prickling, and my—" I stopped abruptly and clutched at my throat.

"All perfectly natural," Uri said, still beaming his megawatt smile at me as several of the attendants rushed toward me. "No, wait for the rest," he said to them.

I tried to respond, but my voice was crushed, and I was only able to emit a few gasping shrieks. Why wasn't anyone helping me? They were all just sitting at the table staring at me with stupid, patient smiles like I was over here just having a temper tantrum or something.

I tried to scream for help, but it came out as a deafening screech like when Jen's goons tried to drag me off back in The Grind.

"Oh! Maybe a hawk?" Sylvie said, pleasantly surprised at the sound I'd just made. I stared at her in disbelief until a searing pain ripped down either side of my back, making me fall out of my chair with the feeling of being yanked backward.

"I think bigger than a hawk," Uri said, leaning forward a little as Leo got to his feet. I stared at them, imploring, but they didn't move. Leo's dark brows furrowed as he crossed his arms over his chest, his jaw clenching. I tried to yell for help, but again, I only heard the ear piercing screech I'd made a second ago.

After a ripping sound and a final burst of pain that radiated down my spine, I was pushed forward, face first into the planked wooden floor. I landed on my hands and scrambled to push up to my knees, stopping in horror as I watched my fingers shifting again, my fingernails growing and curving as the rest of my hand was covered in…*feathers*.

I got to my feet only to fall backward, my center of gravity somehow having shifted like I was carrying a pack full of lead. It wasn't until I was on the ground again that I saw why. The shadow that loomed overhead made me scramble forward, as if instinctually trying to escape a predator.

But the predator was *me*.

Huge, dark brown, half-formed wings folded in around me, stretching out several feet in either direction once I took notice. All the breath left my lungs, and the air suddenly felt thin.

"*What…*" I breathed, and to my utter surprise, I actually heard my strangled voice.

"Eagle," Uri said. "Definitely an eagle. Marvelous. Sylph, then."

I shot him what I was sure must have been a crazed look because I was afraid to move, to speak, to do anything. I was paralyzed by the innumerable possibilities of what the hell was happening to me.

"Leo, give her da water," Sylvie said, prompting him to cross to me with a cylindrical glass bottle. He stopped several feet away from me and splashed the contents of the bottle over my head and face. The water cooled my skin, which up until now had felt like a fresh sunburn. The feathers I'd developed returned to fingers, and it felt like the weight had been lifted off my back several minutes later. When I turned to look over my shoulder, the enormous brown wings were gone.

"You're OK," Leo said, looking at me with an equal mix of pity and apology in his wide, brown eyes as he helped me up.

"*What—*?" I started again, but didn't have the chance to finish my question before Uri came from around the table and took my hands in his. I stumbled trying to move several steps back from everyone.

"There was really no good time to explain everything on the trip here," Leo offered, his expression still pained.

"What just happened?" I finally managed, my throat feeling raw and scratchy.

"The world isn't as you've come to know it, Halsey," Uri said gently. "At least, not for you. Not for anyone on this island. That's why we recruited you."

"What are you talking about?" I nearly yelled, but my throat was too dry and sore to push out the words with any force. Leo handed me the rest of the water in the bottle.

"Drink that," he said with a kind nod. I glared at him, but did as he said. The water was impossibly salty, and I nearly gagged, but in one swallow, the dry, swollen feeling was gone.

"That's seawater?" I glanced up at Leo again, who offered a small smile this time.

"It reverses the change. Makes it dormant again until, well, until you call it back."

"Call it *back*?" I asked, incredulous.

"You've undoubtedly heard of the virus known as Red Fever, haven't you, Halsey?" Uri asked, jerking my attention back to him.

I narrowed my eyes. "Yes, it makes people violent."

"Only those not of the blood." Uri smiled. "Elemental blood—Sylph, of the air, Salamander, of fire, Undine, of water, and Gnome, of the earth."

I looked at him for a long time, waiting for the words he'd strung together to make sense, but they never did.

I shook my head. "I need to know what just happened to me. What were those *wings*!?"

Uri arched a white-blond eyebrow. "It seems you have Sylph blood, Halsey."

Chapter 13

I glanced from Uri to Leo, then to Sylvie. They were all watching me with the same pitiful expressions on their faces, like I'd just missed winning the legacy lottery by a few numbers.

"Very soon you'll feel quite a bit better. In the meantime I know it's a lot to take in," Uri said. "But that's what the honing period is for—a week or so where you'll learn about not only your particular ancestry, but also about the bloodlines of your cousins."

"My *cousins*?"

"Well, not really your cousins, given how many times removed they are, of course, after all these centuries." He chuckled. "But in principle, the newly born Sylphs, Salamanders, Undines, and Gnomes are all descended from the four sisters—the Elemental Queens who preceded humanity here on Earth."

My head was spinning as I looked for the door. I turned to Leo. "Did you drug me? The wings, the way my hands turned into feathers, that was all a hallucination, wasn't it? The antidote was in the seawater? What did you—?"

Leo moved toward me, stepping in front of the others and blocking my view of them.

"I know it all sounds insane, Halsey," he said in a quiet voice. "Just take a walk with me. Let me just give you a tour of this place, and it will all have a chance to sink in, I promise. I went through the same thing—thought the *same* things two years ago."

"*What* was the drug in the food?" I said through my teeth.

"That's just what Hurricane berries do. They strengthen our physical states," Leo said. "It's all part of the honing—you'll learn to control it."

I glared at him. "You *knew* this would happen to me if I ate those berries? You *gave* them to me!"

He lowered his voice again. "They thought it would be better if you had your first transition here with support than in front of mixed company. This is the procedure for all new students," he said quietly, then turned back to Uri and Sylvie. "I'll take her to get settled. She's starting to fade," he added with a nod.

I just stared at him when he turned back to me, his dark brows drawn up, his jaw clenched again, his entire expression almost pleading, and I suddenly felt like I was losing all hope by the time we got into the corridor.

"It wasn't the medicine Jen gave me? It didn't cause the screech, or the running speed, or my hands?" I said to myself, staring at my fingers, which looked perfectly normal again.

"Jicambi can't do that, no," he said, which startled me.

"How did you know about that? You know Jen?" I asked.

Leo took a deep breath and sighed. "They work through several people when they're scouting for potential students."

"She tried to drag me into a van!"

"She is *not* one of their associates," he said, shaking his head. "They just keep tabs on her work like they do for all the medics and researchers looking for a Red Fever cure." Leo checked over his shoulder. "The virus has a catalytic effect on some people, Halsey. People like you, me, and the others on the island. It's why they created this school."

"Catalytic of *what*?" I asked, barely able to accept any of this.

"Like Uri said earlier, in people with Elemental ancestry, it reactivates the dormant genes."

"And in people who don't have the genes?" I asked.

Leo sighed. "The person who bit you had Red Fever, but not enough Elemental blood to shift like you did, Halsey," he said, watching me like he was just waiting for me to figure it out. "For people like that, catching on fire happens when the virus can't push the shift all the way. It gets stuck, kind of. Everyone else just shuts down after a while, their systems exhausted from trying to eradicate the virus."

"She *was* infected..." I finally whispered to myself as the pieces started fitting together. "She caught on fire because of it," I said, then quickly looked up at Leo. "And she *gave me* Red Fever? How many people have this kind of blood? Why is this just now happening if it's in our DNA?"

I pressed my back into the wall, trying to let it all sink in.

"I'm sorry, I don't have all the answers, Halsey." He sighed. "But as far as your bite wound, yes. Your body began transitioning at the cellular level the same day. Her's couldn't, and it just redlined with the effort after a little while."

It all started to make sense, at least, as much as such a thing could. If what Leo was saying was true, it would explain the rest of the physiological changes I'd been attributing to the jicambi bark enzyme.

"Come on, before they hear us. Any minute now, I'm sure you'll feel a lot better." Leo said. "I'll take you to your dorm, OK? It will help to meet Alita, your roommate. She just arrived last week, so it's all fresh for her too."

I wasn't sure what else to say since I didn't quite believe anything he'd just told me. I didn't even believe what I'd seen with my own eyes, but there didn't seem to be another explanation. I needed to talk with Max, to tell him what happened and get his opinion. If nothing else, I needed to let him know my plane hadn't been ripped out of they sky and plunged into the ocean, which we'd both joked about when we learned I'd be flying over the Bermuda triangle to get here.

"I need to let my family know I made it here," I said, hoping dropping the family card would hold more weight than just saying I needed to call my best friend.

Leo looked at me wide-eyed, as if I'd just started speaking in tongues or something. "Oh, well, Tia actually already sent a landing confirmation to your aunt and uncle, so you don't have to worry," he said, and my stomach sank. All right, there was another way to do this.

"Thanks," I said in the most pleasant tone I could muster. "I guess I should just get some sleep then. I'm suddenly really tired," I said, wanting nothing more than to get behind a closed door, away from him. I started walking faster.

"Hey, what's the rush?" Leo called up to me, almost laughing. "Slow down, you don't even know where you're going."

"I need to find a restroom," I said bluntly, not even caring what he might have thought about the urgency in my tone.

"OK, well that's right here," he said, and I immediately turned around. He cocked his head to the door on his right, toward which I made a B-line, and his face lit up again. "Halsey, your queue won't work here," he said softly. "It's the fog around the island. Nothing gets through."

"All right, thanks?" I said, trying to make it seem like I didn't know what he was talking about. The second I was behind the door, though, I touched my temple and scrolled for Max's queue number. I pressed it, and a wave of relief washed over me when I saw the spinning arrow and the word *connecting* appear in my field of vision.

But any hope I had of hearing Max's voice, of getting his opinion on this whole insane thing was dashed when the arrow stopped spinning, and the words *connection failed* appeared in its place.

My stomach sank again, but I took a deep breath and decided I'd try again outside, later tonight after my shadow was gone.

I crossed to the sink and washed my hands, the water feeling like soft fabric running over my skin. It was such an odd sensation I had to look down to make sure it was, in fact, water. I looked around for a dryer, but there wasn't anything like that on the wall, nor were there any towels to be found. How did they expect anyone to dry their hands here? I thought, but as soon as I turned the water off, my hands were immediately dry. I took several steps back from the sink, stopping only when I ran into the divider post of the stalls behind me. I caught my reflection in the mirror and gasped… My short blonde hair was now *purple.*

I pushed open the door and bolted into the corridor. Leo's face was calm, but I'd definitely caught him by surprise.

"Halsey, I told you your queue wouldn't—"

"Why is my hair purple now?" I asked, trying to bite back some of the fury that was surely the result of more than just my stupid hair color changing, but I was too exhausted to rein any of it in.

"I guess it *is* purple," he said, raising an eyebrow. "Though, I've never seen anyone be able to get a gradient like that."

"*Why* is it purple?"

Leo restrained a laugh. "It just happens sometimes after your first shift—eye colors change, hair colors…" His dark brows relaxed as he gave me a slow smile. "It looks good on you," he said, brushing a strand from my eyes. Heat rushed up my throat and into my cheeks, and small tingles started in my fingertips. I pulled back, immediately worried my fingers were shifting back into feathers, and that any second, searing pain would rip down either side of my back again. I looked at my hands, then over my shoulder, but there was nothing there. *Yet.*

"The wings?" I said breathlessly, clawing at the shoulder of my shirt and bringing it forward.

"Whoa, it's OK." Leo let himself laugh this time. "The seawater will suppress any shifts until it's out of your system tomorrow. But we do need to get you a new shirt," he added, nodding to my hand. I reached back and felt my skin through the two holes in my shirt and sighed. Leo looked over my shoulder in the direction we'd just come, then waved for me to follow him.

We went out a different door than the one we came in through at the front of the house, this one leading to a path lined with flowering bushes—the intoxicated, spicy-sweet smell almost too much to handle. The sun was low on the water in the distance, casting a strange glow over everything. It was all so beautiful I almost forgot about the gaping holes in the back of my shirt until I felt the cool breeze darting through them, sending a chill through me.

"This is the way to my dorm?" I asked, wrapping my arms around myself. Leo looked over his shoulder one more time, then nodded to me. He started to pull off his black T-shirt, and I immediately started shaking my head. "No, that's OK," I said. I mean, points for the gesture, but *eww*.

Leo laughed and shoved as much of the shirt into his pocket as he could, the muscles in his chest and arms catching every ray of the setting sun as they jumped.

"Don't panic, all right?" he said, holding out a hand to me. "Come with me."

Do not stare at his abs, I thought. ***Do not stare at—***

"It's OK," he insisted, interrupting my mantra. "I promise I won't hurt you." In the same second, two enormous, featherless black wings unfurled behind him. They looked like the wings of a bat or something —an unfathomably huge bat with armored plating. "Hold onto me, and we'll be at your building before you can ask me why I have wings like this." I shuddered again as my shirt billowed behind me, but I was pretty sure the prickle over my skin wasn't from the sudden breeze. I took his hand, and he pulled me closer. "Sorry, safety first," he said in a low voice, then pressed me against him, his arms folding around me as we rose into the air, the beating of his wings low and so palatable I felt it in my chest. The ground fell away as we rose higher, far above the trees and buildings. I clung to him, suddenly not sure this was the best idea now that the initial shock had worn off.

"Oh my god," I whispered, closing my eyes and turning into his shoulder.

Leo chuckled. "Hold on."

The next thing I felt was a *whoosh* of air, and then we were still. We were on the ground, at least it seemed we were. He released me, and I slowly opened my eyes to find him pulling his shirt from his pocket. His wings were gone.

"What just happened?" I said, afraid to move. His perfect, white smile peeled through the dim light as he put his shirt back on. "How did you do that?"

"Well, I've had a little more practice than you, Halsey," he said, arching a dark eyebrow.

"But your wings weren't like mine…" I trailed off, not even totally sure I hadn't somehow hallucinated mine, and I definitely wasn't sure how to describe his. I shook my head, opting for the obvious. "There were, um, no feathers."

He shook his head in agreement, letting his gaze sweep the ground for a second. "I'm a Salamander Elemental...*fire,*" he said, meeting my eyes again. "My physical shift is a dragon."

Chapter 14

"A dragon? They don't exist," I said flatly, though I didn't know why I wouldn't believe him. I'd just seen his wings with my own eyes.

"A lot of things aren't supposed to exist," he replied with the ghost of a grin. "That doesn't mean they don't."

We walked a few more steps before stopping at a huge, white-brick estate house, this one, two stories high with rows of long, narrow windows on each level.

"This can't be my dorm building," I said in disbelief.

Leo winked at me. "Don't worry. You'll move to a bigger one next year."

I smiled, but the insanity of everything that just happened the last hour prevented me from sharing his levity.

I glanced at the enormous house again, then back to him and shook my head. "Look, I'm not trying to be rude or anything, but I'm still not totally convinced all this isn't the result of major hallucinogenics in my system."

"I felt the same way," Leo said as we started walking toward the iron-framed door. "After my welcome dinner, I tried to queue home just like you did in the bathroom, even though Sylvie told me it wouldn't work—she was my mentor since there weren't really any upperclassmen then."

"What finally convinced you?"

"Meeting my roommate and hearing that he felt the same way—then hearing about his shift," Leo said, glancing at me. "It was a relief to know someone else had been going through the same weird stuff the week before arriving too, not to mention everything with the Hurricane berries." He stopped in front of the door and leaned against the frame, meeting my eyes with another slow smile and a shrug. "It helped not to feel alone." I didn't know what it was about the way he looked at me—like he was looking *for* something—but I couldn't think of anything to say in reply while I tried to figure it out. He sucked in a sudden breath after another few seconds and pushed a hand into his jeans pocket. "*Which is why* it's time to meet your roommate," he added, handing me a key. "Go ahead, that's your copy."

I turned the key in the door and pushed it open. Inside, the foyer was dimly lit and more modestly furnished than the main house where I imagined Uri must have lived. Two staircases wound down from the open second floor, which was lined with doors that seemed to wrap around to the back of the house.

"Are those the dorm rooms?" I asked, immediately feeling stupid because what else could they be?

"Most of them," Leo answered, leading us toward the polished wooden staircase on the left. "There are more on the main level in the East wing. The kitchen and library are in the West wing."

"How many people live here?" I asked just as two girls came out of a room and nearly ran into us.

One of them looked me up and down, raising an eyebrow at my hair. "You a unicorn shifter or something?" she asked, but she and her friend didn't slow down long enough for me to volley a comeback, even if I'd had one.

I *did*, however, risk a glance at Leo to see if there were such things as unicorn shifters, but he'd already closed his eyes in a long blink. I was admittedly a little disappointed.

"Magical mean girls—awesome," I said with a nod.

"That would be Anya. She arrived a few weeks ago." Leo shook his head. "And she wasn't nearly as mouthy when her skin hardened and her tail was flapping all over the dining room floor."

I gaped at him. "What?"

"They're both Water Fae Elementals—Undines." he said with a nod to the pair as they left the house. The confusion I felt must have registered on my face, because the corners of his mouth pulled up when he leaned a little closer and whispered. "*Mermaids.*"

I stared at him blankly for a few seconds, not quite sure if he was joking or not. He didn't say anything else about it, though, and I was honestly starting to feel too exhausted to ask.

"Of course. Mermaids. Why not?" I managed, nodding a few times before following Leo to a door with a bronze number seven fixed to the wall. There was no answer when he knocked, so he fished another key from his pocket and handed it to me. I didn't have a chance to put it in the lock before a girl with red hair came bounding up the stairs, dropping flowers from the enormous bundle in her arms. She backtracked a few steps to try to pick them up, but only wound up dropping more.

"I'll get those," Leo said, chuckling as he darted halfway down the steps to pick up the flowers that had fallen.

"Thanks. Hi. *Sorry*. Sorry I'm late," the girl said, her long red hair falling into her eyes. She tried to blow it clear, but somehow just managed to make more strands fall forward in the process. "Hold these, Leo. Um, please and thank you." She shoved the bundle of flowers into his arms and in the span of about five seconds, she twisted the length of her hair until it looked like rope, then wrapped it into a bun and pulled it into a knot. She picked up the flowers that had fallen, and grabbed the rest from Leo as she made her way up the stairs to me. I was out of breath just watching all that.

"Halsey, this is Alita," Leo called up to us. "Your roommate."

Alita pushed the flowers into my arms this time, but tucked in the ones that were falling out. "Oh!

These are for you," she said. "They sing. Not right now because they need water, but after that they'll sing, and I thought you'd like that because I would have liked that when I got here, but I didn't have a roommate yet who already knew about them," she rambled. "So, I got them. Oh, we can go in. Thanks, Leo. Bye!" Alita added as she pulled a key out of her pocket and quickly opened the door. I glanced down at Leo, whose dark brows were arched in surprise, his wide, brilliant smile beaming up at the door Alita had just disappeared through.

"Looks like you'll be in good hands now," he said, meeting my eyes one more time before he turned to go back down the steps.

"Wait!" I called down to him. He looked back at me over his shoulder expectantly, and my mouth suddenly went dry. "Thanks," I said, more quietly than I had intended.

He nodded and bowed just a little before taking another few steps, swiping up the last one of Alita's fallen flowers and smelling it as he made his way out the door.

***

I followed Alita into the room and closed the door behind me with my foot. The space was bigger than I expected it to be with a small, round table, four chairs, and two full beds, one on each side of the room. A side table and an old fashioned lamp sat along the wall next to each bed, the light filtering through the lampshades filling the room with an orange glow. The embroidered quilts on the beds looked thin, but I imagined it didn't get too cold here, and the stacked, white pillows nearly did me in. One look at them and I was overcome with exhaustion, despite the nonstop adrenaline rush since the helicopter landed. Or, maybe because of it.

"Here you go," Alita said, coming back into the room with a big, clear vase, which she set down on the small table.

"We have our own bathroom?" I asked, assuming that's where the water came from.

"Kind of?" she said, scrunching up her face like she wasn't quite sure. "It connects to the room across from us, but we can lock the doors, or they can, it just depends who gets in there first," she explained without taking a breath. "Here, put those in the water and listen."

She helped me put the flowers in the vase, and to my amazement, different sounds started filling the air like voices. I stepped back, surprised, because once all the flowers were in the water, it really did sound like an actual chorus singing in wordless harmony.

"How is that possible?" I asked, fascinated as I studied the strange shapes and colors—tubular yellow flowers with magenta rings around the edges, and smaller, teardrop shaped flowers that were the same color as a cloudless sky. "Do all the flowers sing on this island?"

"I don't know. But if so, they only do it when you pick them," Alita said, nearly vibrating with energy until she suddenly sobered. "But don't go picking stuff, especially to eat. Nothing that's just growing on a bush or something, whatever you do. Like, not even one berry out there."

"Why?"

"Because anything you eat that's not from the dining hall will make you shift into whatever you are, and you won't be able to ask for help because nobody can talk when they're shifted, and if you're a mermaid, then you're really in trouble because you can't walk, and—oh, hey, what are you?" Alita asked, stopping her barrage of words abruptly, as if the thought just occurred to her.

I shook my head to clear the dizzy feeling listening to her gave me. "Uh, an eagle, I think?" I answered, feeling ridiculous for even thinking it at all, let alone saying it out loud.

"Oooh," Alita said in a low, secret way that made me think an eagle was either really good or really bad.

"So, this is actually real?" I asked." It's not a hallucination, like from drugs they gave us?"

She laughed under her breath, the sound reminding me of tinkling shells. "I thought that too after they gave me those berries and I turned into a fox. *A fox*! And a week before I even knew about

Eden's Bluff, I started *growing a tail*. At least, that's what I saw. After a few minutes, it was gone. I thought I'd imagined it."

"That's *exactly* what happened to me. I thought my hands had turned into feathers." I said, relieved, then explained the unnatural speed and lung capacity I also experienced, the strange screeching sounds…and how I thought maybe I'd become Feral after Lauren had bitten me.

Alita's green eyes widened. "I was sure for like, an entire day I'd somehow contracted Red Fever too, but I hadn't been bitten or anything. Those *things* couldn't get behind The Citadel wall—did they not guard your wall?" she asked, but didn't stop talking long enough for me to answer. "Ours is guarded by live patrols, Tub droids, and an electric field, so it's not like anyone from The Swamp could have even come in and infect everyone. "She wrinkled her nose on the last sentence, and the blood in my veins suddenly felt like it dropped several degrees.

The Swamp. The Grind. It didn't make any difference, and the relief I'd felt just a second ago knowing she'd experienced nearly the same thing I had vanished, replaced by something hollow. Something angry.

We'd may have both left our cities, our worlds, our whole way of life. But *The Wall* had come with us.

Chapter 15

I'd minimized any further conversation with Alita last night by telling her I was tired from traveling all day and just wanted to take a shower, then go to sleep. Fortunately, it worked, and my biggest problem for the rest of the night was trying to decide if I could use the water from the sink as I brushed my teeth, or if it would give me a beak or something.

This morning was another story.

I found my bag and pulled out a bra and a pair of underwear, happy I'd brought them despite being told not to pack a bunch of stuff because there were no replacements here. Apparently everyone just went commando? I put on one of the white shirts in what was apparently my closet, as well as a black skort. It was definitely not my intention to look like I was a runaway server from a wedding, but these were my only options. Ten white shirts, ten black skorts. *Who even wore skorts anymore*?

Resigned that what I looked like today was not going to be high on my priority list, I pushed a hand through my *still* purple hair to keep it from falling in my face. For half-a-second I wished it were long like Alita's so I could just put it all in a braid and be done with it. I settled for pulling it back into a stubby ponytail and anxiously tapped open my queue when I heard the internal ping.

My excitement crashed and died a fiery death when I saw the message wasn't from Max. Uri had sent instructions for anyone who had arrived on the island within the last month to report to the dining hall for breakfast, and then go somewhere called *The Eastern Arena* an hour later. Fortunately, he included a mapping widget, and I blinked twice to start the download.

I wondered briefly if there were any students here who *didn't* have an ocular communication lens, and if not, how they were supposed to find where to go.

Alita gasped, startling me out of my pondering. "We're meeting in an *arena*?" she said, nearly breathless. "Nobody said anything about fighting in my welcome letter," she added, blinking away what was evidently her internal queue screen.

"They *still* haven't said anything about fighting," I reminded her. "Maybe there are just a lot of seats there. It says everyone who arrived within the last month needs to come, right?"

Alita's expression started to relax, then abruptly changed to wide-eyed excitement. "Wait until you try the waffles here," she said, not moving a muscle from the frozen state of bliss she'd adopted upon remembering that island waffles were a thing in this world.

Turn left in ten feet, the map widget said in my ear, making me nearly jump out of my skin since I'd forgotten about the download. I turned it off abruptly and just followed Alita to the dining hall, which she swore was just up ahead.

The island in the daylight was more like a living painting than anything else. The colors of all the plants were more saturated than normal plants, and the grass was thick and plush like expensive carpet. The manicured paths weren't bare dirt like the one back in the woods in The Grind. The one we were taking was covered in dense moss, which was a few shades lighter green than the grass. Every step felt springy under my feet, and I couldn't resist taking my shoes off just to feel it on my skin.

It felt like walking on carpet, at least, what I imagined walking on carpet would feel like. Living in the woods, floors were far less expensive to maintain, so that's what we had.

"What are you doing?" Alita said over her shoulder. She chuckled, but her bold, red eyebrows darted together in a look of judgement I knew well.

"It could be carpet," I answered, then remembered she was from the interior in Florida, and carpet was probably everywhere inside their Citadel wall. She would have no idea what this feeling was like.

She shrugged and turned around again just as a flock of huge, multicolored birds with long, white tails few overhead. I watched them glide gracefully across the sky until they disappeared over the treetops.

"Halsey, *what* are you doing?" Alita called to me, and to my surprise she was several yards ahead. I jogged to catch up to her, still surprised by how fast I could move now.

"Did you see those birds?" I asked. "The flock of colorful ones with the long tails?"

"They're seniors," she said matter-of-factly. I squinted at her. "No, really. Their physical shifts are birds of paradise. They fly overhead everyday to get to the dining hall."

She turned down another path, which was covered in cobblestone instead of moss, so I put my shoes back on and tried to make my brain accept the fact that those were *people* flying above me a few seconds ago. I remembered the feeling of the wings on my back from last night, heavy and cumbersome, and I had no idea how they could ever be used for flying. *Wait, could I actually fly*? I thought, feeling a little stupid that this hadn't occurred to me already.

A few minutes later we came upon a building that must have been the dining hall. It was simply structured, but not industrial looking at all. Instead of the cement and steel I was expecting, this building was made of whitewash brick like my dorm house with a terra-cotta roof.

Inside, normal looking students filtered through various lines, some featuring buffet bars and others with attendants dishing out selections. I scanned all the different bays in the vicinity of the foyer. They had every fruit I'd ever seen and several I never had, like bananas that were about as big as my thumb with vertical purple stripes.

"We don't have a card or anything. How do we pay?" I asked Alita, who was already a few steps ahead of me surveying our choices.

"You don't," she answered. "Just pick out what you want and sit down with it."

I couldn't do anything but blink at her for a few seconds. I knew my scholarship came with room and board, but I wasn't accustomed to anything being free. Ever. So I was surprised all over again. Apparently, everyone who was here also must have received a full-ride scholarship because Alita was right. There were no pay stations anywhere to be found.

The fruits and vegetables in the fresh bar I walked up to were mostly familiar, but they were much larger and much more richly colored than the ones I'd seen at Mr. Burke's grocery. The strawberries were the size of plums, and the plums were the size of oranges. I spooned a scoop of mixed fruit into a little bowl, nearly spilling it when Alita almost ran into me with her plate full of thick, blue waffles covered in what looked like strawberry pieces and whipped cream.

"These are not from Earth. I'm telling you," she said, completely straight-faced.

"Are they blueberry flavored or something?" I asked, studying her stack of electric blue Belgian style waffles.

"Something called figberry," Alita answered, shaking her head at her plate, seemingly in awe of her masterpiece. "I can't even explain the flavor. You'll just have to get some," she added, nodding to the baked goods bay just behind us.

"All right then." I said, about to turn and grab a plate when I saw Leo already watching me from the other side of the room. A table of others who were definitely *not* first-year students surrounded him, and my heart started pounding in my ears. I managed to return his smile with a weak one of my own, then quickly shifted my attention back to the bright blue waffles at the baked goods bar. I put a plate on my tray and added one of the waffles to it, trying to pretend that I couldn't feel his eyes burning holes into me like laser beams. *Just focus on the food,* I told myself. *Not his abs. Not his shoulders. And definitely not his eyes...which were staring at me right now. Carbohydrates. I needed to focus on carbohydrates.*

Every kind of pastry imaginable flanked the tray of waffles, their bright blue color outdone only by the various tubs of syrups directly in front of them. Brown, which I imagined must have been maple, but also chocolate, something called *Faya*, which was bright green with what looked like finely chopped nuts mixed in, and a golden syrup called *Mana*. I thought it might have been butterscotch until I stirred it with the spoon and swirls of red and orange appeared in the wake of the ladle. *Whoa.*

I had no idea what to choose, so I just opted for a little of the strawberry syrup Alita had on her waffles. I turned to ask her if she'd ever had the Faya or the Mana syrup, but she was already gone. I scanned the room for her, which was starting to get crowded, and after several seconds, I saw her waving me over to her table.

I only had time to blink before realizing it was also Leo's table, and he was still watching me.

Chapter 16

I took a deep breath and crossed quickly to the juice station, too nervous even to see what I'd poured. It was thick and yellow, thicker and lighter than orange juice, but at this point I didn't really care.

I started to make my way over to Alita, who finally stopped waving her hands in the air like some kind of red-headed windsock, and Leo got to his feet. *What was he doing*?

As I approached the table, he pulled out the closest empty chair for me, much to the surprise of the cat-like blonde sitting on the other side of him. Her electric green eyes looked me up and down a few times before she was able to manage the ghost of a smile. Her long hair was so shiny it almost seemed like a mirror as she flipped it off her shoulder and rested her pointy chin in her hand.

"Figberry waffle. Good choice." Leo smiled and gave me an approving nod. "Have a seat."

"Thanks," I said, a little embarrassed that literally every person at the table was now staring at me.

"We didn't have waffles like this in the Miami Citadel network," Alita said. "I mean, we had waffles, but just the normal color. We did have the strawberry syrup though," she added, then studied my plate. "Did you have strawberry syrup in your Citadel network in Portland, Halsey?"

I almost choked on the gulp of air I sucked in at her question. "Yeah, of course," I said, reasonably sure they had it behind The Citadel wall. I mean, if we had access to strawberries in The Grind—albeit not to any as big as the ones here—they had to have them there.

A smile pulled at the edge of Leo's mouth as he met my eyes again, and after a knowing look, he cleared his throat. "Halsey, this is Rhea," he said, gesturing to the mirror-haired cat-girl to his right. "This is Alec," he added with a nod to a very pale, blond guy who was shoveling food into his mouth like he was being timed. Leo held out a hand to another boy who was intently reading a tablet in front of him, barely picking at his food with the other hand. "And the professor reading the tablet there is Bryce," he said, waiting for the boy to look up from under a wing of black hair, which was bleached near the ends. The boy casually raised a fork and wagged it back-and-forth a few times, which I presumed meant *hello*. Leo chuckled.

"Nice to meet everyone," I said, quickly taking a drink of the juice on my tray. I startled a little, expecting orange juice flavor, but it tasted like peach and something tart that I couldn't identify.

"It's *mango*," Rhea said, staring through me without even blinking.

I startled again, surprised she'd been watching me, and shook my head. "Oh, I know. I just thought I'd grabbed orange juice," I added, which wasn't *totally* a lie.

Rhea raised a golden eyebrow before returning her attention to what looked like an omelette on her plate.

"So, you're a freshman like Alita?" Alec asked, then took a bite of the pastry he was holding.

I nodded. "We're roommates. I just got here yesterday."

Alec's face exploded in a wide smile as he cut a glance at Leo. "We heard…" he said. Leo rolled his eyes.

"What's your new little job title again? *Transportation* babysitter or something?" Rhea asked, squinting at Leo.

"*Transition assistant*, thank you very much," he answered. "And you're just jealous because you don't get to ride in private cars and jets."

"Why didn't *we* have that?" Alec asked. "They just put us on a boat. And by the way, for a place that gives out so many scholarships, somebody tell me where the funds for private cars and jets are coming from?" He looked around the table, but everyone just stared at him.

Leo shrugged. "Obviously, there are some donors now or something. Anyway, are we still going tonight?" he asked, then nudged Bryce, jostling his tablet.

"Going to what?" Alita asked around a mouthful of waffles as she leaned in.

Bryce finally looked up and pushed his bangs out of his eyes, the shade of gold so light it was almost yellow. I gasped.

"We're going to the cliff," he said absently to Alita, then shot a glare at me. "And before *you* ask, yes, I'm Chinese, and yes, I still have yellow eyes. Thank you, hurricane berries. Did you land here with purple hair, or are you a peacock or something?" I opened my mouth to respond, but nothing came out except half-words and squeaks.

"Mine just got darker red," Alita interjected.

Bryce shook his head impatiently. "A bluejay? What?" He pressed his lips into a flat smile, daring me to respond.

"Um, an Eagle," I finally said abruptly. He squinted at me, taking another look at my hair, but then he quickly shook his head again and held up his tablet screen to Leo. "So, you need to take off from the north end and fly south this time."

Alita nearly choked on her waffles. "Take off from a *cliff*?"

"He *flies*," Rhea groaned. "*Freshmen…*"

Alita raised her chin in protest. "But I *can't* fly."

"Then maybe you can just scurry around and look for some rodents to eat." Rhea gave Alita a sardonic smile.

"Says the Djin snake." Bryce chuckled, then turned his yellow-gold eyes back to Alita. "You don't have to fly to come with us. Not *everyone* here is Sylph or Salamander Fae."

"Which are you?" I blurted, wishing with every one of the *eternal* next few seconds that I hadn't. I cleared my throat. "I mean, if you're not Sylph or Salamander Fae... And *Fae*, isn't that like, Faeries?" I managed, then took another long gulp of mango juice.

"Faeries are the genus—the *family*, like Homo Sapien." He sighed, seemingly already exhausted by this discussion. "I'm *Gnome Elemental Fae*. My shift is a wolf," he added with an expression that seemed to dare me to laugh. "*Not* a werewolf. Those are Lycan and a completely different thing from us," he added, his tone now abrupt and biting.

"Uh, all right." I nodded slowly. It made sense that he shifted into a wolf. I could see it in his face—in his eyes, *of course*, and in his long, narrow nose. I wondered if I resembled an eagle in the same way and made a mental note to check a mirror later. Almost immediately, I felt compelled to roll my eyes at myself for the thought. *Was I really starting to believe all this?*

I turned to Alec, but didn't dare repeat the question to him. Fortunately, he answered it anyway.

"I'm an Undine—water Fae," he said without ceremony, then turned quickly to Bryce." And I will be a hundred percent useless to this mission, professor. Nothing but rocks on the southern end of the cliff. I can't navigate that in this body, and that seawater will burn off my shift just like everyone else's."

"Rhea or Leo will have to carry you out past the rocks so you can swim wide then. No one else can hold their breath as long or manage a rip current, which there will probably be, and we need to know if the tear is underwater," Bryce said.

Alita and I exchanged confused glances. "Tear in what?" she asked very loudly, which made all four of the others stop and stare at her in shock.

Rhea gathered her tray and stood in exasperation. "Leo, when you're done babysitting, let us know. See you all at the arena," she added to everyone else except Alita and me. She didn't so much as look at us.

"They just got here, Rhea," Leo said. "Been a little busy!" he called after her as she walked away, then sighed and met my eyes. "The tear is in the veil."

I tried to keep my expression neutral, but I had no idea what he was talking about.

"She doesn't know," Bryce said, putting his tablet on the table, then glancing at Alita. "Neither of them know."

"Neither did we until the end of our first week here," Leo chided, his voice quick and impatient as he got to his feet and collected his tray. "So they'll know by the end of the honing, just like we did."

***

Alita and I walked with Leo, Bryce, and Alec to the arena, which I very much hoped was chosen as our freshman class meeting spot because of what must be its ample seating, and *not* so we could participate in some kind of *battle royale* hazing ceremony.

My thoughts were racing about whatever Leo meant by *the veil* just now, and how they were going to try to find a tear in it, even *underwater*. There wasn't enough time to ask questions now, though. I didn't know where this arena was since I was just following the others, but we'd definitely already walked the ten minutes it was supposed to take to get there.

"Wait," I said, suddenly remembering that Leo, Rhea, Alec, and Bryce were all returning students, and this meeting was for anyone who had arrived within the last month.

I turned to Leo because we *did* have time to get an answer to this question. "Why are you going to this thing too? You've been here way longer than a month."

"Extra credit," Alec answered without hesitation. "They want camaraderie...moral support or something for you all. Tell you what, we didn't get any of *that* either," he added with a huff.

"Where are you from, Alec?" I asked.

"The Seattle network," he answered. "Had a swimming scholarship to The Pacific Northwest Citadel and everything."

"Wow, what made you come here instead?" Leo immediately winced and gave me a pained look. "What?" I asked quietly, but he just shook his head.

Alec laughed wryly. "Why did I come here…let me see," he started, his voice thick with sarcasm. "Because I was set up," he held up his hand and began counting off on his fingers. "And because of that, I lost my scholarship. And finally, did I mention *because I was set up*?"

Leo rolled her eyes. "Nobody *made* you take the supplements. That's on you."

"If they were only supplements…" Alec started, turning to walk backward to face us as he talked, "…they wouldn't have given me webbed fingers and toes, now would they?" he asked, wiggling his fingers and looking at me for the answer.

"Um, no," I said, not knowing what else to say with the intense way he was staring at me. "Wait, so you took a supplement and it made you change?"

"Yep. Got the letter for Eden's Bluff the same day I got my *rescinded offer* letter from The Citadel."

"Was the supplement in a vial?" I asked. "Red, blue, or yellow?"

Alec narrowed his gray eyes at me. "No, a blue syringe."

"And you?" I asked, turning to Leo. "Why did you come here? What made you start changing?"

He immediately looked uncomfortable and forced a laugh. "It's a long story," he said." Remind me and I'll tell you later. The arena is just up there."

And it was. A few hundred feet in the distance, a small stage with a lectern was set up in the middle of a combed sand circle. Bleachers full of people rose up all around, and I breathed a sigh of relief that apparently it *was* because of the seating that we were called here today.

"Shit, we need to hurry up," Alec said as Sylvie and Uri climbed the small set of stairs leading to the lectern.

"You're in my section—the green rows on the left," Bryce said to Alita. "Sit near the front so you don't have to navigate everyone to get your tie."

"My what?" she asked.

"Your—never mind. You'll see. Just sit close," Bryce repeated, then started jogging to catch up with Alec.

"Sorry, we have to be on the stage," Leo said to me, raising his dark brows in apology. "You're in the white section, dead center. Try to sit close," he added as he started jogging after the other two toward the stage. Alita and I exchanged confused looks.

"They're giving us *ties*?" she asked. "As in neck ties?"

"I have no idea, but I guess we're about to find out."

Chapter 17

Alita and I made our way to our assigned colored sections, and I started to feel a little self-conscious that out of the several hundred people who appeared to be lining the stands, I didn't see one other person with wild purple hair like I had. There were so many with the spectrum of red hair, ranging from intense, like Alita's, to a strawberry blond. The other spectrum ran jet black to white, even a mix of the two like Bryce, but no one had an unnatural color like I did.

I wished Leo were still close by so I could ask him why exactly that was, but he was already on the stage with Alec, Rhea, and Bryce.

"Thanks for coming everyone—just a reminder, to sit in the colored section designated by your transition assistant. Check your queue in-boxes if you have no idea what I'm talking about," Bryce said, pointing to his temple. I stifled a laugh.

After a few minutes of organized chaos, people finally settled into their sections, and Leo stepped up to the microphone, his black hair loose now and falling in shiny waves at his shoulders.

"Welcome to paradise, class of 2127!" he said, then flashed one of his million dollar smiles as everyone exploded in cheers.

"All right, first thing is first, my name is Leo Red-Cloud—" he said, which garnered another explosion of cheers. He laughed and waved his hands in an attempt to get everyone to quiet down. "If you're also a transition assistant, please stand," he added, and several students seated in the front rows all around the arena got to their feet. "These are your Gnome, Sylph, Undine, and Salamander mentors here at Eden's Bluff," Leo continued. "And they will be the ones distributing your colors today." He gave all the mentors a nod, and they each picked up a large shoulder bag from under their seat and began handing out differently colored striped neckties. *Wow, they really were giving us actual neckties.*

A very tall girl with long, silver hair and the same white shirt and black skort as mine approached the microphone next.

"Undines, we're house blue!" she shouted, flipping her own royal blue and black striped tie in the air as those mentors passed others out to the cheering students.

The Undine mentor made way for another girl, this one very tan with thick, dark brows and choppy brown rockstar hair. She was wearing the same style white shirt—though, tied around her tattooed midriff —and instead of a skort, she wore the black utility pants the boys wore. *How did she get pants? I wanted pants...*

"Hello, kitties," she said in a soft, teasing voice. The entire other side of the stands got to their feet and began hooting and cheering louder than the Undines and Leo's fans put together. After another few seconds, she gave the crowd a slow, easy smile and moved in closer to the microphone. "Those of you with Gnome blood will proudly represent...house *green*!" The entire side of the arena erupted in shouts and cheers again, led by the mentors passing out the green and black striped ties.

She stepped back and blew everyone a kiss, her arm flying high and wide to the crowd, which provoked yet another wave of deafening cheers. Next, a tall, lean boy seemed to glide from the group of representatives on the stage as he made his way toward the podium. His slim, T-frame build reminded me of Max, and I felt a pang in my chest at the thought of him. His reddish-blond hair flew loose in the breeze, along with the tails of his unbuttoned shirt, and when he spoke, I was surprised to hear a thick, Scottish accent.

"How do ye, Sylphs?" he asked, his voice rich and lyrical, which garnered cheers from everyone around me. At their response, he flashed a dimpled smile that rivaled Leo's. "Is that so? Weel then, lemme hear ye!" The cheers exploded again as people rose to their feet, and for the first time, it occurred to me that Leo was a *Salamander*, but also my transition mentor. Why wasn't I assigned a Sylph mentor? "Lads and lassies, will ye join me in representing house white?" he asked, throwing his arms back just as huge wings that ran the gradient from purple to yellow unfurled behind him, the same colors as the birds of paradise flying overhead this morning. His shirt floated overhead, landing a few rows up, and I couldn't hold onto the thought about Leo with the chaos that erupted around me—not to mention with the wave of white and black striped ties quickly washing up through the stands. I grabbed one and tied it in a loose shoelaces knot around my neck as I made my way to the end of my row, out of the way of all the flying elbows as everyone put on their colors.

"Oh, it's like that!" Leo said over the roaring students and held out a hand to the Sylph mentor. "Well, two can play at that game," he added, winking to the crowd as he unbuttoned his shirt, making *everyone* from all the sections cheer. A gust of wind kicked up and blew his black, wavy hair off his face and shoulders, which only made him smile. Every muscle in his chest, arms, and stomach flexed as he maneuvered out of his shirt and threw it into the crowd without looking. In seconds it was torn to shreds by people trying to grab it, which made the Sylph mentor shake his head and chuckle.

"Uri will have our hides." He laughed again and shook his head as Leo walked into the wind. He pulled something out from behind the podium, then turned to face the crowd.

"You might want to stand back," he said, waving away the Sylph mentor, who played along and exaggerated an eye roll. "OK, suit yourself." Leo shrugged and dropped his chin to put a red and black striped tie around his neck. As he did, his armored black wings expanded, stretching far beyond the edges of the pop-up stage in the sand. The Sylph mentor laughed as he was forced back down the steps in order to avoid being knocked off. When Leo looked up, he cinched the tie with glowing red eyes and smirked. "Salamander Fire Fae, welcome to house *red*."

Everyone, not just the Salamander block, cheered again, and I was sure my ears would be ringing for the remainder of the week. I stared at Leo, marveling at the ridges and curves of his wings in the daylight. The breeze that had been blowing on him before kicked up again, blowing his hair in every direction until he looked straight up and started moving his wings. The familiar, low thrum of it reverberated in my chest from several rows away, and in seconds he was in the air. Everyone gasped, then shouted again as he blew a cloud of fire over our heads, which quickly snapped out with a loud crack.

Everyone around me was going insane. One girl a few rows down got so excited she passed out and fell into the row ahead of her. Three of the others in the row quickly helped her to her feet, and by the time I looked back up at the stage, Leo had landed again.

The Sylph mentor returned to the stage as well, his hand raised as he approached. Leo's wings quickly folded in as he turned, receiving the high five, and then took a seat again with the rest of the upperclassmen mentors.

The aftershock of Leo's performance rippled through the stands until Uri, dressed in a white suit that almost seemed to glow in the sun, made his way behind the microphone. The commotion died down in under a minute in anticipation of what he was going to say.

"Well, it will certainly be difficult to follow that!" He grinned, earning a roll of laughter from the crowd. "But in all seriousness, the masterful displays you just witnessed are only a sampling of the miraculous transformations you will come to learn how to control in your time here at Eden's Bluff. They are gifts of your Bright Natures—the bloodlines of Sylph, Salamander, Undine, and Gnomes, The Elemental Fae who were the original inhabitants of this beautiful world." Uri paused for a wave of applause.

Sylvie approached the microphone dressed in a breezy green dress and brown sandals that laced in criss-crosses over her dark skin. She stopped at Uri's side and leaned closer to the podium to speak, the tinkling sound of the beads in her hair rapping against the lectern. A chill ran down my spine, but I wasn't sure why.

"Dis week, my children, we begin da honing process," she said, her hypnotic, tropical accent rolling off her tongue like the waves breaking on the shore. "Several of de faces ya seen here today will be part of yer schooling. Some ya haven't met yet, but when yer ready, da career programs dat'll show ya how to make da world a better place will be waitin' fer ya. And togedda, my loves, we gonna fix every-ting."

Chapter 18

We were introduced to the teaching staff for the remainder of the presentation, but I couldn't focus on anything they said after Sylvie spoke. The clouds overhead had started to darken and roll in the distance, so I attributed my sense of unease to the looming storm.

The air was still charged as we all made our way to the respective honing areas they told us to find. Mine was at the top of a stupidly high cliff, which I didn't quite understand with a storm brewing in the distance. But I didn't get paid to make these decisions. The surf was breaking hundreds of yards below, and I wondered if this was the cliff we were supposed to meet at tonight.

I didn't notice anyone as we all walked, so when someone off my shoulder started talking to me, I jumped right out of my meandering thoughts.

"Tried yer wings yet?" the Sylph mentor from the stage said, his Scottish accent warm and comforting. Now that he wasn't several yards away, I could see a smattering of freckles over his nose as well. His piercing blue eyes twinkled as he smiled widely at me

"Ah, no—no test flights yet for me," I said without hesitation. "And from the look of that drop, I hope you're not taking us up here for a maiden voyage."

He laughed and jogged a few steps to catch up to me. At my side, he was about the same height as Max, and his kind eyes only reminded me of him that much more. I *had* to get my queue to connect somehow.

"Dinnae fash. All ye birdies are still too wee to be tossed outta the nest like that." He gave me an easy smile, then offered his hand. "Ma name's Ian."

"I'm Halsey."

"A pleasure," Ian said with a nod.

"Can I ask you a question?"

He winked conspiratorially, which made his clear blue eyes seem to sparkle even more. "Fire away."

"Well, this is awkward maybe, but do you know why Leo Red-Cloud was my transition mentor even though I'm not a Salamander? I mean, shouldn't it have been a Sylph mentor if I'm supposed to be a Sylph?"

Ian's ruddy brows drew together. "Reckon wires must've crossed somehow once ye hit the radar."

His words were like an abrupt punch in the stomach, and I stopped walking. "Wait, what?"

He looked at me, surprised. "Yer assignment— which bloodline ye belong to. *Wires...*"

"No, I mean about the radar," I spluttered, remembering what the officer from The Grind, *Eve somebody*, had shouted to me as Max and I ran from Jen's exam room.

"Oh..." Ian chuckled low in his throat. "That's somethin' tae do wi' us sensing our own kind," he said, pausing for a second to study my face. "Speakin' of—what's yer shift, if ye dinnae mind? Mine's that ridiculous pelican flying to breakfast ahead of the crowd each morning—well, one o'em anyway."

"Oh, yeah…I saw you!" I managed, trying to get my bearings again. "My roommate said you're a bird of paradise?"

"Guilty." Ian nodded to the ground and slipped his hands into his pockets. "And you then?"

"Uri said my shift is an eagle."

He nodded slowly. "Weel, I s'pose we'll get tae see soon enough."

We started to approach the rest of the group, but another unsettling feeling came over me. Ian hadn't said he didn't believe me, but it was clear he didn't with the vibe between us cooling just like the breeze coming off the ocean.

"You don't think I shift to an eagle?" I asked, hesitantly.

Ian laughed out loud this time. "And why wouldn't I?" He smiled broadly at me, but it didn't reach his eyes this time. He *didn't* believe me, and he also didn't answer my questions. "Twas good tae meet ye, lass. I best get tae ma perch." He winked again, the sparkle in his eyes having changed to something knowing, something guarded, which I didn't understand.

He crossed to stand next to a woman with cascading waves of blonde hair that were blowing all around behind her, along with her light blue, flowing sun dress. Her angular face and wide eyes were kind, almost maternal, though at the most, she couldn't have been more than ten years older than the rest of us. As I approached, she held my gaze a few seconds longer than a wordless greeting would have normally been, and again, I had the feeling that I was being evaluated somehow.

The woman finally looked away and smiled kindly to the rest of the group as we all took seats on the rocks surrounding her.

"Welcome, to your first honing session," she said, folding her hands in front of her. "My name is Midori, and with the help of your transition assistants," she added with a gesture behind her to the mixed group of upperclassmen sitting with Ian, "we'll begin."

Midori went on to explain that before humans, the earth was populated by beings called *The Elemental Fae*: Sylphs, who governed the air, Salamanders who routed the sunshine and sparked the fires, Undines, who engineered the seas and rivers, and Gnomes, who tended everything on land. Uri had mentioned as much to me when I arrived, but Midori elaborated.

The Undines were responsible for connecting and directing all the water in the world so that it flowed in a consistent cycle. The Sylphs brought the water into the sky and changed it into rain to support all the plants and animals, and the Salamanders were in charge of making sure the fire at the center of the earth and in the sky never went out.

Midori went on to explain how this system evolved over thousands of years, and eventually, The Elementals became so efficient at helping each other, the Creator of All Things asked the Gnome Queen, *Ghob,* to grow a beautiful Garden.

Save for a few giggles from the crowd at the queen's odd name, Midori explained how Ghob called up fruit bearing trees, vegetable vines, and flowers in every imaginable color. She asked her sister Necksa, the Queen of the Undines, to route streams and waterfalls through The Garden, and her sister was happy to help. Her other sisters, Paralda, the Sylph queen, made sure the water from the evaporated sea fell from the sky, and Djin, the Salamander queen made sure the sun shone and the weather was always warm.

"And all was well when The Creator of All Things brought forth Adam and Eve from The Garden," Midori said in an inspired tone. At this, several people started whispering their surprise that the pair had actually existed. This made me roll my eyes. We'd just witnessed two people literally sprout wings and breathe fire, and *Adam and Eve* was hard concept to swallow? "The Creator of All Things adored the new humans," Midori added. "And because The Elemental Fae lived in such harmony, they were asked to help the humans—to teach them and protect them. But the Gnome queen quickly saw that all things began to revolve around the humans," she went on, her voice growing more ominous. "The Creator had given Adam and Eve permission to kill and eat the animals, which was unthinkable to Ghob. They cut down the trees she had made, burned the wood and cooked the flesh of the animals they'd killed with the fire the Salamander queen was ordered to provide."

"Why didn't they just stop helping them?" a girl several yards from me asked.

"That's exactly what Ghob asked Necksa, the queen of the Undines, to do. *Dry up the streams and stop the waterfalls*, Ghob had asked her sister. *We are enslaved and must break our chains.* Necksa agreed to stop delivering water to the Garden in solidarity with her sister, but when The Creator of All Things learned of their plotting, he banished Ghob and all the Gnomes from the Garden they'd created. He permanently returned the Undines to the sea, and worst of all, those who were still on land working to remove the remaining brooks and ponds from the Garden were stranded on two legs, never again to return to their lives under the ocean."

Midori heaved a heavy sigh and finished the story by explaining that the Sylph queen and the Salamander queen were so heartbroken for their sisters that they sneaked Ghob back into the Garden after Adam dropped the forbidden fruit. She took it and created an exact replica of the Garden from the seed—the island we were standing on now.

"Wait, so this is The Garden of Eden 2.0?" a silver-haired boy near me asked through a laugh. A few others also laughed, but everyone waited for the answer.

Midori smiled gently and nodded. "Our school is named for this cliff—*Eden's Bluff*. The double meaning is ironic, no?"

Everyone began to chatter, and I'd likely have done the same if there would have been anyone familiar nearby. This island was an exact copy of the *actual* Garden of Eden? But then a thought crossed my mind.

"What happened to the original Garden?" I asked. The chatter died down immediately, and Midori met my eyes, and for the second time, the air seemed to chill between us.

"Djin, the Salamander queen was ordered by The Creator to bring forth great gates from the molted iron deep in the earth, and an archangel with a flaming sword was posted as a sentinel. The humans, the Gnomes, and the Undines were forbidden ever to enter again." Midori didn't look away after answering my question, even though several others resorted to raising their hands to get her attention.

Finally, another girl just spoke up. "So, where is the real Garden now?"

At this, Midori finally looked away from me, a gentle smile blooming on her face as she found the source of the question. "It lies somewhere behind the veil—the divider between this plane and the next," she said, now looking around at everyone. "All Sylphs and Salamanders who were on this side of the veil when the Gnomes and the Undines were banished from The Garden were given something of a dual citizenship. They were allowed to pass between worlds—the physical and the ethereal. All other Elemental Fae were trapped behind the veil in their Bright Spirit form, as things can only be on the other side."

"So *we* can't go to the other side?" I asked, trying to figure out why Leo and the others were so bent on finding the tear in the veil somewhere up here tonight.

"The Blood has been diluted over the millennia… mixed with that of humans, and until the Red Fever catalyst, we weren't even able to access our physical shift forms or our Bright Spirits," Midori started, her gray gaze again filling me with a sense of vastness— of an emptiness that sent a shiver through me. "The influx of Elemental blood on this plane has torn parts of the veil all over the world. It is our hope that through training you at Eden's Bluff in the ways of your ancestors, you will become a new generation of Elemental Fae, capable of helping mankind heal *this* world." Midori's voice was melodic like someone reading a bedtime story, and I felt a sense of calm fall over everyone when she finished talking. That is, it fell over everyone except me because she hadn't actually answered my question about if we could pass through the veil to where the rest of the Elemental Fae apparently were, and from the way she just stared at me, unblinking, she seemed to know it too.

Chapter 19

I knew I wouldn't make it back to the dining hall in time for lunch because I didn't want to follow the rest of the Sylphs. It wasn't that there was anything nefarious about them, but the feeling that they didn't think I belonged with them was all too palpable.

Instead, I sat near the edge of the cliff and watched the storm gathering over the ocean. I wondered if it were one of the hurricanes that was supposed to start hitting the islands soon, and if so, why no one had said anything about it yet. I hadn't even been here two full days, but I had the sense there weren't really any rules except a few absolute ones like don't eat anything that's not from the dining hall. I was really starting to hate that rule as I looked around at the strange, beautiful fruits hanging on nearly every tree in sight. Skinny, bean-like, purple fruits and bunches of shimmery, golden berries that looked like grapes were both within arm's reach, and my stomach had started to growl.

I got to my feet before I was tempted beyond my willpower to try them, remembering what Alita had said about potentially being stranded out here as an eagle. Though I had to wonder if that would be so bad? I could always fly back to the main house, couldn't I? And there had to be some way to un-shift, at least partially, as I'd seen both Ian and Leo do this morning.

I looked at the shimmering berries that cropped up in front of some of the larger rocks facing the horizon, but the visceral, drumming sound in the distance pulled my attention away. Something was flying in the distance, diving, then rising again in a huge, looping arc.

My heart pounded in my ears, the same sense of panic flooding my bloodstream as when I saw the shadow of my own wings overhead—an imminent predator just waiting to snatch me up and swallow me whole.

Tingles pricked my shoulder blades and ran down my arms to my fingertips. The same feeling made its way to my lips as I tried to focus on the ominous, dark mass getting closer to land with every pass. Almost immediately, my vision sharpened, and the creature closing in wasn't a freakishly large bird as I started to suspect. The huge, black wings raised and lowered slowly, effortlessly, carrying the creature whose neck was nearly as long as its tail, and I quickly made my way into the thick brush to my left.

In what seemed like just a handful of seconds, a deafening *whoosh* rippled through the air, followed by a thunderous sound when the creature actually landed. The impact felt like a small earthquake under my feet, and I gripped the tree I was hiding behind so I wouldn't be thrown to the ground.

The creature's scales shimmered in the sun, partially blinding me with every step. Whatever it was, it sounded like an enormous horse snorting and forcefully exhaling in short gusts that shook the branches all around me. Different kinds of fruit rained down on me from overhead, driving me out of my hiding place. I stumbled over the collection of them underfoot and landed in the clearing.

Scrambling to my feet, I desperately tried to cover my eyes from the glare shooting in every direction in front of me, but I just wound up tripping and falling again over the fruit on the ground. The glare finally started to dissipate, and when I could finally open my eyes, Leo was crouched in front of me wearing *nothing* at all. His huge, black wings slowly began disappearing behind his back, and his horns carefully receded into his forehead. In seconds, there was no trace of his dragon at all.

I gripped the grass and branches all around me, pulling myself to my feet only to stumble over yet more fruit on the ground. I didn't fall again, but only because a boulder just behind me was close enough to catch and then steady myself. I moved behind it, and Leo met my eyes.

"Well, this is awkward," he said, quickly covering his more decorative parts as he flashed a genuine smile at me. Every muscle in his body tensed, keeping him fixed in his stance. "Could you throw me my pants?" He nodded to the boulder just to my right, a pile of clothes folded neatly on top of it.

"Um, yes. Yes, I can do that," I said too quickly and tried not to trip again as I grabbed the stack of clothes and brought it over to him, keeping my eyes on the ground the whole way there and back to my boulder. After a second, I risked a glance to see if he was done getting dressed, but he'd only managed to put on underwear that looked like biking shorts. He'd turned around to face the horizon, and I watched the columns of muscle shift in his back and legs as he stepped into his dark cargo pants. After another few seconds, he turned back toward me and walked with such purpose, I had to fight the instinct to run. Heat pushed through my chest as he got closer, the hard curves of his stomach, his chest, and shoulders shifting and rolling with each step. He pulled an elastic from the pocket of his pants and raised his arms to tie his dark hair back, which made his biceps jump. I was frozen where I stood.

He stopped abruptly and smiled at me, then stepped into his sandals at the foot of the boulder. He pulled his shirt on and started to button it up, offering me an arm when he finished.

"I promise I won't bite," he said. "Despite the rows of enormous razor teeth I'm sure you just saw."

I hadn't, in fact, seen any rows of razor teeth, and suddenly knowing he had such things didn't do much for my current levels of anxiety, nor for…whatever else this feeling was. I wanted to run as fast as I could in the other direction only slightly less than I felt compelled to stay with him. To get and stay as close as I could to him.

"So, that was your dragon," I said stupidly, which made him laugh.

"You'll see this for yourself soon enough, but if you go awhile without fully shifting, it starts to make you restless," he said, glancing over at me. "It's almost like the animal inside is trying to get out."

"I've felt like that a few times in the last week or so," I said. "It's been a little worse since yesterday— since the hurricane berries."

Leo nodded, pushing his hands into his pockets and raising his shoulders against the cold breeze coming off the ocean.

"It'll get worse now that your eagle is awake in there," he said, the concept of an actual eagle living inside my body sending a jolt of fear through me. "It's all right, though," Leo continued, chuckling a little." It's just another part of you, that's all. The sooner you accept that, the easier shifting back and forth will be."

I looked up at him, suddenly not as anxious. "How did you know it bothered me when you said that? About the eagle living inside me?"

He looked up and scanned the hillside in the distance, then gave me a side-smile." I don't know, I just felt it I guess. Like, the temperature around you just changed, if that makes sense."

It made more sense than he knew. Or maybe he *did* know? I wasn't sure if the sense of comfort I had around him was because he was the only other student on this island who knew I didn't come from the interior wall of my city—that I came from the outside, from The Grind, just like he'd come from The Ridge. Or at least, that's what he'd told me, and I didn't know why anyone would confess a thing like that when they had the chance to start fresh with new people.

I'd only known Leo a few days, but the pull I felt to him was the opposite feeling I'd had with the Sylphs. With people who were supposed to be just like me. I couldn't even get past the initial stranger-awkwardness with them to find out where they were from…if they'd come from outside the walls of their own cities too. We never even had a chance to find out if we were alike or not, and it struck me that this was the same feeling I had back at Portland Prep. A distance of some kind that kept me back, apart from everyone else there except for Max.

"I didn't feel right today with the Sylphs," I confessed." I don't think they believed that I was a Sylph."

Leo's brows drew together. "What makes you think that?" he asked as a flash of lighting ripped across the sky, and seconds later, thunder cracked in the distance.

"I don't know, it's just how I felt around Ian and Midori. And being around the other Sylphs felt like a blank feed channel, all static and noise. Not actual noise, just the feeling you'd get if there *were* too much of it, you know?"

Leo nodded and smiled widely. "I do," he answered. "Spent my first year here feeling that way, but being able to help other people transition has helped a lot."

"Why is that?"

"It just undoes the knots I guess—whatever they are from day to day." He slowed our pace as we approached the dining hall, which came into view in the distance at the bottom of the hill.

"I know what you mean. I want to be able to help people too—help them solve their problems."

"How so?" he asked.

"I want to be a psychologist," I answered. "After taking the intro in high school, I just kept taking independent study classes with the teacher so I could learn everything I could."

Leo smiled just a little. "No wonder you're already in my head," he said, and I wasn't sure if he meant what it *seemed* like he meant, or if he was just trying to make a joke. "Anyway, sounds like you're probably halfway to being an expert already."

"Not even close," I chuckled. "But I like puzzles, and that's all problems are. You can't always change your circumstances, but you can change your perception of them with the right arrangements in your head. Feels like the same thing then, I guess."

Leo looked at me like he was trying to decide something, then seemed to come to a conclusion after a few seconds.

"You're shift may be a Sylph, Halsey, but there's a fire inside you."

I smiled awkwardly at the combination of the look he was giving me and the intensity of his words.

"Thanks," I managed, which sounded pitifully inadequate the second I said it. My mind completely blanked after that, and heat filled my chest, rushed into my cheeks, and made it that much harder to think. I opened my mouth, hoping something would come to me, but I didn't have the chance before Leo's fingers brushed my cheek. They moved slowly into my hair, and as he took a step toward me, he brought his other hand to the back of my head.

When he moved his hands back into view, he was holding two pieces of plants that looked like bright green, unwound twine.

"Ripple Moss," he said, twirling the pieces in his fingers. "Must have fallen from one of the trees somewhere on the walk back."

"Oh..." I said, a little relieved and a little disappointed. Prickles ran over every inch of my skin and I felt my body stiffen with the fear that wings and feathers would appear again right now, at *the worst* possible time.

I took a deep breath to steady myself, the smell of him rich and comforting like a campfire. I smiled to myself because *of course* he smelled like a campfire. I took in another deep breath, the warm scent of him chasing away the last of the prickling sensations I'd felt.

"What's that look?" he asked, a smile lacing his voice.

"Nothing," I said, shaking my head. "Um, OK, that's a lie." I laughed. "I just panicked a little for a second because everything started to prickle like it did after I ate the hurricane berries, and I was worried about…well, shifting again."

I took a step back, feeling awkward and embarrassed. *Why* did I even say anything?

"You don't have to worry about that," Leo laughed a little. "It can be controlled with some practice. You just have to find a way to connect with it," he said taking another step toward me to close the distance I'd just created. "Otherwise, the build-up will just gatecrash you."

I started to reply, trying to keep my voice steady, but he was so close to me that I could feel the heat radiating from him. "H-how do you connect with a tidal wave like that?" I swallowed, then took another breath as I stepped back again before I completely lost my composure.

"It's funny you put it that way," he said, clearing his throat. "When it first started for me, when I first started feeling the fire building, I'd lose control because I'd try to fight it. It just took me over until I got here, and by watching the ocean, I realized it was more like water than fire. It built the same, like a swell that comes on gradually until suddenly it's just on top of you." He shook his head and turned to face the ocean beyond the edge of the cliff. "So I decided that you just can't fight a tidal wave. You can only watch it coming, and then find a way to ride it."

Chapter 20

Leo and I walked down the hill and through the orchard on our way to the dining hall, and I didn't ask him anything else about what he meant when he said he'd *always lose control*. But I hoped he would tell me.

The dining hall was buzzing with even more people than there were this morning at breakfast. I scanned the faces for Alita, or better said, I scanned for her bright red hair. She was sitting at the same table we were at for breakfast, along with Alec, Bryce, and Rhea, none of whom I'd seen since we all went our separate ways for the welcome assembly. I wondered if Alita's first honing class was like mine—if her Gnome teacher had told her the same story about how their queen got them all kicked out of The Garden of Eden.

"Well, well, well," Rhea said as Leo and I approached the table. She shook her head and looked us up and down. "And where have you two been all afternoon?" she asked, raising an eyebrow. "*Somebody* missed third year Fire and Flight Prep."

"I think I showed everybody this morning that I don't need that class," Leo said, returning her taunting tone.

Everyone else at the table whistled low, stopping only when Rhea stared daggers at them. She eventually laughed it off and turned to me with a wink. "Just because he's an expert at bagging new blood he thinks he's an expert at everything."

Alita immediately sucked in a breath and covered her mouth, her green eyes suddenly wide as she jerked her attention to me.

"No way…" she gasped, risking a quick glance at Leo.

Both Alec and Bryce gave each other knowing grins, then Alec slapped him on the back in some kind of congratulations.

"Uh, no guys…" Leo started with a raised hand, but I cut him off, furious.

"Are you actually kidding me? I've known him two days," I said, consciously having to control my volume.

"*That* long? Wow…" Rhea said, mocking me with feigned surprise. "He must be thinking about proposing then." She laughed low in her throat until Leo picked a grape from Bryce's plate and tossed it at her. He laughed out loud when it went down the front of her shirt, and just that fast, the tension in the air was broken.

"OK, so seriously did you and Leo—" Alita leaned in and whispered to me as I took a seat.
"No!" I said loudly. Too loudly for as close as she was to me, and she visibly jumped.

The whole table laughed even harder as she looked at me in shocked amazement. "OK, OK, all you had to do was *say* so."

"I *did* say so...about ten seconds ago. You just—oh my god, never mind," I said, fighting to keep from calling her out for being so vapid. It's a good thing she had a Citadel wall to protect her from the real world her whole life.

Leo must have seen me fuming because he quickly interjected. "Let's get a plate," he said, brushing his hand over my shoulder as he stood. Surprised looks ricocheted around the table, and heat rushed through me all over again.

"Great idea," I said, glaring at everyone as I turned to head to the pasta bay, which was on the other side of the dining hall. Leo walked with me and handed me a plate once we arrived.

"Sorry about them," he said, spooning ravioli into a bowl. "Rhea can be...*petty*."

And there it was, the secret key that unlocked Rhea's apparent problem with me since I met her this morning. They had history.

"How long have you two been broken up?" I asked, scooping spaghetti with the pronged ladle.

"*What*? No," he shook his head adamantly. "No, we've never been a thing."

"Well, she probably wants to be a thing in that case," I said, my stomach in knots about how to make this all go away because it was only my second day here. Rhea obviously had issues with me, and they were the *instant-onset* variety, so there was probably very little, if anything, I could do about them. I moved to the other side of Leo and put some steamed broccoli in a bowl.

"I don't think jealousy is her problem, but I'll have a talk with her and find out what is," he said, adding a roll to his plate. "She shouldn't have set you up for all that back there, whatever her motivation was."

"You don't have to do that," I answered too quickly. "I mean, thanks, but I can fight my own battles. Almost every girl I've ever known has been like her. She's not my first *jealous-for-no-reason* mean girl experience."

"Well, if your suspicions about her are right, then I wouldn't say she has no reason to be jealous," Leo said, giving me one of those smiles that lasted a few seconds too long to be casual.

I didn't understand how anyone could have the kind of timing he had. Every word he said either put me at ease or made me feel like at any second I was going to shoot into the sky like a rocket. And I wasn't sure what I thought about that. I'd never made time for dating with trying to get into The Citadel, not that I'd have *wanted* to date any of the guys in The Grind anyway. But maybe this was just what it felt like when...you *did*.

I tried my best to shelve everything about that entire topic for now. I'd only been here two days—wait, *two days*? I let the reality of how much time that was sink in. What was I doing? Getting caught up, that's what. Getting distracted from the real insanity of finding out I had some kind of pre-human blood running through my veins. Blood that had been unceremoniously activated by a girl who took a drug, got a disease, and then passed that disease onto me when she *bit* me!

That's all this was, then, I'd decided. Distraction from the upside-down new reality I was living. In psychology class back at school they'd talked about latching onto something else in times of stress—just something to take your mind off reality. That's how addictions started, as little escapes that just built up over time. And with as much as I was obsessively aware of Leo's presence, maybe I was well on my way to becoming addicted to him.

"Halsey?" Leo said, which startled me out of my thoughts. I turned to him, surprised that we were already halfway back to the table. "There you are." He smiled. "You OK?"

"Fine, sorry," I said, shaking off the web of thoughts I'd just tangled myself in. "My mind was just wandering."

"Yeah, it's been a busy few days," he added. "And I have a feeling your week leading up to them was probably pretty hectic too."

"Definitely an understatement," I said, letting myself laugh about it now that everything with Lauren and Jen was all really in the past.

"Well, I probably didn't help all that earlier," he said, then cleared his throat and slowed his pace.

"Oh, don't worry, no... That was—" I started, but he stopped me.

"You don't have to do that, it's OK. I just got ahead of myself. I know that sounds like an excuse, but I'd like to get to know you. And I want to do it right." Leo came to a full stop and met my eyes. "Will you meet me tonight, before everyone else gets to the cliff? I want to show you something." I stared up at him, dumbfounded for several seconds. He suddenly dropped his eyes and started again. "I understand if you don't want to, I just thought..."

"No!" I interrupted. "I mean, it's OK. That would be, if you want to, um—" I babbled like a *full-on* drunk person and had to suck in a quick breath to stop the deluge of nonsense coming out of my mouth. "*Yes*, is what I'm saying." I winced, pressing my lips into a hard line to prevent any more felony class dumbassery from escaping.

Leo's mouth quirked as he nodded. "All right then. I'll come by around seven."

"All right, it's a date," I somehow said, my blood instantly freezing in my veins. *Why would I say that? It wasn't a date. It was just, meeting...together. Romantically. Maybe. But—*

"It's a date," he repeated with a little nod, effectively stopping my runaway train thoughts with a slow, impossible smile.

"Halsey! You *are* screwing Leo!?" Alita literally yelled halfway across the dining hall, which made me jump so abruptly it nearly resulted in a meatball storm for everyone within a five-foot radius of me.

The entire dining hall froze in a coordinated, gaping stare at us. It was like a flash mob, but instead of dancing, it was staring. Then it was laughing with the staring. And then I was dead.

I sent Alita an *I-will-kill-you-with-your-own-hair* look, which I maintained without blinking the entire, double-timed walk back to the table.

I put down my tray and sat about an inch from her face. "Are you *actually* high right now? Did you snort some kind of fake Garden of Eden stupid fruit and just yell that shit over like, *five* lunch lines at me?" I hissed every word through my teeth.

She didn't have a chance to say anything before our own table erupted in laughter, and I wanted to kill everyone with my spork.

I had no choice but to make a hand cave and put my head in it, and there, quietly wait for the fatal dose of embarrassment to smite me from existence. Rhea started laughing herself into a coughing fit, but I secretly hoped she was choking on her cabbage roll.

In that moment, with that realization, the aftermath of the adrenaline started to kick in—the fear after the *fight or flight*, and I felt my throat closing with the imminent threat of tears. They stung my eyes the second I started to panic, and then the floodgates opened thanks to my *acute* awareness that the only thing worse than what Alita just shouted in front of everyone would be if I sat here and *cried* about it in front of everyone.

But oh, there was something even worse than that.

My wings snapped out and cleared the tables on either side of me, and at least a dozen magical lunch eaters were all swatted to the floor, their various entrees falling like a food typhoon all around them.

When I realized what had happened, I lost all control. My hands curved into feathers faster than they had even after the hurricane berries, and the burning sensation in my throat and eyes intensified until I couldn't see at all. Pain ripped through my whole body, sharp and abrupt. I screamed, but it wasn't my voice anymore. It was the eagle screech.

I fell to the floor and tried to find my bearings, but no matter how many times I blinked, I still couldn't see anything but black all around me. I screamed—no, *screeched* again, but this time, the ear-piercing sound somehow brought my vision back. It was blurry at first, but at least I could see. I blinked several more times, and then I could see better than I ever had in my life—the individual eyelashes of everyone staring at me...each freckle, each hair follicle from clear across the room.

I had to get up. *Up...get UP,* I thought, wanting more than anything to run out of there as fast as I could. I searched for the door, which in that second pulled open as someone rushed out. *Get up! Run! Go, before it closes!* I thought again, and the next thing I knew, I was moving fast.

But I wasn't running.

Chapter 21

I darted through the closing door just in time. The only thing I could think to do was run to my dorm and lock the door behind me. Maybe I'd even wedge a chair under the handle so Alita couldn't get in. I reached for the key in my pocket, and immediately face-planted in the grass. I rolled over and over for several seconds until I finally stopped and tried to get to my feet, only I was already upright, and already on my feet. Everything in my head was on a weird five-second delay.

"Halsey!"

"Halsey, wait!"

I heard a few different voices call my name. And then I heard their footfalls over the grass as they began running in my direction.

I didn't think beyond getting away from them, so again, I ran as fast as I could.

And again, I wasn't running. I was *flying*.

It only lasted a handful of seconds before I crashed into the ground again, but I'd somehow managed to make my way over the orchard trees. I was expecting a hill past the orchard, but instead I found the beach. I must have taken a wrong turn somewhere, or maybe it was a different orchard?

Take a deep breath… I remembered Leo saying. *You can't fight a tidal wave.*

"The seawater!" I said out loud, and although the words sounded strangled, at least they were words instead of the screech. I took another deep breath, but the fear of being discovered in whatever half-state I realized I must be in was terrifying. No matter how many times I tried, I couldn't calm down long enough even to try to reverse the sensation of my skin being set on fire. I couldn't retract the feathers I saw in place of my fingers, and I couldn't stop the blood-freezing horror I felt at the sight of something new—a bony ridge had developed all the way up my arms, and dark gold feathers began creeping over my shoulders like they were trying to close the gap with the partial wings on my back.

I had to get to the water. It had stopped my skin from burning after I'd eaten the hurricane berries. It has stopped the shift altogether and reversed it.

"Halsey! Stop!" Leo shouted behind me, but I was only a few yards from the water. "*Halsey*! It's not the same water!" he shouted again, but it was too late. The surf washed over my feet, but instead of it alleviating the burning feeling like it had before, it made it *worse*. Ten-thousand times worse.

I screamed, a mangled half-screech sound, and stumbled backward. As I scrambled back from the water, I turned to see Leo lowering himself to the beach. His arms just seemed to pull out of the black, armored wings that were kicking up sand and debris as he touched down. They disappeared the second he landed, and the final *whoosh* of air blew what was left of my shirt in every direction. I looked down and wrapped my deformed arms around myself upon realizing the buttons of my shirt had all been torn off and the sleeves had split all the way up each side.

"You found her!" Rhea said, but when I looked up, it wasn't Rhea I saw. At least, not completely.

Her long, blonde hair started to reappear over the armored gold scales that had just been covering her head, throat and torso. They caught and reflected the last of the setting sun in the same moment her red and gold shimmering wings also began disappearing behind her. But before they were gone, I could see they were feathered like mine. She stood there bare chested and completely unfazed by it as she pulled a wadded tank top from the pocket of her skort and slipped it over her head. "Is she all right?" she asked as Leo scooped me up and carried me back from the surf toward her.

"I think so. She just got caught mid-shift."

"Oh no, her legs…" Rhea said blowing out a breath. I couldn't see what she was talking about, but at the mention, the searing pain ran through me all over again.

"Go to the admin house and bring the water," Leo said, and before he could finish the sentence, Rhea was already taking off her tank top and shoving it in her pocket again. I watched in fascination as her skin hardened into the shimmering golden scales it had been a minute ago, her hair disappearing in the same interval her beautiful red and gold wings appeared. In an instant, she shot over the trees and out of sight. She was the most stunning thing I'd ever seen, except for Leo's black dragon—but I'd only seen parts of that through the trees.

I was suddenly very much aware of the gnarled, monstrous appearance of my arms, and I was paralyzed with fear for what my face must look like because my nose and mouth tingled, and I could breathe like I never had before. Each inhale felt like five, and the surge of energy after each one was almost too much to bear.

"Don't...look at me," I said, my voice hoarse and strained as it tore from my throat.

"Stop, Halsey..." he said, pulling me against him as he kneeled beside me and buried his face in my hair. He kissed the top of my head, lingering there as heat radiated from him, and with everything feeling like it was already on fire, I pulled away before I changed even *more*.

I looked down at my legs for the first time, and saw that my feet, ankles, and halfway up to my knees were covered in burns. *How could that have been just from the seawater?* At the sight, the intermittent feathers over my thighs and shins started to recede, and the tingling in my lips and face stopped. I held out my hands, which were also no longer covered in feathers, so I immediately brought them to my face to make sure everything was the same.

No beak…no feathers except for what felt like a few near my temples, but even those were receding.

"What's happening to me?" I said, my voice breaking on the last word.

"The shift recedes if you're hurt so it can heal you from the inside," Leo said. "It channels it's energy to repair your injuries."

"*What*?" I asked, breathlessly watching the grotesque ridges in my arms get smaller until they disappeared entirely. I gripped my elbows, pressed my fingers into the joints to feel for the bones that were just there, under my skin. They were gone, and so were the burns on my legs, feet, and ankles.

A sudden gust of wind came off the ocean, blowing the shreds of my shirt back, and my bra was gone! I pulled down the pieces of my shirt and crossed my arms over them, all at once feeling my center of gravity shifting again like that night with the hurricane berries.

I stumbled backward and fell, the weight of my wings too much to stay upright.

"It's OK, Rhea will be here with the water soon. You can put my shirt on then." He smiled. "Don't worry, it's clean. Dragons are *obsessive* about hygiene."

A laugh bubbled in my chest. "How…?" was all I managed to say before the threat of tears closed off my throat again. My sandals were gone, and in an effort to regain my composure, I tried to occupy my mind with pinpointing when I must have lost them. Oh, and when my *bra* had disappeared. I would be instantaneously struck dead of embarrassment if it were hanging off the dessert bay in the dining hall right now.

"Your wings just shot out pretty fast, and they're sharp at first..." Leo said, running a hand between the tatters of my sleeve. "The first time I shredded a shirt to ribbons, I had no idea how it happened either." He went on, and I looked at him, amazed again at his insight as to what to say to me right now. He pulled in a long, easy breath. "*But*...you don't have to be embarrassed, I mean, if you are. I was just going by the way you're clinging to the scraps of your shirt like that." He nodded to what was left of it. When I risked a glance at him, he was smiling, and his eyes warm and kind. He raised his brows and nodded. "Hey, Sylphs and Salamanders walk around the island topless all the time. Nobody cares. The only reason it's not happening now is because it's honing week. New Bloods have enough to stress about without adding public nudity to the picture."

At this, I *did* laugh, and after a deep breath, I felt like I might be able to say more than one word at a time without bursting into tears.

"Why won't my wings turn back like everything else?" I managed, glancing at the lower half of them reaching several feet into the sand. "And what's wrong with them?"

"They're just stuck. You started to shift, but...just got caught in the tidal wave." He winked. "You don't lose your arms to them until you completely shift. It started to happen here," he added, moving his hand over my bared shoulder.

"Then those bone ridges..." I shook my head, barely able to bring back the image without shuddering.

He nodded. "It's the bridge of your wing—kind of like a frame, or a rudder. It's how you move them up there." Leo looked to the sky, then back to me. "But you can have both arms and wings if you know how to stop your shift." His dark eyes shadowed, and a few seconds later, his wings slowly emerged again, first the bridging bone he'd just mentioned, but this one stopped at his shoulder. Then, the smaller network of bones branched out behind him until it looked like a matrix of webs.

"Oh my god," I gasped, watching the velvet black skin appear at each joint, then spread over the expanse of interlaced bones until finally, the armored, black-mirror plates appeared over the jointed area like vented shields, which expanded until all the small bones were covered too. The last pieces to form were the serrated edges, long and elegant like feathers, but visibly sharp on both sides.

"See? You're normal...for being *abnormal*." Leo slowly moved his hand to my face, tracing his thumb over my cheekbone.

He leaned in slowly and pressed his lips to mine, transforming the prickling stabs of heat I'd been feeling into a warmth that flooded my whole body. The campfire smell of him filled my lungs as his other hand moved through my hair, and I couldn't get close enough to him.

"*Really*?" Rhea's voice was a rock through my small window of calm, and instantly, the little stabs of heat returned over every square inch of my skin. The ridges also appeared in my arms and shoulders again, and pain rushed through me.

"No...no, no!" I stuttered, trying to press the ridge back into my skin, but it didn't work. I scrambled to my feet, but the wings were too heavy, and I fell backward into the sand again. I clutched at my shirt as everything started going black just like in the dining hall.

"Halsey! Halsey, take a breath!"

"Move, Leo!" Rhea shouted.

A second later, I felt the cool water on my skin and the sense of relief was so strong that tears burned my eyes again. Rhea was behind me in an instant gripping the back of my hair.

"Hey! Stop!"

"Leo, I will neuter you—shut-up and stay back! Halsey, open your mouth!" she yelled, but it wasn't until she jerked my hair that I really heard her. "Open your mouth, Halsey! You have to drink this!" I did as she said, and she tipped the bottle to my lips. I swallowed giant gulps of the water, choking on the last one. But the burning everywhere was instantly gone, and I felt like a hundred pounds had been lifted off my chest and back. "There, you're fine now. Take shallow breaths," Rhea added, letting me go. She straightened and rounded on Leo. "And you… Don't *even* look at me like that. Did you think you were going to kiss her broken shift all better?"

Leo snapped his wings out, creating a shadow over us all. "Why do you have to be such a *bitch*, Rhea?"

"This *bitch* just saved her ass, you dickwhistle. She doesn't know shit about shit yet and you're all over her. Just do your job!" She launched the glass bottle of seawater at him. It thudded as he caught it against his chest before she turned to run up the beach. She pulled her shirt off, and in seconds, her brilliant wings exploded to either side of her. They caught the next gust of wind that hit us and carried her halfway to the cliff in the distance before she even had to begin flapping them.

Leo turned his back to me and yelled after her, his wings fully extended as a stream of fire shot several hundred feet down the beach, and a roll of thunder filled the red, darkening sky.

Chapter 22

Leo flew me back to my dorm in what seemed like only seconds so I could change out of my tattered shirt. He said it would probably be better if I didn't show up on the cliff wearing his after all, and I knew this had everything to do with Rhea.

He also opted to wait outside so nobody passing by would see him coming out of my dorm room, especially after Alita's idiotic *and untrue* declaration in the dining hall that we were sleeping together. And speaking of her, I hoped she wouldn't be inside when Leo and I landed in front of the white-brick dorm house because I *did not* want to see her face yet.

I fished my key out of my skort pocket—silently thanking the inventor of zippers for it still being there after the frenzy that caused me to somehow even lose my *bra*—then I occupied my mind with thoughts of putting the key on a chain as I went inside to dig out the spandex racerback tank-top I knew I'd packed.

I also took off my stupid skort and put on a pair of black leggings that had a zippered pocket on the side. I dropped my key into that and again, thanked the zipper guy. After a little digging in my bag, I found a pair of socks and my boots, but the passing glance I caught of myself in the mirror stopped me in my tracks.

I took a long, hard look at the apocalypse that was the state of my hair—four shades of long, purple bangs blown in every direction. It was even purple where it was nearly shaved around the back and sides, so it was now apparently growing straight out of my head this color. I ran my fingers through the top a few times and straightened it out enough that the zig-zagging layers looked intentional and edgy. But reality seemed to slip a little as I watched my hands move through hair that *wasn't* my hair. Or, so it seemed.

Maybe this wasn't me. Maybe I wasn't here, I thought.

I stared into the mirror for several more seconds seriously considering the possibility that I was actually in a Red-Fever induced coma. Maybe I'd been dreaming everything that had happened since I found out I didn't get into the Citadel? Maybe I'd just had a psychotic break because of it?

I mean, it would explain why there didn't seem to be any way off this island. Why was no one talking about that? No one had even said a word about going home for breaks. Did we even have any breaks at this school?

It would also explain why there was no way for me to queue anyone from home. I could only talk to the people here on this island.

"Wake up," I said with *one hundred* percent certainty it would work, and I'd find myself in a hospital bed or something. "Wake the hell up right now, Halsey."

Nothing. Not a single thing happened other than my edgy unicorn hair falling into my eyes, and I pushed it back in frustration.

I heaved a long, pained sigh and suddenly remembered something from psychology class. If this really were a dream world, the *facts* would only be facts if I said they were, right? So, if I'd blocked out the real world because it was too hard to know I didn't get into The Citadel, I was here in this fantasy world because I thought I could control it.

All right. Then it was time to start trying.

***

Leo had put his white shirt back on and was standing with his hands in his pockets, the bottle of shift-neutralizing water under his arm. His black hair was blowing off his shoulders like some kind of brooding vampire from a gothic novel, and the air was starting to feel heavy with the pending rain.

"Wow," he said, apparently surprised at my outfit change. "I was expecting just another white shirt."

"The last one didn't hold up too well," I said, pushing away the constructed humiliation I'd let myself fall into before. If this were a dream, I reminded myself, I wasn't going to *choose* to feel embarrassed in front of him.

"Well, not that I'm advocating for the white shirt over your current selection, but we have a little insurance now at least," Leo said, holding up the bottle of seawater.

I smiled at him. "Sorry about all that by the way," I said, walking confidently toward him. "It all happened so fast, and I couldn't stop it."

"Halsey..." he laughed. "You don't have to apologize about any of that. I'm the one who should apologize to you."

I darted a glance at him and huffed out a breath in disbelief. "For what? You just *helped* me."

Leo shook his head and lowered his eyes. "Rhea was right. You wouldn't have needed any help like that in the first place if it hadn't been for me. Alita wouldn't have had anything to yell about in the dining hall."

"If anyone is to blame for that, it's *Rhea*," I said, anger sparking in my chest again. "Alita hadn't thought anything until Rhea started taking jabs at us."

He raised his chin in the direction of the setting sun and let out a long, slow breath.

"That's actually true, but even so, it's still my fault." He shook his head and studied the ground again. "On the beach back there... I didn't plan it like that, you know? It wasn't the right time. You just got here and have enough to adjust to without me complicating it all even more."

I let the anger fall away. If this were a dream reality, it was tricky, and I needed to be careful not to let myself get caught up in its machinations again. I needed to act, not react.

I looked over at him as we walked. "You know what, out of all the things I wish I *could* erase from reality today, nothing you did is on that list." The corner of his mouth turned up, but he still watched the ground as we made our way to the cliff to meet the others. I had an idea. "We can start over if you want," I said. A curious smile spread over his face as I held out my hand to him. "Hi, I'm Halsey Rhodes. What's your name?"

He took my hand, laughing a little at first, but then he shook it gently. "Leo Red-Cloud. Really nice to meet you, Halsey."

"Is that a Native American name?" I asked. He nodded slowly, smiling at my sudden interest. "I read somewhere that in some tribes, mothers named their babies after the first thing they saw when the baby was born. Is that true?"

Leo took a deep, thoughtful breath. "I've heard that too, but it's more common to be given a name after your personality starts showing," he explained, but then seemed suddenly impatient. "Anyway, we have lots of names—some we earn over time, some we inherit, and some we never say."

I knew he'd put it that way to sum up his answer, but all it did was make me have more questions. "So, given those three options, did you earn *Red-Cloud* or inherit it?"

"Both," he finally said just as we reached the cliff where Rhea, Alec, Bryce, and Alita all turned their eyes to meet us.

"Halsey!" Alita shouted as she ran up to me. A rush of anger pushed through me upon seeing her, but before I could say a thing, she'd thrown her arms around my neck and started gushing apologies for being so *epically* thoughtless. I closed my eyes and tried to let my insta-rage slide over me.

"It's all right," I said, maneuvering to step out of her shockingly strong vise grip. After the eighth time repeating it was *really* OK and I wasn't mad anymore, she finally let me go.

I looked up at Rhea, who was watching the scene with Alita play out.

"I didn't get to say thank you for helping me," I said. "For making me drink the water. I know you flew back and got it."

She shrugged, but the corner of her mouth twitched upward for just a second. "Half-shift constipation sucks," she said without a second thought, and the ridiculousness of that phrase made me laugh without warning.

Rhea didn't laugh at all, and instead, turned to Bryce. "All right, he's here, so are we ready now or what?" she asked.

Bryce punched a few things into his tablet, which generated a 3-D layout of what looked like the immediate area. I could see the cliff edge, the ocean, and even the surrounding forest on either side of us all meticulously etched in glowing, green lines. All green except for the hazy red bubble a good way down the shoreline.

Bryce turned to Leo. "That's where the tear is supposed to be, at least, that's where it was supposed to be an hour ago. If it moved since then, it can't be by much."

"The veil, as in…the divider between planes?" I said, trying to play along with what I'd heard this morning. "They were talking about that today in my honing class."

"In mine too," Alita said. "I can kind of see Ghob's point, though. I mean, going from having the run of a place to being servants?" she added.

"Humans have been a disease here ever since," Bryce added, which was about the last thing I expected to hear.

"You know, you're still human too, right?" I clipped, taking more than a little offense.

Bryce blew his two-tone hair out of his eyes as he studied the 3-D hologram. "And tell you what, if I could choose one or the other, I'd take Gnome Immortal Fae any day."

"You'd *actually* pick—" I started, then registered what he'd said. "Did you say *immortal*? Midori didn't say anything about being immortal."

Bryce sighed and scrubbed his hand over the broad planes of his face, finally resigning to look at me. "OK, only the queens are immortal, but we might as well be too. Elementals live for centuries. Humans get one, if they're lucky. So yeah, getting sick was the best thing that ever happened to me."

"You had Red Fever?" I asked hesitantly.

"We all did," Rhea said, unbuttoning her shirt. "That was the catalyst. I thought you said you went to your honing today?"

"I did, but—what are you doing?" I asked as she got close to the last few buttons.

She looked at me like I'd just asked her to throw me off the cliff. "Did you forget what happened to *your* shirt when your wings came out?" she asked, raising an eyebrow. "Leo has to scout the tear, and someone has to watch his back to make sure he doesn't get sucked in or something. We don't know what will happen that close up."

Everything was going too fast. There were answers here…and more questions, but I couldn't slow it all down enough to separate them. I just had to start where I was.

"Why are we trying to find the tear in the veil?" I asked, hoping this would at least give me a starting point. Alec laughed like I'd missed the most obvious answer in the world. I glared at him. "What? Why is that funny?"

He let his laughter dissipate and gave me a conciliatory look like I'd just spilled my ice cream onto the sidewalk.

"Oh, these kids…" he said, shaking his head as he sighed. "To go *through* it, Halsey."

Chapter 23

"Then I'm going too," I said. "I'm going to see what's on the other side of the veil too."

Rhea laughed so loud it echoed, and I glared at her. She opened her mouth to no doubt tell me how delusional I was since I had demonstrated exactly zero control over my wings thus far in our relationship, but that was a simple matter of cause and effect, which I was sure could be remedied. Instead of telling me this, though, she just held up her hands and shook her head at Leo.

"You're up—this is your fault," she chuckled, a look of exhaustion on her face.

Leo sighed and put his hands on his hips as he studied the ground again.

"Halsey…" he said, meeting my eyes.

"Is there a time limit before the tear disappears or something?" I asked. "Like in hour from now, it's gone?"

Leo's expression shifted to surprise. "No, but—"

"Then take me up right now. Show me what to do."

"Halsey, it's not that simple," Leo answered. "You have an entire class dedicated to nothing but mastering how to fly. You're not going to learn how to do it in a night."

Rhea, Alec, and Bryce all started to snicker, and even Alita hid her laughter behind a ridiculous throat clearing episode when I locked eyes with her. Anger rolled in my chest again, and I remembered my theory.

Stop reacting, I thought. *Stop reacting, and act.*

If this was a dream, then I was going to fly, damn it.

I started running as fast as I could toward the edge of the cliff. Leo called after me, then Alita. After a few more seconds, the rest of their voices clanged together shouting all kinds of warnings in inevitabilities if I didn't stop.

Stop reacting, and act.

I saw the edge of the cliff approaching and the deep purple sky beyond. I saw the whitecap waves rolling and growing until they spilled onto the shore, powerful in their element. Air was my element, wasn't it? If I was an eagle, then I was meant to fly.

I leapt from the edge and held out my arms, expecting the searing pain of the wings opening, but it didn't come. My wings didn't open. My hands were still hands, and I was falling not toward waves, but toward rocks—jagged and layered as if the cliff had teeth.

I was wrong. This wasn't a dream world I'd created so I could control it. My theory was wrong, and now there was nothing left to test.

I shut my eyes and instinctively tried to brace myself for the impact…like it would have made any difference on the terrain I was heading for.

But I didn't hit those rocks. I hit something solid that knocked the wind out of me. I couldn't breathe, and for a fleeting second I was sure I'd hit the water. It had to be the water because what else could it be?

I forced my eyes open, but couldn't see anything until a few seconds later when the wind and the pressure relaxed. Leo's arms were wrapped around my ribs and legs, and I would have given almost anything to rewind the last five minutes so I could make a different choice.

"Have you lost your mind!?" Leo shouted. "Are you trying to get yourself *killed*!?"

"I thought I could…" I started, but embarrassment crashed into me so hard the physical pain in my side —a tightening, followed by a relentless stabbing sensation—halted my words. "I thought…my wings would work," I managed, but the pain got so intense I started to feel lightheaded. My head was too heavy suddenly, and I let it fall against his shoulder.

"But why would you—*shit*," Leo interrupted himself. "Hold on!" The wind picked up again, and the pressure on my stomach and chest made the sharp pain worse.

"Leo!" Rhea yelled, and in the same second, everything was quiet. The wind had completely stopped, and the pressure on my chest was gone. The pain was still there though, and I was sure we'd stopped moving.

"What happened?" I asked as Leo put me down, and pain ripped all the way up my side again. It was foggy and damp, and all the beautiful flowers and foliage, not to mention the *ocean*, were gone. "Where are we?" I said, clutching at the sharp stabs over the left side of my ribs.

"I think we're inside the tear," Leo whispered, then turned to me. "Your head is bleeding," he said, then sighed. "It must have happened somehow when I caught you. Does your side hurt," he asked, glancing at the way I was holding my ribs.

I nodded. "Feels like I swallowed a stick or something."

"That's probably my fault too… When I caught you. The cut through your eyebrow is on the same side." He took a deep breath and let it out slowly. "I'm sorry."

I shook my head at him, which made me dizzy. "It's not your fault. You saved my life. I shouldn't have jumped, but I was just so sure," I added, marveling at how *wrong* I was. And that could only mean one thing… This really wasn't a coma dream.

Leo angled his head toward a collection of large, jagged rocks. For a second, I thought they were the ones I saw from the top of the cliff, but none of this fog was surrounding them ten minutes ago. "You need to relax to heal, and then we'll try to find our way out of here," he said, moving to my injured side and putting his arm around me.

"Where's Rhea?" I asked, remembering her calling to him.

"She must not have made it through."

"How did we make it through?" I turned toward him and immediately winced.

"All right, just a few more steps," he said. "I think you have some broken ribs, but they shouldn't take too long to repair. Just try to relax."

We moved into a little cove of rocks, jagged all around. They butted up against two flat pieces, the arrangement made the whole damp, dim place seem like a secret fort a kid might build.

"These look like the rocks at the bottom of the cliff," I said. " But where's the water?"

"Don't think about any of that right now," Leo said, then ran several fingers through my hair. "Just lie back for a few minutes so everything can heal."

I lay on the flat rock and closed my eyes, listening to the absolute silence. How could anything be this quiet? Not a bird, not a frog, nothing.

My heart jumped when I realized this was the same kind of complete and utter silence that happened in the eye of the forest back in The Grind. Was that spot another tear in the veil? Midori said there were several around the world. As I let myself wonder, the pain in my side started to dissipate, and I sat up.

"Leo, I think—" I started, but he stopped my words with a finger raised to his lips. It was then that

I heard the voices in the silence. Uri's voice, and another I didn't recognize, though the accent was similar to Sylvie's.

"She ain't been seen in Jordan fer centuries," the woman said. "And dat Cave of Wonders dried up centuries before. Nah, angel. She on da mainland now. Lured Knox Ryder straight off ma' boat in Portland. Who ya got searchin' der?"

My eyes flashed to Leo's, which were wide with surprise.

"She's mortal, Ghob. She doesn't have the power to do that. *Jordan* is her last known record," Uri said. "I don't know what else to tell you."

"What I say ta call me, angel?" The woman, apparently named Ghob, said, her voice slow and full of contempt.

Ghob…was that…? No. It couldn't be, I thought.

Uri sighed, exasperated." *Luz…* I'll have a trained team as soon as honing week is over and the new bloods aren't constantly in their shadows," he started.

"Who ya got fer me den?" she asked. "Which of dem first-year babies all grown up now and ready ta bring me dat woman?"

"Leo Red-Cloud is ready."

"Dat de boy who killed yer hunter?" Ghob—er, *Luz* said, which made Leo's previously surprised expression harden into anger.

"Yes, he's the one," Uri said. "Ian MacTavish is also strong enough now, but his Sylph nature gives me pause. He leans toward the humans' plight."

"Den we need *anodder* Sylph. We gotta have one each of da four Elementals."

"I have another Sylph in mind, but I need more time to see which way she leans," Uri added. "She's already the strongest in this wave."

"See dat she gets schooled up in a hurry, den." Luz started laughing after several seconds. "All dem wild bloods can pick da low-hangin' fruit fer now. But we gonna have *five* continents needin' generals soon, and Eve *has my fifth*!" Luz barked, all traces of laughter gone from her voice as it reverberated all around us.

Uri cleared his throat, and when he spoke again, his voice was steady and ominous. "I'll *find* Eve. She'll be sent back to the dust to join that *prating* Adam once and for all," he said, grinding the words through his teeth. "If she's hiding Knox Ryder, we'll find him."

"Ya betta, angel," Luz said, the deep laugh returning to her voice. "Because if ya don't, my sista gonna cook ya in yer soulless skin when I tell her who got her snakes stripped of der eart'ly plumes… When I tell her who's ta blame fer dem bein' made to crawl on der bellies… When I tell her it was *you, Uriel,* who let Lucifer into *my* Garden."

The silence returned, but the fog didn't lift. The searing, sharp pain I'd felt had finally subsided, though, and I started to get to my feet. Leo crossed to me shaking his head, then took a seat at my side as he stared past me into nothingness.

"Stay here until we're sure they're really gone," he whispered, his normally tan complexion now seeming pale in the filtered light. I looked over his shoulder beyond the jagged rocks, but all I could see was dim glow through the dense fog.

"Leo, are you all right?" I asked, wondering why he wasn't moving.

"Uri called her *Ghob* at first," he said quietly. "The Gnome queen."

"She's the one who turned on Adam and Eve, and was then kicked out of Eden with the Water Fae queen..."

"Necksa." Leo nodded slowly until he pushed his hands back through his loose, black hair and took a deep breath, still not meeting my eyes.

"Eden…wait," I said, remembering what Ghob had said. "Leo, she said *Eve* from The Garden of Eden was in *Portland*. And Uri is—"

"I know—just give me a second, OK?" Leo interrupted me, his voice clipped and tight. After a few more seconds, he sprung to his feet. "We have to get out of here first. Wherever *here* is."

"You are in the fold, fire child…" a low, male voice said, but there was no one else around. The beating of quick wings sounded somewhere above, but we couldn't see anything flying.

"Who said that?" Leo asked the gray, opaque sky above, then he sucked in a gasp when a huge, black bird swooped into view from the fog. "You're *Raven...*" he whispered with what sounded like the last of his breath.

"And you're in The Fold between the pages of this world and that," the raven said, soaring and diving in and out of the fog. "The neutral ground. The meeting sky..." it said, its voice now echoing in every direction.

"Show us how to get back!" Leo shouted to the bird.

"It's not the same now," it answered. "Not for you. Not for the moth in the flame—go between the empty places."

"What was that? What did it mean?" I shouted, but Leo just shook his head.

"He's a spirit guide to my people back home, but he'll only talk in riddles if you ask for clarification. The only thing you can do is listen. Or sometimes, tell him what you need, and he'll give you a message...a warning or a blessing."

"And that was a warning?" I asked hesitantly.

Leo nodded slowly as he searched the cloudy sky again, but the raven seemed to be gone now. "Yeah," he said with a sigh. "That was a warning."

Chapter 24

Leo and I walked through the fog in silence for what seemed like an eternity without going anywhere. We could only see about ten feet in front of us, above us, behind us, and wherever the light source was coming from, it had to be far away.

Leo's shirt hung from his pocket as he walked with his thumbs hooked in his back belt loops. If I were to glance at him quickly, it almost looked as if he were being marshaled somewhere by a Sweeper droid.

I had so many questions, but I didn't know if he was ready to give me any answers. I risked a glance at him and looked away quickly when he turned to me at the same time.

"I didn't have a choice," he said after a few more seconds, surprising me. I knew he was talking about the hunter he'd apparently killed. I wanted to ask him more about it, but I also didn't want him to feel obligated to tell me.

"Leo, you don't have to—"

"I'd been gathering wood," he continued, ignoring my protest. "I had it packed in a few bundles on my back and just needed to cross through the woods to get to my village on the other side." Leo took a deep breath and let it out slowly. "As I got closer, I felt something out there. I couldn't hear it, but I knew it was watching me. Have you ever felt that…where you just knew someone was watching you even if you couldn't see who it was?"

"Yeah, definitely," I said, knowing the feeling exactly from the eye in the woods back in The Grind.

"Anyway, I grabbed one of the branches I'd broken up, just in case, but I still wasn't ready for as hard as it hit me. I thought maybe it was a bear, but it was something else. Half a bear, or maybe a wolf, and the other half was a man." He lifted the back of his hair and showed me several dark, shiny scars evenly spaced from each other at the base of his neck. "It tried to *bite my head off*," he added, laughing humorlessly. "I ran the stick through its chest, which was just stupid luck since I couldn't see anything, and we both fell to the ground. I got to my feet trying to see what the hell it was. But it was just...*gone*."

"What? How?" I asked almost immediately.

"I don't know. When I got back to my village, they sent a hunting party out for the bear they were sure it was based on the bite mark, but they came back the next morning with nothing."

"Oh my god, Leo..."

"I know I killed it though—whatever it was. I felt its life slip away. All the anger and hate it held," he said, then turned to me, his dark brows drawn together. "I felt it slip into *me*, Halsey." He looked away again and after a few more seconds, he cleared his throat. "My mother said I was asleep for three days, so the village elders sent for medicine men from three different tribes, and after trying everything they could to wake me up, they all said the same thing… that the lives of my ancestors had swallowed me. That the Red Cloud had come for me, and I would never be the same."

"That sounds terrifying," I whispered.

"The people in my village had mixed ideas about it. Some of the people who knew my father's family said it was a blessing. Others said it was a curse. All I knew after I woke up was that my blood felt like it was boiling, and if I didn't leave, I was going to hurt people. So I left."

"Where did you go?"

"To a cave until I could figure out what was happening to me. But a few days later, Sylvie showed up out of nowhere and told me about this place where others were like me—others who had beaten the *trickster*—and how I'd been chosen to lead them."

"You just trusted her?" I asked, remembering my own suspicions about Eden's Bluff.

"What choice did I have, Halsey? I thought I'd kill everyone I knew."

"And they fixed that here?" I tried not to sound like I doubted him or disagreed with his choices.

"They taught me it was just the dragon, and they taught me how to let it out safely. Once it came out, the hate and anger turned into…I don't know, just… power, I guess."

"Have you been able to tell your mom? Your family?" I asked. "I mean, do they still think you're living in that cave?"

Leo shook his head and studied the ground again as we walked. "They aren't worried about me anymore."

"How do you know?" I asked. "Maybe you could queue them?"

Leo narrowed his eyes at me and gave me a flat smile. "The medicine men don't exactly put in communication chips for people in the villages, Halsey," he said, letting the flat smile turn upward. "I didn't get one of those until I came here."

"OK," I raced to think of something else. "A package? Maybe you could send them—"

"No addresses. They're not part of the system there," Leo answered, then gave me a quick, hesitant glance. "And, Halsey, even if they were, we can't connect to anyone from that world now. At least not in that way."

"What are you talking about?" I asked, slowing our pace as the fog seemed to get thicker all around us. My heart started pounding against my ribs. "Are you saying we can't go home?"

He stopped and turned to me, lowering his eyes to meet mine. "We were all furious when we found out. It was right after we first got here too. We've been trying to find the tear in the veil ever since, and we're finally close now," he said, taking my hands. "There's a path home, or at least somewhere close to home for each of us somewhere through the tear." Leo glanced over my shoulder toward the direction we'd just come. "We didn't know about The Fold, though. We've never gotten this far." He looked back at me with hope in his eyes. "Bryce has been researching it for the last few years—ever since we found out we couldn't leave. The tears are like doors, Halsey. We just have to find the ones that open up to where we're from, and we can go back and forth. We can put things right."

I stopped walking and pulled my hands from his. "What do you mean?" I asked, shaking my head. "Why won't they let us go home the normal way? My aunt and uncle will want to know why I'm not queuing or coming back for holidays…*Leo*!" I shouted when he only looked at me.

He took a deep breath, then sighed. "No, they won't," he said, lowering his voice. "Right about now, they're being told your helicopter disappeared somewhere off the coast of Florida en route to Eden's Bluff," he said calmly, then took a deep breath and sighed. My mouth fell open, and it felt like my blood was turning to ice.

"No, they can't—"

"It's just what they do, Halsey. They get us here, isolate us, and then they make us forget where we came from because it's easier than letting us go back and forth. Humans *can't* know about us."

"But I didn't forget—*you* and the others didn't forget, Leo. Why can we remember?" I felt my chest tightening with every word, and it was getting harder to breathe.

"The water that first night was supposed to make you forget everything about where you came from, but it didn't," Leo said. "You wouldn't have kept asking all those questions, and you wouldn't have tried to queue home there in the bathroom if the water had been working. It was the same for me. That's why they started training me to be a transition assistant."

I suddenly started to feel dizzy, so I sat down. The ground was rocky, but dry, and I pressed my fingers into the cool, rough, stone surfaces.

"They all think I'm dead…" I said out loud, though not to Leo. "*Max…*" My voice cracked, and burning tears began flooding my vision.

"I'm sorry, Halsey," Leo whispered, moving to sit next to me. He wrapped his arm around me and pulled me in, and for a second, the campfire smell of him was comforting. But then I remembered that he was the one who gave me the water back in the dining room my first night here. I pushed his arm off my shoulder and got to my feet.

"You were the one who gave me the water!" I shouted. "You knew it would make me forget everything about where I came from!"

Leo flinched and held out his hands to me as if they could stop my accusations in mid-air.

"And do you know how much I hated that? Do you know what it's like to watch someone's face go from terror to peace, but only because they've just left behind an entire life there on the floor?" Leo pressed his lips into a hard line and pulled in a quick, sharp breath. His hands moved to his hips, and his eyes once again found the ground. He shook his head. "I was so happy when you wanted to call home, Halsey," he said, risking a glance up at me. "It meant you were like us…like *me*."

My head was spinning and my chest ached. "Rhea —she gave me that water again. *You* told her to bring it."

"Because I knew if the water didn't work before, it was never going to work. I told her to bring it because it *does* reverse a shift. You saw that happen, Halsey."

Leo started to walk toward me, but I stepped back and held up a hand, stopping him in place.

"Why didn't Alita say anything to me about this?" I asked, waiting for the lie I knew I could catch him in if I just kept asking questions. The lie that would somehow be the excuse I could use not to believe anything he said.

"The water only mostly worked on her," Leo answered, scrubbing his hands over his face, then pushing them back through his dark hair. He heaved a breath, and in that moment, let his arms drop to his sides, seemingly exhausted. "She remembers where she came from, but only on the surface. She doesn't remember her family, her friends, nothing personal. We just keep watching her to see if something will leak back in, but so far, it hasn't. Not like you."

"Why, then? Why do I remember? Why do you and the others remember? Does Uri know about all of them?"

"OK, slow down." He smiled. "I want to answer your questions. We're on the same side." Leo raised his palms toward me again as if he was trying to get me to lower a weapon. "Uri only knows about me. We've been keeping Alita close so he doesn't find out about her," he explained. "As for why the water didn't work on us, we don't know. But I've brought most of the students to this island, and you've been the only fully lucid one aside from the ones up on that cliff with us."

"This is too much," I said, shaking my head and turning my back to him. I started walking again, trying to process it all—that Red Fever had activated some strand of DNA in my body that wasn't even *human*, then hearing what Uri was saying about killing Eve...actual *Eve* from *The Garden of Eden*. And now, not only were my family and best friend being told that I was dead, but I was never even supposed to remember any of my life before coming to Eden's Bluff.

I felt like I'd been hit in the stomach. My throat felt like it was closing up.

And then, I was falling.

Chapter 25

I heard Leo call my name from far away, and then I heard Rhea.

"They're here!" she called, and a second later, I was yanked upward by an arm around my stomach. My arms and legs were dangling, but I couldn't even turn a fraction of an inch in the vise grip to see anything other than the whitecap waters reflecting the moonlight below.

It seemed like I only had time to blink before I was falling again, but this time only a few feet. I rolled a few times before coming to a stop in the cool grass.

"Damn, Rhea—she's not even shifted!" Bryce yelled.

"If she's hurt, she'll heal. I need to go back for Alec."

I looked up with enough time to see the back of Rhea's red and gold wings arc wide, then bend in as she darted out of sight. She quickly reappeared after Leo in the night sky, barely visible save for his silhouette in the moonlight, the light and shadows outlining the curves of his wings and the outline of his cheekbones, chest, and shoulders. Alec had hooked his arms over Rhea's, letting go when his feet were close enough to the ground.

Leo's wings collapsed and folded in immediately when he saw me, then ran to kneel next to me.

"Halsey!" he looked me up and down. "Are you OK? I saw Rhea grab you. Are your ribs—?"

"She's *fine*," Rhea sighed and rolled her eyes. "What happened? You both just fell into, and then out of the fog. Did you find the tear in the other side?"

Leo turned to her, then to everyone. "No. We got stuck somewhere called *The Fold*. It was like, a neutral space or something—just all fog in every direction—but the other tear had to be close by."

"Are you sure?" Alec asked, pushing his hands through his wet hair. "There was nothing in the water except for rocks." I couldn't help but watch the intricately woven muscles of his torso move as he put on his dry clothes—there wasn't even an ounce of fat on his entire body.

"A raven messenger was in there with us," Leo answered. "That's where it said we were—in *The Fold* between the worlds."

"What's a *raven messenger*?" Alita asked, hugging her knees.

"Kind of like a living map," Leo said, turning to Alita. "A guide that tells you where you are...if you can figure out what it's saying."

Leo went on to tell the others that we'd overheard Uri talking to Ghob, who was now going by the name *Luz*. He explained that they were talking about Eve— the *actual* Eve—and how Uri intended to make Leo one of the generals in charge of killing her.

"Wait, Uri is *Uriel*? The *archangel*?" Bryce laughed, incredulous. "*Uriel*…who guarded the gates of Eden after Adam and Eve were kicked out?"

"How do you even *know* that?" Alita asked, surprised.

"The professor is a wealth of knowledge," Rhea grinned. "How many times have you read that Bible?" she asked, glancing at Bryce.

"It's research." He leveled his gaze at her. "And this is serious."

"Why would he just *let* Lucifer in?" Alec asked, now totally dry somehow. "And how is Eve still alive?"

"I don't know, but Uri is working with Ghob to kill her. They're talking about a war," Leo answered.

"And how convenient that *you*'re one of the generals in that war," Bryce said accusatorially.

Leo glared at him." You think I *asked* for this?"

Bryce put his tablet down and got to his feet. "Why else would Ghob want you instead of a Gnome?"

"She wants a Gnome *too*," I interrupted before they could escalate anything. "Ghob said she needed one of each Elemental type. That's why she wanted another Sylph when they wrote Ian off for being too supportive of humans. There have to be four, plus whoever Knox Ryder is," I insisted. "She said he was the fifth general, and they seemed to think he was the one who could lift the veil."

Alec laughed out loud. "If that veil comes up, there will be no more separation between the Elemental world and this one. Not to mention whatever else is locked behind there."

Bryce shrugged and shook his head. "Would that be so bad?" he asked. "Then we wouldn't be stuck on this island. We could go anywhere we wanted without having to hide what we really are."

"Wait, five generals for five continents," Leo said to himself, seemingly oblivious to the rest of the conversation. "So Ghob and Uri must be the other two," he added, then finally looked up at the rest of us in realization. "They're going to start a *world* war."

"Or a war on the world," Rhea added a few seconds later.

"Then we need to find Eve before Uri does," I nearly shouted. "Ghob said she had somebody named Knox Ryder, and that she'd lured him off her boat in Portland." I cleared my throat when everyone's eyes fell on mine. "I'm from Portland, and I think there's another tear in the veil there. It's in the woods near my house."

Alita nodded and forced a laugh. "Oh, our Citadel complex has woods too."

I shook my head at her before I turned back to the others. "I meant if there's supposed to be a tear close to each of our towns, I think I know where the one in Portland is. I think I know where to find Eve."

I stopped feeling so confident in my information with everyone staring at me. Maybe I was just in shock…had I babbled any of that?

"Even if you do know where Eve is, so what?" Alec shrugged. "It's not like we can get there. Once again, there's *no* gateway underwater. Leo and Rhea can't take on Uri and Ghob alone, and they can't carry all three of us through the tear you just found."

I glanced around at everyone to see if they agreed, but no one's expression changed. "I…could carry someone," I finally said, and now everyone except Leo started laughing again. "I *can do it*," I insisted, which, to my surprise, stopped their chuckling. "I just need some time to learn."

They all stared at me blankly until Leo spoke up. "I'll work with you up here at night then." He nodded, then turned to the others. "She'll be ready."

"Whatever," Rhea said, which seemed to set the tone for everyone else, who also unceremoniously agreed.

"Well, if everyone is done leaping off cliffs for the evening, I'm going to go see what I can find out about *The Fold*," Bryce said, picking up his tablet and slipping it into his bag. "I'll let you know when we have enough information to try again."

Alita got to her feet and dusted off to follow him. "See you at home," she said to me, which made my chest ache all over again. This place wasn't home, even if she couldn't remember why.

Alec slipped an arm around Rhea's waist and nuzzled her neck, then said something about *hitching another ride.* She elbowed him in the ribs and laughed as he feigned injury all the way down the hill.

This left Leo and me standing in awkward silence. I didn't know how to remedy that since my options were either to scream at him for deceiving me, or run into his arms for saving me, so I left him standing there and started the long walk back to my dorm. If I were to take a clinical look at everything, I'd have to start with a baseline of what was known: I wasn't completely human, a war between worlds was coming, and if I ever wanted to go home again, I needed to learn how to fly.

***

I'd skipped breakfast the next morning mainly because I just couldn't bring myself to get out of bed, despite Alita's nauseating enthusiasm about waffles. It felt like my mind was still rejecting everything that had happened since I left The Grind, even though I didn't need any more proof it wasn't a Red Fever coma dream, and none of this had been a hallucination. If I was ever going to get home again, I needed to start playing by the rules of this reality.

I made my way to my honing session the same way I'd gone before, but this time I wasn't talking with Ian and could pay attention to the impossibly surreal plants and insects that lined the route. Flowers with dark green stems and leaves that curled in on themselves, the buds a deep red with bright blue plumes in the centers. Not even a few feet farther up the path, magenta butterflies with long, feathered antennae fluttered over another patch of flowers, these like carnations, only purple and orange with variegated leaves.

But it wasn't until I saw the tail end of something climbing up the white, birch-like bark of a tree that I stopped, completely in awe. An armored, bright yellow snake with actual horns appeared from behind the thick trunk, and I nearly fell backward when I saw that it wasn't a snake at all. Whatever this was, it had arms and legs like a lizard and red and gold flowing wings like something in a fantasy drawing. As it made its way up the trunk and onto an extended branch, I realized it must have been at least six feet long with the girth of a softball. Each of its armored plates caught the sun as it moved, reflecting hypnotizing, iridescent rays in its wake.

"Wow…" I said under my breath, mesmerized by how beautiful it was.

"That's a Djin snake," Leo whispered, which was ironically more startling than it would have been if he'd just used his normal voice. I sucked in a quick breath, fortunately managing not to scare the animal in the tree away. Leo took a few slow steps toward me and stopped at my side. "I don't think it's a student either—no one really moves into their full shift unless they don't have to come out of it for the day. And everyone is doing something now during honing week."

"A Djin snake..." I repeated, then remembered this was what Bryce had called Rhea that first day in the dining hall. This was her shift. "This is what Rhea becomes?" I asked, glancing at Leo.

"If she wants to," he answered, his eyes widening as the snake-like animal unfolded its wings in the rays of sun falling over them. "But she doesn't like it —says it feels too confining—so she usually shifts just enough for her wings to come out."

"That's why her skin turned into the armored plates, and her hair..." I trailed off, amazed all over again as I remembered.

"This is the serpent Lucifer pretended to be in the Eden story with Eve."

I remembered what Ghob had said about them all being punished for it—they'd lost their wings, arms, and legs—and I was suddenly struck with anger.

"Why were they all punished? It wasn't their fault."

Leo shrugged. "It's just the way it was," he said, tilting his head to admire the glittering wings as they soaked in the sunlight. "But they're in their original form here, since this island is basically a replica of Eden. You won't see them like this anywhere else in the world."

We started walking towards the honing grounds, and I felt something light inside me. This injustice was no different from the power dynamic in The Grind where the innocent were punished and the guilty—the ones who were really guilty—went free.

I had to learn to fly. I had to find my way home to my family and Max. And I *had* to warn Eve.

Chapter 26

Leo walked me to the Sylph practice field, still apologizing the whole way for trying to make me forget where I came from. I didn't know if I forgave him yet, but whether I did or not, we had to move past it so we could find our way home.

"I'll make it up to you," he said, stopping just before he went ahead to help with the Salamander honing session. "If you'll let me."

"Teach me to fly, and we'll call it a good start," I answered. The corner of his mouth tacked up, and he gave me a little nod.

"Meet me on the cliff tonight. Just before sunset."

"All right," I said. He nodded one last time, then turned to make his way over the hill to his training session.

I had been expecting to see Midori on the Sylph field, but Ian was leading our group today. And apparently, I was late.

"Nice a'ye tae join us, Halsey," he all but shouted across the field of Sylphs in white, racerback tank tops, who were practicing some kind of breathing exercise. I jumped when two of them closest to me suddenly disappeared in a puff of air strong enough to blow my tie over my shoulder. Each of their clothes fell to the ground in a heap, but no one seemed to pay any attention.

"What the hell!" I shouted involuntarily, my heart instantly pounding like I'd run all the way here. Several of the students started laughing, and Ian did little to deter them.

"Jes workin' on transmutation," he said casually, like I was supposed to have *any* idea what that meant. "It means how tae *shift*. We introduced it at the beginning of class. A half-hour ago." Ian added with a flat smile. "Get'che a place then."

A hummingbird and a huge, yellow moth fluttered back into the space where the two other students had just been, and with another gust, they both reappeared. The girls grabbed the other's arms and started jumping up and down in celebration, each of them squealing and laughing until they realized their clothes were currently being trampled under their own feet. They screamed and scrambled back into their skorts and racerback shirts.

"Well-done, lassies." Ian nodded at them, and their instant, obvious mortification was palpable. I turned away quickly in order to be *one fewer* set of eyes on them and waited for my instructions. *But...* Ian didn't say a thing.

"Hey..." I glanced at the tall, dark-haired boy next to me. "How do we shift?" I whispered, completely unprepared for the death glare he gave me in return. Instead of just his lips frowning at me, his entire face seemed to turn down as he opened his mouth to answer me. The corners of his eyes, the muscles in his cheeks, even his dark hair, all of it almost looked like it was *melting*.

I stumbled back again, nearly falling into the person behind me as I watched the boy's nose and cheekbones sharpen and his black hair grow down his arms. I only had time to blink before his shoulders arched, and the lengths of black hair gave way to black feathers that shimmered blue in the sunlight.

"I did it!" he yelled and started flapping his huge wings. They took out the girl behind me, whom I'd almost stumbled into a few seconds before.

"Indeed, ye have, lad!" Ian said, moving toward us clapping. He leaned in when he was close enough. "But listen, ya wee doo, mind yer wings, aye?" He winked to the girl behind us, then slapped the boy on the shoulder. As if he'd hit a button, the huge, black wings retracted, and Ian nodded to me. "Yer up, lass."

"Oh, no… I don't know how to shift on purpose," I said, shaking my head. "And…I wore the wrong shirt for, um, my wings," I added, looking down at my striped tie and white button-down.

"Highly advisable ye keep 'em tucked in, then. Go on wi' the rest, though." Ian folded his arms and shifted his weight to one hip, apparently waiting for me to partially shift.

I shook my head at him. "Like I said, I don't know how to do it."

"Shore ye do." He nodded adamantly, then reached into his pocket and, to my horror, pulled out my *bra*. "Ah believe that belongs tae ye, no?" he asked, tossing it to me. I snatched it out of the air, and felt heat rush into my cheeks. Sharp prickles ran down my arms, and I started to panic that my wings would tear my shirt to pieces in front of everyone just like last time.

"No…no, stop!" I said, frantically studying my hands, which were also starting to prickle.

"Let it come," Ian ordered. "But only tae yer hands. Reroute each wee stabby like a leaf in a current."

I tried to do what he said, to imagine water pulling each of the prickles to my hands as I tried to swallow the panic welling up in my chest. I pictured a rushing waterfall at the top of my head washing the prickles down my shoulders, then I pictured a crashing wave at the small of my back sending the prickles up and over my shoulders, down my arms, and finally, into my fingers.

It was working. The sharp little points that were everywhere a second ago were actually rerouting to my hands, and when I looked down, the feathers were only appearing there, stopping halfway up my forearms.

"It's working…" I said with the last of a breath. The rush of excitement broke my focus, though, and prickles started traveling higher up my arms, soon followed by feathers and the grotesque raised ridges. "*No, no…no,*" I said, consciously trying to channel the sensation back to my hands, and while the feathers didn't recede, to my relief, the ridges finally did.

"That's braw," Ian said. "Weel done!"

"It worked!" I gasped. "You were right, I just had to think of the water pushing the—"

"*Water*?" Ian interrupted, raising an eyebrow. "Is that what ye imagined?"

I studied his face for a second, confused.

"Yeah, you said to imagine the *wee stab* or whatever like a leaf on a current."

His eyes widened a little. "An' *water* is what came tae mind—nae air…" he stated rather than asked, then nodded slowly. "Weel, tae change back, push th' stabs oot yer fingers an' toes."

I did as he said, imagining the prickles running out of the ends of my fingers. To my amazement, the feathers that covered my hands started to recede.

Could it be this easy? I just somehow trigger a rush of emotion to create a flood of heat, and then just imagine that heat flowing to a particular place to control the shift? This must be how Leo and Rhea were able to stop right after their wings appeared.

"Thanks for—" I started to say, but Ian had already made his way to the other side of the field to help someone else. I stared at him, astonished that he had silently covered so much ground in a matter of seconds. In fact, when I looked around for the other Sylphs who were just here training next to me, they'd also drifted several yards away. I was standing far from the group, and I hadn't moved at all.

"Wonderful job," Uri said, nearly startling me out of my skin. The feathers on my arms quickly ran up my shoulders, and I closed my eyes for a second to imagine the flow of water pushing them to my fingertips, and then out into the air—gone. When I opened my eyes, my hands were back again.

"Thanks," I said, smiling at my little victory. "I think I'm getting the hang of it."

"I'm not surprised in the least," Uri said, taking a few steps toward me. "Leo tells me you're a quick study."

Now that the imminent panic of my wings tearing my clothes off in front of everyone had subsided, a new sense of dread came over me when I remembered Uri's conversation with Ghob last night in The Fold.

"I'm trying," I said, scrambling for smalltalk. "He's been a good mentor."

"He's one of our best," Uri added, studying my face without so much as blinking. He suddenly took in a quick breath and glanced at the rest of the Sylphs across the field. "Look how they've drifted…" he said, smiling. "That's, of course, completely normal for a new Sylph…they tend to get caught up in each other's momentum the first few weeks. In another twenty minutes, you'll likely find them right back here. Interesting you weren't pulled along with them."

He studied me carefully again, tilting his head to one side as if contemplating something.

I cleared my throat. "Well, I was a little late," I confessed. "So I probably didn't have time to get in sync or something."

He nodded in placation. "Of course, that must be it," he said dryly. "You seem to have adjusted well to island life, Halsey. Quite a change from Portland Prep, I imagine." He fixed his eyes on mine again, the intense, unblinking blue reminding me of a cat waiting to pounce. As far as he knew, I didn't remember anything about my old life, and I needed to make sure he didn't find out otherwise.

"Um, where?" I said, trying my best to keep my expression as blank as possible. He lowered his eyelids, scrutinizing for another several seconds, but then seemed to relax. He flashed another smile, this one wide as he chuckled. "Be sure you're drinking enough water." Uri nodded and slipped his hands into his white pants pockets. "It's the best thing you can do for yourself here," he added, then started making his way down the field until he disappeared over the hill—exactly where Leo had gone.

***

Since Ian was clearly not interested if I stayed with the rest of the Sylphs or not for the day, I'd stopped back at my dorm and looked in my closet for the white racer-back tank top everyone else had been wearing. I found about five of them shoved to the far right on the hanger bar, and quickly changed.

Before I knew it, I'd spent the entire day on the opposite end of the field from the other Sylphs, trying to open and close my wings without allowing the feathers or ridges to spread to my arms. It wasn't perfect yet, but by the time I was supposed to meet everyone else for dinner in the dining hall, I'd managed to keep the wings separate from my arms, save for feathers over my shoulders. I couldn't wait to show Leo what I'd learned, but these thoughts went out the window when I opened the door and the smell of garlic bread wafted over me. I quickly loaded a plate and made my way to the table with Alita and the others.

"Wow, have some spaghetti with your meatballs," Bryce said, eyeing my plate as I sat down.

"You're eating that again?" Anita asked.

I shrugged. "I like pasta."

"Where were you all day? I didn't see you at breakfast or lunch."

"Practicing on the Sylph field," I answered her, forking an entire meatball into my mouth.

"You've been out there since this morning?" Alita watched me, wide-eyed. "Are you even chewing?"

I swallowed. "Yes, and yes," I said, eating another whole meatball.

Rhea laughed. "She'll get two more plates before she stops eating like that. Flight school is no joke."

"I still eat like that," Alec said. "Before and after learning to shift—that's just swimming."

"You're all animals," Bryce said, finally looking up from his tablet. "Speaking of animals, where's Red-Cloud?"

"He was at the fire field before lunch, but then he went somewhere with Uri," Rhea said.

"Well, get word to him to meet on the cliff tonight after sunset. I found the tear to Portland."

Chapter 27

After dinner, I thought it would be a good idea to at least try to fly before meeting Leo on the cliff. If everyone else was coming after sunset, we wouldn't have a lot of time to practice after all.

I tried to recall the feeling I had when Ian threw my bra at me earlier this morning. The rush of embarrassment that crashed into me as I imagined him retrieving it from wherever it had been flung in the dining hall, then actually putting it in his pocket for safe keeping or something. *Ugh.* Suffice it to say, it didn't take long before I felt the prickle racing up my throat and into my cheeks, and I imagined it being washed to my shoulder blades. A few seconds later, my wings expanded behind me, and I imagined the rest of the prickles flooding out, dripping from the ends of my fingers.

I flapped my wings a few times, laughing out loud that I managed to stop the rest of the shift, then startled when my feet left the ground. I quickly stopped my wings and felt the grass tickling my ankles again, then blew out a long, slow breath. I hadn't tried to fly earlier today when I was practicing, but the cliff was a good ten-minute walk…and no one was around.

I started running in the direction of it, flapping my wings a few times until my feet left the ground again. I started gliding, but after a second, a pocket of wind pushed my left wing down and I started to drop. I tried desperately to flap my way free, but it only made me start spinning.

In a matter of seconds, I'd crashed headfirst into the ground—well, more like elbows first since I'd hidden behind my arms. I rolled a few times, and noticed my knuckles and elbows were bleeding when I finally righted myself. Without even trying, my wings started to fold in, then shrink until they were gone again, and in the same moment, the scrapes on my hands and arms disappeared. *The shift channels its energy to repair your injuries,* I remembered Leo saying, and smiled to myself.

When I stood up again, the main house I'd been taken to when I first arrived was in sight, so I'd flown at least halfway to the cliff. That moment of satisfaction faded quickly, though, when I heard raised voices coming from inside, though the house was several hundred yards away.

I made my way up the steps and slipped through the front door only to realize it was Leo who was yelling, but I couldn't make out any of his words. I moved quickly toward the closed door where the voices were coming from and stopped abruptly when a sharp pain jabbed my left ankle.

"Ow!" I said too loudly and quickly covered my mouth. When I looked down, my ankle had two puncture wounds, each of them dripping blood. In the corner, a yellow, horned Djin snake was coiled in the dark, its wings extended and shaking like a rattlesnake at me. It hissed, and I slowly moved backward, accidentally running into an end table and knocking over a lamp. "Shit," I whispered. The snake hissed at me again, and the yelling behind the door stopped. "Shit...shit! *Shit*!" I whispered under my breath again and tried to rush back toward the front door, but it was too late.

The doors swung open, and Uri came through. I stopped where I stood and put my left ankle behind my right leg so he couldn't see the bite mark, which was starting to itch.

"Halsey, what a pleasant surprise," he said, clearly *not* pleased to see me. "Is there something I can do for you? Oh..." he added, looking at the floor where I stood. "Are you hurt?"

I looked down to find that the blood had run forward over my foot and sandal straps, and now the whole injury looked much worse than it was. "Um..." I said, scrambling for words. "I was taking a walk on a trail...and...I don't know...I think something bit me?"

"Indeed," Uri nodded. "Jeanette! A first aid kit!"

Within seconds, one of the gray-uniformed, silent attendants came rushing in the room with a small, white box. She knelt by my side and took off my sandal, then just started dabbing a cold, wet cloth all over my foot. I sucked in a breath through my teeth when I felt the sting of the other little cloth she'd ripped open and pressed over the bite on my ankle. It couldn't have been a handful of seconds later that the bite had healed, and my sandal was already cleaned and back on my foot. She started tapping on my shin with her leathery hand, forcing me to step back so she could clean the floor where the blood had dripped. I looked up for what just seemed like a few seconds, and as fast as she'd arrived, she was gone again.

"Wow…" I said, in a little shock. "Thank you. I'll just head back to my dorm then."

"I'll escort you," Leo said, storming through the doors Uri had just opened. I forced myself to swallow the gasp in my throat when I saw the small, black horns slowly receding back into his forehead, his dark hair pulled into a ponytail with several loose strands framing his angular face.

"Oh, OK," I said, glancing at Uri, whose bright blue eyes were narrowed and his lips were pressed together in a rigid smile.

"I'll have the mentors made aware, and thank you, Mr. Red-Cloud," Uri called after us as we made our way to the door.

Outside, Leo pulled off his shirt and jammed it into his pocket. His wings shot out what must have been fifteen feet in either direction, and I didn't have any time to react before he threw his arm around my waist and took off straight into the sun. I turned my head into his shoulder to shield my eyes, then risked a glance at the ground that was quickly starting to look like a collection of toy trees and houses. But Leo just kept flying higher and higher until wisps of white clouds started to obscure my vision.

"Leo! We're too high!" I finally said, holding onto him so tightly now I was afraid I might leave marks on his skin.

A few seconds later he leveled out, then started to dive. I buried my face in his neck and tried not to scream, but the whistling air and sense of falling were almost too much. Finally, we slowed, and he leveled out again. I took a deep breath and risked another glance toward the ground, but there was no ground this time. We were flying over the ocean. Behind us, the cliff rose up from the rocks far below.

"Hold on," Leo said, slowing until we were nearly stopped, his arm tight around my waist as his other hand moved to my face.

"Leo, what happened?" I asked, his black horns now extending into a twist near the ends. His eyes were a golden brown, like the darkest part of a fire. "Leo...?" He leaned me backward, his wide, black wings slowly moving over us, pushing the air and catching it again.

"Put your arms around my neck," he said close to my ear. When I did, he moved his lips over mine, softly at first, but then more urgently as his hold tightened around my waist, and his other hand pulled my leg over his hip. A rush of heat rose inside me as he trailed kisses down my throat and chest, then back toward my ear again. "All the heat, push it to your back...your shoulders...show me your wings, Halsey," he said, his voice low and rough.

I did as he said, channeling it all until my wings unfolded, and he rotated us so that I was above him. His hands moved to the small of my back, and we started falling.

"Leo!" I said, feeling the cold wind rush up from below.

"Use your wings!" he said. "Hold them out...catch the air!"

Again, I did as he said, and the second I extended my wings all the way, I felt the air like giant hands pushing them up—pushing us up.

"It's working!" I shouted.

"Go higher! Push higher!"

I pushed against the air, which sent us lofting upward each time, and when I felt the next breeze, I extended my wings again and let the air carry us. *I was flying...*

Leo let go of my waist and fell several feet before rolling to his stomach and extending his wings. The air caught him, too, and sent him soaring upward until we were flying next to each other.

"Now follow me..." he called just before darting forward. We flew at full speed for several more seconds until the fog cleared just long enough to show a curtain of raging fire coming out of jagged rocks.

"Leo!" I shouted to him as we went into the fire, unable to stop in time, but the very next second we were surrounded by silence again. Deafening silence. He collapsed his wings and landed on his feet, but I realized this too late and couldn't close my wings all the way before I crashed into him. He caught me around the waist and steadied me until my feet found the ground. "Thanks," I whispered, feeling my heart pounding against his as he loosened his hold on me, his hands moving from the small of my back to my hips before he let me go. His horns were starting to recede, but his chest was still heaving, and all his muscles were tensed. "Leo, what happened back there with Uri?" I asked, surprised at how difficult it was to talk.

He took a slow, deep breath and let it out through his nose in two streams of smoke, both of which disappeared into the fog that surrounded us. His horns receded the rest of the way, and his black hair fell in soft waves around his shoulders, the ponytail apparently a casualty of his aerodynamics just now.

He let his gaze fall to the ground and shook his head. "I'm sorry," he said. "I never should have brought you to this island." When he looked up at me again, his eyes were dark again, but now also glassy and bloodshot. His heavy brows were drawn together, and his jaw was clenched like he was in physical pain.

"Leo…what *happened*?" I asked again, moving my hand over his shoulder.

"The Sylph Uri was talking about last night—the one he was looking at to replace Ian on the mission to kill Eve," he started, then took another deep breath. "He wants you, Halsey."

I stared at him for a second, then stepped back. If I was the Sylph Uri had been talking about with Ghob, he'd clearly missed something. I *definitely* sided with humans. This had to be a mistake.

"I can't be the one he wanted," I said. "He didn't want Ian because he was too partial to humans. *I'm* partial to humans, Leo. And I would assume you are too?"

"It doesn't matter," he said. "I think he told her that to buy some time, but she didn't take the bait after all. He called me in there this afternoon and put it all on the table."

"If it doesn't matter, why doesn't he just ask Ian?"

"I *don't know*, Halsey. Midori told him you were the one." Leo pushed his hands through his dark hair. "She doesn't think you're a Sylph," he added. "She told him as much after that first honing class."

"Then what the hell am I? Uri is the one who said I was a Sylph in the first place."

"He still believes you are," Leo answered. "But the fact that Midori doesn't think you're like the others is exactly why he wants you to go with us. I told him you weren't ready for this."

"*Us*?" I asked, studying him.

Leo sighed and moved his hands to his hips, then let his eyes fall to the ground again. "I don't have a choice. I have to lead a group to find Eve and kill her, just like we heard him discussing with Ghob last night," he said, then met my eyes again. "We're leaving in a week, Halsey."

Chapter 28

I stared blankly at him, hoping this was all just a bad dream.

"We can't, Leo. You heard them say that Knox person she's protecting will lift the veil. With Eve gone, they'll take him and then attack everyone."

Leo gave me a pained, knowing look. "Not everyone," he said quietly. "Uri said the Gnomes would protect the people who never hurt the earth."

"Everyone has hurt the earth!" I shouted. "They'll kill everyone!"

"*No*. He promised me. Ghob told him herself."

"We can't do this." I shook my head. "If we don't, that guy can't lift the veil, and whatever is behind there can't kill anyone. We just refuse."

"Halsey…" Leo sighed. "If we don't, they'll kill the rest of my tribe. And yours…all of the people each of us on the team cares about. The original Elemental Fae like Sylvie who can cross between the planes have already started setting traps near the tears in the veil —luring the people we care about with echoes and glimpses to the other side so they'll be marked."

"My aunt and uncle barely leave the house, but Max…" I whispered.

"Uri said he's been coming to those woods of yours since they told him your helicopter went down. There's another tear right there somewhere," Leo explained. "Every time you thought about him, reached out like that in your mind, Sylvie made it so he'd hear you better the closer he got to that spot on the path, and when he was close enough, she marked him."

"No..." I said, tears burning my eyes as my voice broke on the word. "I didn't know. I didn't *know*, Leo..."

"None of us did," he said, his voice full of anger, but not toward me. "That's how Uri wanted it, and we don't have a choice now that our people are marked. We have to protect them."

My mind was spinning with indecision, and I was doubled over with guilt and anger. No matter what I did or didn't do, someone was going to die because of me—either the veil would be lifted, and the war on humanity would begin, or Sylvie would make sure everyone we cared about would pay the price. There had to be another way.

"Leo, you said there were others," I remembered. "Who? An Undine and a Gnome, right? Ghob said there had to be one of each bloodline."

"I recommended Alec and Bryce. Uri doesn't know we've already found a tear on this side of the veil."

"Do they know you put them on this team? Bryce just said he found the tear that leads to Portland. We're supposed to meet on the cliff after sunset tonight."

"When did he tell you that?"

"Tonight at dinner."

"Then they don't know yet...I don't know when Uri is planning to tell them."

"You said we're not leaving for a week. We have time then. We can still sabotage it somehow like we were talking about last night," I said, trying to pace myself. "We can go tonight and warn Eve, and maybe she can protect the people who are marked. She has to have some kind of power or they'd have killed her by now."

"Bryce will never agree to that."

"Then we won't tell him. Someone *has* to be helping Eve, Leo. She has an archangel and an Elemental Fae queen trying to kill her, and they haven't been able to do it yet."

"Halsey…"

"Do you really want to be responsible for killing most of humanity? We *have* to try," I said, moving deeper into the fog.

Leo followed me. "Where are you going?"

"To find the way out so we can get back to the cliff," I said, trying to push the fog out of the way.

"No, Halsey, listen. You can't just go wandering around in here. Bryce said The Fold is—" Leo started, but his voice quickly faded as I toppled down and landed on something hard. Water splashed me, and I panicked that it would burn my skin, but it didn't.

The fog was several yards above my head against a backdrop of gray, overcast sky that met the dark lake surrounding me. Everything was deadly silent except for the sound of the calm water below. I looked down and found myself sitting in a rowboat, which I nearly fell out of when *another* rowboat came out of the fog. As it came closer, I saw a vacant-eyed, older woman inside paddling slowly. Before I could say something to her, dozens of other rowboats appeared in the fog, each of them carrying a person who seemed to be in some kind of trance too. "What is this place?" I whispered to myself, watching the boats slip in and out of the fog that was now seeming to close the gap from the sky to the water.

"Halsey!" Leo shouted as he descended from the fog above, his dark wings sending currents of air that rocked my rowboat. I reached for the sides to keep from falling overboard, but Leo's arms hooked under mine as he lifted me out of the boat and back through the tear.

We toppled to the rocky ground that we couldn't see, and I was confused about why we were both desperately out of breath.

"Where…was that?" I gasped.

Leo's wings snapped closed, then disappeared. He dropped to his hands and knees, trying to suck in slow, deep breaths.

"Limbo," he finally said. "For human souls—it's their world between planes."

"Are you talking about Purgatory? People riding around like zombies in rowboats on a foggy lake?" I asked, then coughed and sucked in a breath.

"It's just another tear, Halsey. I was trying to tell you…The Fold *is* the veil."

"Bryce told you all that? That's what he found out in his research?" I said, getting to my feet.

"As of this morning, yeah," Leo nodded. "The raven messenger just called it The Fold because everything has to be a stupid puzzle," he said, rolling his eyes. "It extends out past this island—it's the fog, just like by the cliff, and it's the reason why planes and ships go down if they don't know how to avoid the tears like the one you just fell through. The Bermuda Triangle is just a bunch of tears in the veil."

"But you said they were doors. You said we just needed to find the right ones to go back and forth between home and here," I said, confused.

"Yeah, *doors*, whatever, they're just more tears in the veil," Leo agreed. "But we don't know which ones lead home and which ones lead to the fifth ring of Hell, or Limbo," he added, throwing out a hand in the direction we'd just been. "That's why Bryce was researching."

"OK…" I took a deep breath. "Then we go back to the cliff and fly the others back here. And Bryce will show us where to go. We'll talk to the others about warning Eve, and Bryce can just think it's the day trip he's been trying to make happen all this time."

"We can try it," Leo said, resigned. He sighed, and his wings slowly extended behind him. I watched the shadow grow under him as they unfurled again, his shoulders, chest, and stomach flexing to balance the weight.

The sight of him was enough to send a wave of heat through me again, and I quickly channeled it to my own wings. I closed my eyes for a second once they were fully extended and pushed the rest of the prickles out through my fingertips. When I looked back at Leo, he was smirking at me and shaking his head.

"What?" I asked, curious why he wasn't elated for me.

"I was hoping I'd have to kiss you again to get that to work," he said, his dark eyes flashing a deep golden glow.

***

The sun had set while we were in The Fold, but only recently judging by the simmering purple on the horizon. Leo and I glided to the cliff edge, where Rhea, Alec, Alita, and Bryce were just coming over the ridge.

"Perfect timing," Bryce said to me as we landed. "I guess you really are a quick study."

"Wow!" Alita rushed over to me and ran her hand over my left wing. "These are huge! And soft."

"Halsey said you knew where the tear was that led to Portland?" Leo said, folding in his wings as he turned to Bryce.

"The tears seem to be aligned with the constellation Orion. Our tear here is lined up with the star *Mintaka* on Orion's belt," Bryce said, typing something into his tablet. When he finished, a green series of lines and dots projected into the sky, one of the dots in the center shining brighter than them all. He typed something else into his tablet, and a red line shot downward, stopping in the middle of the fog. "That's our tear."

"When you get close, it looks like burning rocks," I said, glaring at Leo. "Which would have been nice to know."

Leo smiled. "I didn't want you to chicken out." He winked, then turned back to Bryce. "And the tear that leads to Portland?"

"It's north—aligned with the star *Betelgeuse*, Orion's sword shoulder," Bryce answered, typing another combination into his tablet and making a star to the upper left of the other shoulder light up." The tears in the veil move, though, because of the earth's rotation. I was telling Red-Cloud it's actually amazing you haven't wound up in Limbo with your free dives since it's right there next to our tear—aligned with the star *Alnilam*." Another red line shot down from the highlighted, projected star in the center of Orion's belt. "You fly forty-five degrees to the left, and we're suddenly a long way from home."

Leo and I exchanged knowing looks. "We'll be careful," he said. "How do we get to the tear lined up with *Betelgeuse*?"

"Go in through our tear and just keep going north forty-five degrees. We should run right into it. Space is compressed in the veil, so it shouldn't take nearly as long as it would to fly to Portland from here, even if we could get through the tear landmines around the island."

"How did you find all these tears?" I asked, amazed, but at the same time, confused. "How did you even know about them?"

Bryce exchanged looks with Leo.

"It's all right. It won't matter if she knows," Leo said.

Bryce looked back at me carefully. "Uri's *Book of Muzaloth*." He waved his tablet in the air. "I digitized it after I found it one day while I was looking for the generator he had to have for the island. I was going to shut it down and kill the firewall I thought he had running, and then I could queue home."

I looked from Bryce to Alec and Rhea to see if they were trying not to laugh, but their faces were serious.

"You saw the tears in a *supernatural world divider* in a *book*?" I said, incredulous.

Now the others started chuckling.

"Halsey, it's the book the archangel Raziel—the angel of mysteries—wrote about the eighth level of

Heaven." Leo said. "We don't know how, but Uri... *Uriel*, must have taken it."

"Sorry, the what? There are levels of Heaven?" I asked, then turned to Alita. "Did you know about this?" She shook her head, looking as utterly confused as I was.

"We don't really have time for this," Bryce said, checking the Orion projection. "The stars are shifting as we speak, but OK, crash course because I love this stuff: There are ten levels. The eighth level governs the different realms: Limbo, all the other nine levels of Heaven, the constellations, wormholes, dimensions, astral projection, whatever. Raziel wrote a bunch of books, even gave one to Adam and Eve after they got kicked out of Eden so they didn't walk off a cliff or try to pet a tiger or something."

Alec shook his head at Bryce. "Oh my god, can we go now?"

"And it's just written in this book that the stars aligned with the tears?" I asked. "I mean, if you've been reading that book for a few years how are you just now figuring it out?"

Bryce sighed. "OK, this is going to sound stupid, but new pages appeared. I don't know how to explain it," he said, holding out the tablet that was still projecting the constellation of Orion. "I think after we finally found the first tear, it like, *knew* we were ready for more information or something. I don't even know how new *digitized* pages appeared because it's not like this is the physical, angel-touched book or anything."

I looked skeptically at Bryce, but Leo refocused everyone's attention when he started talking again.

"If anyone would like to go home, then we need to leave before the tear moves again. I don't want to hit Limbo instead," he said, meeting my eyes, and all the overwhelming new information I'd just learned was washed to the back of my mind. We needed to warn Eve about Uri's and Ghob's plan. *Now*.

Chapter 29

I carried Alita since she was the lightest of the three. Rhea carried Bryce, and Leo carried Alec as we made our way toward the fog and what we hoped would be the right set of flaming rocks. We followed Bryce's red grid lines in the sky, and I held my breath when I finally saw the flames.

"Halsey!" Alita screamed.

"It's all right! It's supposed to be there. Close your eyes!"

Seconds later, we were through the tear, the familiar white fog and rocky terrain beneath us... *which* I only discovered because I still couldn't seem to land on my feet. Alita and I crashed to the ground and rolled a few times before everything finally stopped spinning. I got to my feet. When I looked up, Rhea was slowly clapping.

"Oh, I forgot...you could fly into a flaming tear in the veil and stick the landing when you first got to the island, right?" I snapped. She raised a finely penciled eyebrow and sneered at me, but she also *stopped* clapping. Granted, it was only to punch Bryce in the arm for snickering, but I'd take my victories where I could get them.

"Keep laughing and I'll drop you in the ocean on the way back. You can dog paddle to shore," she said. Bryce just rolled his eyes, unfazed.

I turned to Alita to help her up. "Are you all right?"

She nodded and looked around, wide-eyed. "Wow, it's just all fog everywhere," she said, taking a few steps in the opposite direction. All at once, Bryce, Leo, and I all screamed for her to stop. "Whoa! *OK*," she said, holding up her hands.

"Limbo, remember?" Bryce's eyes widened like this was the most obvious thing in the world. And I mean, we *had* just been talking about it. "It's literally like, twenty steps in the direction you were just heading. Come on," he added, waving for her to follow him.

"How far away is the Portland tear supposed to be?" Alec asked, holding out a hand and watching the fog move through his fingers as we walked.

"It's a straight shot northwest," Bryce answered, checking his tablet again. "No other tears for about an hour unless we get wildly off course."

Leo dropped back and walked at my side, slowing our pace a little to let the others get ahead.

"I talked with Alec and Rhea," he whispered. "They'll help us warn Eve about next week. But Halsey... Next week, we won't be able to pull any punches. Uri and Sylvie will be watching everything we do then."

"Then they can watch us look for someone who's not there," I said without taking my eyes from the empty fog path ahead of us.

"What about Alita?" he asked, lifting his chin to her back, several feet ahead of us.

"Maybe talk to Bryce about taking her under his wing? To look out for her, you know?" I said, turning toward him so there was no chance she could hear me. "I think he likes her. But she's kind of scattered. If she knows what we're really doing, she might slip and say something. It's better they stay together."

Leo nodded. "So where's the first stop when we come out the other side? How will we know where to find Eve?"

"She works behind The Citadel wall as the Crisis Management Director. I used to have a card with her queue code, but I can't find it."

"Should be easy enough to track her down with a title and a location, don't worry," he said. "But we'll need to get in and out. We can't afford to have all of us turn up missing tomorrow for the closing of honing week."

I nodded. "That's fine. I just want to let Max know so he can stay close to her, help her keep that Knox guy safe so the veil stays down."

"All right, we'll find him too. I'm going to tell Bryce to keep Alita close." He angled his head toward the front of our group, then raised my hand to his lips and kissed it before he walked ahead.

I took a deep breath and tried not to think of Max, of the danger he and my aunt and uncle were in now because of me. If this didn't work, Uri and Sylvie would kill them, and they would never know the truth about anything.

I wasn't sure how long I was caught up in those thoughts, but I was startled out of them by Bryce's excited shouts.

"It's there! Just ahead!" he barked, holding out a hand to stop everyone's progression.

"What's on the other side?" Rhea asked. "Water, what?"

"I don't know, Halsey said woods?" Bryce answered, glancing at me with raised eyebrows for confirmation.

"If a tear is supposed to feel like the one we went through back there, where all noise is swallowed up, then yes, this will come out in the woods."

"All right, then look out," Alec said, making his way to the front of the group. "Wait, unless...is it like, a drop out of the sky?"

Rhea rolled her eyes. "Come on," she said, extending a hand. "We'll go together."

Alec bounced his nearly white eyebrows at us and took her hand. They started walking slowly, but didn't seem to be getting anywhere.

Rhea turned back to us. "Where is it supposed—" She didn't even have the chance to finish the sentence before they both disappeared into the ground in a swirling cloud of fog, which made the rest of us jump.

"*Oh my god,*" Alita gasped. "Are they all right?" We all exchanged glances until Rhea's head and shoulders appeared near the ground in exactly the place she'd just fallen through.

"No wings necessary. It opens about a foot off the ground next to a giant rock wall," she said, then disappeared again.

"All right," Bryce blew out a breath. "Shall we?" He offered an arm to Alita, who flipped her long, red braid off her shoulder and gave him a huge smile. She took his arm, and in a few more steps, they, too, disappeared into the ground.

"Our turn," I said, moving toward the spot where everyone else went through.

"I'll go first and catch you," he said, smiling.

"It's just a foot off the ground..." I trailed off, wondering why Leo was already several steps in front of me.

He turned to look at me. "I'm sorry, Halsey..." he said, his expression falling.

"For what?"

He sighed. "We aren't leaving in a week. This is the strike team...here, now. We just needed you to find Eve."

I swallowed hard to push down the tightening feeling in my chest as my heart pounded in my ears.

"What the hell are you saying?"

"We can't risk warning Eve. You said it yourself, everyone has hurt the earth. They all need to go, Halsey," Leo shook his head. "Humans had their chance."

The pieces finally started coming together, and panic welled in my chest. "No, Leo, *you're* still human. What about your *tribe*!"

"*My tribe*..." He laughed, but without humor. This laugh was full of regret and pain. He scrubbed his hands over his face and pushed them back through his loose, dark hair. "Halsey, I already killed most of them...all of the ones I loved. I'm not human anymore. I'm a monster."

"*What*? But the cave?"

"Oh, I *did* leave to go there..." he added, his eyes searching the ground before he found mine again. "But then I went back. I tried to stop myself, but it was like I was just watching from the outside—a passenger in my own body." I stared at him as the scene played out in his expression, his eyes distant and vacant. "Sylvie found me back in the cave, covered in their blood. She took me in as I was then, a *monster*. She saved me. Eden's Bluff saved me. And now I need to save the others like us."

"Leo, listen to yourself! You're just perpetuating more violence, don't you see that? They'll *kill* all those people! You heard what Ghob and Uri said. You know what will happen if they lift the veil. The rest of the Elemental Fae and whatever else is behind it will—"

"Look what they've all done with what they've been given." Leo interrupted, unblinking and soulless. "Maybe they deserve to die. Goodbye, Halsey."

"*No!*" I shouted.

"Seal it!" Leo took a step backward and dropped through the ground. I rushed into the cloud of swirling fog he left, but nothing happened.

"Leo!" I dropped to my hands and knees feeling around for an opening, but all I felt was more of the same cool, rocky terrain. "*Leo!*"

*****

I walked back and forth over the space where the others had disappeared, half-convinced that any second I would fall through like they did into the eye of the woods. I could almost hear the chirps and rustles all around it, almost felt the anticipation I always had that everything would stop suddenly, and I wouldn't be able to pinpoint when.

Bryce had said there were no other tears between here and the one back at Eden's Bluff, but he didn't say anything about there being more from this point forward. I was suddenly careful where I stepped, not wanting to accidentally fall onto the front porch of Hell, or who knew where else.

Maybe I could make my way back to Eden's Bluff? Take my chances with flying to the coast of Florida? If I crashed through another tear, couldn't I just fly right back through it like Leo and I did in Limbo?

Leo... The pain that tore through my chest at the thought of him again flooded me. Feathers appeared quickly all up and down my arms, and at first I just let them come. I sat on the ground and felt the stabs of heat race up and down my back, over my lips and throat until it became harder to breathe. I knew if I just waited a few more minutes, I'd breathe easier than I ever had just like before, but I didn't want to change. I didn't want to be something else. I just wanted to be myself, in my own body, in my own world again.

I took a long, strangled breath and tried to channel the prickling sensations to the tips of my fingers and toes, to push the Sylph in me away because I didn't want to have anything to do with them...with any of the Elemental Fae who would rush through the lifted veil and slaughter the human race.

And it was all my fault.

I'd led them right to Eve.

I raised my knees, buried my head in my arms and just let the tears come. It was pointless, but so was everything else I was doing right now. I was lost, and so was anything I'd ever loved.

Chapter 30

I jumped and scrambled to my feet when I felt something huffing next to my ear. As the fog cleared, Fate and Draco, the huge, black guard dogs from Mr. Burke's grocery in The Grind were both sitting there staring at me.

"*What...*" I gasped, then tried to rub my eyes to make sure I wasn't hallucinating. Out of shock, I wound up poking myself in the face with the feathers that had emerged over my hands again. I shook them immediately and let the water flow through my fingertips and out into the nothingness all around us. *Was I back? Was I back in The Grind somehow?* I dropped to my knees and held my hands out for the dogs. "Come here, guys..." I said, expecting them to nuzzle my hands like they had outside Mr. Burke's store.

But that's not what they did.

"All is not lost." A low, male voice came from one of the dogs.

"Wh—Are you *talking*?!" I pushed backward from them. "OK...OK what's happening...is this a raven bird trick or something?"

"We are Foo guardians," a female voice came from the other dog. "Do not fear us, Halsey Rhodes."

"You're really talking to me...I saw your mouth move."

They exchanged looks and at the same time, began growing until they both towered over me. Their heads morphed into that of lions with tightly curled manes and thick, downcast eyebrows. Their arms and chests both became rippled with muscles, and I stumbled backward. I squinted as a bright light reflected off the gold pendants that had been their dog tags, now hanging like clock pendulums from thick, intricately woven chains that were also made of gold.

"This is our spirit form, Halsey Rhodes. Our true form," the male lion said. "We are entities of the spirit world. You know us as Draco and Fate, and may call us this still."

I opened my mouth to say something, but it was as if I'd forgotten how to speak standing before them. Their faces were full of expression with kind, enormous gold eyes and wide, smiling mouths, though each of their teeth were easily the size of my entire arm.

My wings flew out behind me, making me fall to the ground. Feathers had completely covered my hands and arms, and I forced my eyes closed to push them away.

"You are more than you know yourself to be," the female voice, which must have been Fate's, said, her voice gentle and maternal. I noticed in that moment her glinting medallion was actually a miniature lion, a baby curled into a little, sleeping ball. Tears pricked my eyes, and I blinked them back.

"I don't want to be," I said, forcing my voice to stabilize. "I just want to go home and have everything go back to the way it was. They're going to kill everyone," I said, the tears coming too fast for me to blink them away now.

The medallion on Draco's neck detached itself and floated under his paw, slowly turning into a blue globe swirling with clouds. I was mesmerized as they slowly wove themselves into and out of each other like embroidery.

"There are many holes between our worlds," he said as I watched the clouds turn into cords and create patterns of perfectly knitted, hollow triangles. "But there are also many points that connect them." The hollow triangles almost disappeared from view as the woven strings of cloud became brighter, and soon, I saw those outlines instead of the hollow places inside.

"Like us, you are both the physical and the spirit." Fate's calming voice washed over me again. "Thus, you may travel as we do. But be warned. To embrace both your natures means you will see the dual natures in others. To pass through the realms, you must accept this as it is, and you must do what you can to restore balance where the scales have slipped. This is the charge of all those with Bright Natures."

"I don't understand," I said, shaking my head. "Are you saying I can just go back? I don't have to find the tear?"

"The veil is only as opaque as the strength of the denial we weave..." Draco said, his eyes lowering to the clouds stitching more tightly, covering the blue and green globe underneath until it was completely hidden. "We're in denial when we choose to see only our physical self, and only that of others."

"I still don't understand how accepting both parts of myself will help me get home," I said, studying the disappeared globe, swallowed by the woven cloud strands. Draco stepped back from the globe, and it started to grow as tall as he was.

"To accept your dual nature is to accept your Bright Nature," Fate said. "Not one or the other, but two in one. As two strands appear to exist from one. It becomes the filler of empty spaces." The cloud unravelled, revealing the globe again, and when the knitting was completely undone, there was only a single length of string. It folded over on itself, made loops and darted in and out of them again to create the same open triangles as before. The same connected points of *solid* triangles.

I understood.

"We don't need a tear…" I whispered, mesmerized by the fabric being woven before my eyes. "We can go between…*through* the weave." I looked up at Draco and Fate, who were both smiling at me as they spoke at the same time.

"If you accept that the two strands are an illusion, because they are one and the same. Just like you, Halsey Rhodes…The Moth and the Flame."

The tapestry globe shrank again and returned to the golden necklace that rested on Draco's chest. Both lions turned around and started walking away, with each step shrinking back down to the size of the dogs I'd come to know. I followed them, and my wings receded, though not because I was fighting for control over them. It felt more like they were healing something in me, just like when I'd burned my ankles on the beach with Leo, which seemed so long ago now.

When the fog cleared, I was standing on the sidewalk in the middle of The Grind. It was night time—the worst possible time to be in the valley, and *snowing*? I hadn't been at Eden's Bluff that long. It shouldn't be later than the end of summer here. *How much time had gone by*?

Draco and Fate walked in front of me, people made way in the distance, but as they passed me, some of their faces shifted on one side to brief flashes of snarling monsters with bared fangs.

I looked away and saw a shivering man with a normal face sitting near the edge of an alley. He took a small, red vial from his torn and dirty shirt pocket and removed the lid with a shaky hand, then brought it to his lips and drank the contents. When the liquid was gone, he shook the last drops onto his tongue just before throwing the empty vial into the dark. He sighed and closed his eyes, letting his head lean back on the stone wall behind him. Within seconds, half of his face, too, became that of a snarling beast, its eyes glowing red behind the man's skin. His shivering had stopped.

I sucked in a sharp breath and tried to fight the urge to run. *You will see the dual natures of others...* Fate's words came back to me, and I remembered the man in the woods who offered me the vials before I left The Grind.

This has to be what happened to Lauren. The vial gave her Red Fever, and it activated something else in her just like it had in that man back in the alley. But what about all these other people with half monstrous faces? Did they all have Red Fever but didn't know it yet? Had they all taken that drug in the vial?

A smiling man knelt up ahead as Fate and Draco approached, startling me out of my thoughts.

"They're absolutely beautiful. What are their names?" he asked, blinking away the snowflakes falling into his eyes. He held a hand out to the dogs, and I had to consciously stop my mouth from falling open. Instead of the bones of a snarling monster, his eyes glowed a soft, light blue. The color extended all around his head and hands when I smiled back at him.

"Um, Draco and Fate..." I said, and both dogs nuzzled his hand. He pet the tops of their heads, beaming rays of warm, light blue and now pink light in every direction, and I was filled with a sense of ease and happiness I hadn't felt for a long time.

"Those are great names," he said as he rose to his feet. Thanks for letting me pet them. I'd say be careful out here, but these guys are probably keeping the riff-raff at bay. This weather is crazy, isn't it?" He smiled one more time at Draco and Fate before he nodded at me, then crossed the street and turned around a dark corner.

Not five seconds later, a group of younger men rose from the stoop of a building like shadows come to life. I couldn't see their faces right away, but when I channeled the tension I immediately felt upon seeing them to my eyes, my vision became twenty times stronger. It was as if they were just standing a few feet in front of me, even with the curtain of snow falling between us.

Behind half of each of their faces was a deformed, fanged beast with red-eyes—all except for one of them. His eyes and surrounding space just glowed a dark, muddy green, like a bruise trying to heal. I watched him walk backward in front of the others, his hands extended like he wanted them to stop. He started chuckling, trying to cajole them, but they just shoved him out of the way as they turned to follow the man who had just pet Draco and Fate.

"No…" I said out loud. "They're going to hurt him." Draco and Fate turned to me, and I could feel them restraining themselves, ready to sprint off the curb. They wouldn't move a muscle, but I knew they wanted to make sure I'd be all right if they left—that they wouldn't leave me if I felt I couldn't find Eve on my own. Though, I wasn't alone. I had the eagle. I was the eagle. There were magical, otherworldly things *within* this world, and I was one of them. "It's OK, help him!" I said, and in the same second, both dogs bolted across the street, snarling and barking like an entire pack of raging hellhounds.

Chapter 31

It was hard to see all the people on the streets of The Grind in the snowfall, but of the ones I did see, several had faint monsters inside them while a few had bright, vivid ones. I didn't know what that meant. Maybe the brightness correlated to when they might change, like Lauren did. Or maybe the monsters never came out and saw the light of day, and that's why most Feral attacks happened at night, when they could hide their true forms behind the thin skins of sick people. My blood ran cold as the idea that my parents may have had monsters like these inside sapping their lives away in their final days.

Occasionally, some people sleeping on benches or walking aimlessly didn't have any monsters behind their eyes at all. Only muted colors like the bruise-colored man, drab and cloudy, which seemed to pull the energy right from my bones when I saw them. Again, I thought of my parents and...hoped.

I shook the thoughts away and tried to focus. I needed to get behind The Citadel wall before Leo and the others could. As good of a hacker as Bryce was, I didn't think he'd be able to short circuit the entire system from his stupid tablet...but then again, he had managed to project an astral map of the supernatural tears between worlds into the sky from it.

I wrapped my arms around myself and scanned for Max's house, which wasn't far from The Citadel wall. I was tempted to run to it and pound on his bedroom window like I did when we were kids and I wanted him to come out and play. I'd lived just a few houses down from him then, with my parents before the wasting sickness took them. My mind slipped back to them again, to what their colors might have been, or if they had monsters inside because of Red Fever too.

I heard a pinging sound in my ear, and was confused for a second until I realized it was a queue notice. *The communication block from the island was gone, of course!* I tapped my temple and blinked to view my inbox. There were half-a-dozen messages from Max, more from my Aunt Alice. I was afraid to open any of them right now because if I did, I knew I'd lose my composure and I had to get behind the wall to warn Eve. When she was safe, I'd let myself read them.

I blinked at the snow whipping into my eyes and accidentally closed, then reopened the inbox several times until I tapped my temple for an open line.

Queue Eve Adams, Crisis Management Director, I thought, hoping I could still access the public directory. My heart almost leapt out of my chest when I saw the spinning arrows and the word *connecting.* I held my breath, hoping I wouldn't get the same error message I got when I tried to queue Max in the bathroom back at Eden's Bluff.

Instead, the queue connected, and I heard Eve's voice coming through loud and clear.

"You've reached Eve Adams, Director of Crisis Management for the Portland area. I'm sorry I can't respond to your queue right now, but please leave a message, and I'll get back to you as soon as possible."

The disappointment hit me in the chest and made me feel hollow for several seconds, but at least I could leave her a message.

The tone sounded, and I started babbling.

"Eve, this is Halsey Rhodes. You tried to warn me when you arrested Jennifer Kwan—you said I was on the radar. I didn't know who you were then or what that meant, but I do now," I said without taking a breath. "Uriel has sent a group of people to kill you. You have to get out of here right now. They're coming tonight. They know your name and your job title. Please just get—" I was cut off by another tone, and promptly disconnected.

It wasn't enough to leave her a queue message. I had to find her before Leo and the others did. I doubled back, away from The Citadel gate and the horde of Sweeper droids patrolling it. Maybe I could fly over the side, where it was hopefully less populated. I clenched my teeth against the cold and walked backward to try to get a better look, then turned to run when I was sure of where I needed to go. I didn't get three steps before I crashed directly into someone, nearly knocking us both to the ground. Strong hands gripped my arms, steadying me.

"Whoa, are you OK?" he said, and I stopped breathing.

I looked up into his blue eyes, which widened, despite the blowing snow, when he saw me. "*Halsey*?" he whispered.

Draco and Fate trotted to a stop at either side of him. I beamed my widest smile at each of them, hoping they could feel how grateful I was. Max's eyes glowed a soft blue-green, brightening into a turquoise when I nodded at him.

"It's me," I said, barely able to get the words out. "I'm back. I'm back and I have so much to tell you, Max."

Heat radiated through me in spite of the chill all around. It channeled to my shoulders automatically as I'd practiced so many times now, but I didn't stop it this time. I felt the weight of my wings slowly unfurling behind me, and I took a step forward so I wouldn't fall.

Max let me go and stumbled backward, his bright, glowing eyes dimming.

"Halsey…?" he whispered, clearly in shock. Draco and Fate moved quickly to him, pushing their heads into his hands. He started absently petting them and dropped to his knees as both dogs wedged under his arms as if to hold him up.

"Like I said, I have so much to tell you," I tried to laugh, but it came out like a hiccoughed sob.

"How? Are those...from the bite?" he managed as snow dusted his blond hair.

"I'll tell you everything I know, but I need you to come with me right now, OK? We need to find Eve Adams. Remember her? She's not who we thought, Max. She's Eve. Like, *the* Eve from The Garden of Eden. And she's in trouble."

"*What*? But that's imposs..." he trailed off and dragged a hand over his face as he studied my wings again.

I looked at Draco and Fate. "Can you make sure my aunt and uncle are OK? Can you keep them safe?" I asked. Max looked at me like I was insane, then did a double take when both dogs barked in reply and took off running. Max got to his feet and took a few more steps away from me. "OK, listen," I nodded, then moved toward him. "Do you trust me?"

He gaped at me, but shook his head quickly as if to clear a fog. "Halls, *why* do you have wings? Why did you just talk to those dogs like people? And *why* did they listen to you? Is the snow because of you too?"

"I'll tell you all of that—what? The snow? *No*," I shook my head to refocus. "Max, do you *trust* me?"

His eyes brightened again, and the turquoise light started to glow all around him. "Always," he said, then swallowed hard as he nodded. "I trust you."

"OK, then hold onto me."

I wrapped my arms under his and jumped, pushing against the cold air with my wings until the ground fell away.

"Halsey, *shit!*"

"It's OK, just hold on!"

"Yeah, not gonna be a problem!"

We rose over the side of The Citadel wall, which seemed about a hundred feet high. A platform around the top held multiple snow-dusted cameras, and I was utterly amazed that the Sweeper droids didn't see us. I focused my eyes and saw several sets of emergency doors at different intervals surrounding the interior city, Sweeper droids stationed at each one just like at the front gates.

I landed in the shadows on the wide ledge, my arms still wrapped around Max's ribs as I looked up at him.

"Are you all right?" I asked, his turquoise glow mixing with rays of red now. He moved his fingers over the feathers on my shoulders like he didn't believe they were real, then met my eyes.

"Yeah," he said, his voice cracking a little. He immediately cleared his throat. "What are we doing again?"

I smiled at him. "We have to find Eve Adams."

"Why? She wanted to arrest you. And why do you think she's *the* Eve?"

"Let me tell you when you have your feet on the ground, OK?" He opened his mouth to say something, but only wound up blinking at me several times before he shut it again and nodded. I hugged him, resting my head on his chest for a second before I moved another inch. "I missed you so much," I whispered.

"I missed you more, Halls," he said, then took a deep breath and let it out, slow and controlled as he rested his chin on the top of my head. I looked up at him, and he ran his thumb over my cheek. "I thought you were gone, and I—"

An ear-splitting alarm sounded, which startled us both off the ledge. We were falling forward toward the interior of The Citadel wall, the glaring lights in every direction making it hard for me to tell which way was up and which was down. I held on tightly to Max and just started flapping my wings, but we'd fallen too far and too fast for me to stop our momentum entirely. We crashed to the ground, but not hard enough to keep us there.

"I'm OK—are you all right?" I asked between the siren blares, scanning Max for any visible signs of injury.

"Fine, I'm fine—come on!" he said, nodding to a searchlight that was heading right for us. We started running, and I pulled in my wings because there was no room to extend them between the buildings we were weaving through.

I could hear the Sweeper droids exchanging communication codes even though none of them were in view. Everything was louder, clearer, and quickly getting closer.

"We can't stay out in the open like this," I said, finding a series of buildings across the street. One of them looked like a restaurant, or maybe a club. "That place, see where everyone is going in with the big gilded door?"

"You can see the door details *from here*?" Max said.

"Eagle eyes... Comes with the wings."

"Eagle?" he darted a glance at me. "You turn into an *eagle*?"

"Kind of. Come on."

We walked as casually as we could across the street, and I fit myself under Max's arm so it would look even more normal. We filtered into the crowd of people making their way through the door and quickly slipped into a table near the back. "Shit, they're in here too," I said through my teeth as I spotted the hovering metallic discs floating from table to table.

"No, wait. Those aren't Sweepers. Watch." He nodded to the one hovering over a table about twenty feet from us as it lowered a pitcher of beer. The arms retracted inside and reappeared with four glasses, one for each person at the table.

"It's a waiter," I said, amazed. "Those are all waiters."

Feed display holograms hovered in every corner of the room, most of them showing sports, while the rest showed either emergency weather feeds or the same woman's picture flashing with the caption, *Frankie Mason, CPC Researcher, Back from the Dead to Cure Outlands Disease: Red Fever* at the bottom of the display.

A bunch of shouting from down at the bar pulled my attention away from the feeds.

"What?" A man stood up and held his arms out to his side like he was surrendering to a droid. "I'm just saying, it's just natural selection. More time for the rest of us, you know? Who would miss them out there?" A woman stood up in front of him and threw her drink in the man's face, then stormed out. He started to follow her, but his friends held him back, laughing and pushing napkins at him. Half his face flashed the same ghostly-boned monstrosity with bared fangs and glowing red eyes that I'd seen on the streets in The Grind.

"Halsey, what's wrong?" Max asked, gripping my hand. I turned to him quickly, trying to shake the image from my mind.

"The man down there, the one who just got a face full of beer... He has Red Fever, Max."

"How do you know that? The lady is the one who got aggressive."

"He did something to provoke her," I said, scanning the room to see if there was anyone else in here with demonic half faces glowing inside them.

There weren't, fortunately. Just different shades of colors, some bright, some muted. Those with darker colors gathered around the ones who glowed in bright pinks and greens, some of whom brightened even more, while others faded until they moved away from the newly gathered crowds. I squeezed my eyes shut and tried to imagine the water washing over them, but when I opened my eyes again, the colors were all still there.

"Halsey, you need to talk to me here," Max said. "What is happening? What's with the *wings* and superhero vision, and *why* is it snowing?"

Chapter 32

I had my own questions about the snow, but as I started to explain what I could about why I knew the man near the bar had Red Fever, one of the waiter droids hovered over to us. It looked like a floating plate with metallic arms holding two glasses of water underneath it. The arms extended, lowering the glasses to the table.

"Hello, Maxwell Barrett" it said in a friendly female voice as it scanned a light over Max's face. "Welcome to Ivy's. Welcome to The Citadel Academy." The waiter droid's green light moved over my face, and I froze while it seemed to be thinking. "Hello...Unregistered. To be served, I will need your guest clearance code. Please press your thumb into the imprint disc on the table in front of you."

Max and I got up at the same time, and I pushed back the prickles running up my arms. "Um, we're good. We're actually late for something else. Thanks anyway," Max babbled to the hovering droid.

We moved quickly toward the door but were forced to stop and turn around when four live patrols walked through with a Sweeper droid in their wake.

"Shit!" I said under my breath as they split up and aimed their handheld scanners at everyone they passed.

The Sweeper droid sent a thin ray of light over the entire room, obviously scanning for whoever set off the perimeter alarms. Max rushed in front of me, moving me quickly into the corner of the shadowy wall.

"Don't punch me when I do this," he said, moving close to me and slipping his hand into my hair. Before I knew it, a wave of heat rushed through my chest and forced my wings to bump the wall behind me, which pushed me into him. Max blinked at me in surprise, but then tightened his arm around my waist and quickly pressed his lips to mine. It only lasted a few seconds before I broke away from him, afraid my wings would expand beyond the initial fold if I didn't get control of my sudden deluge of emotion. Confused, he frantically searched my face until he glanced over my shoulder at the tops of my wings. "*Oh*. OK, I'm sorry. I wouldn't have done that, but I thought you'd read the queue I sent right after you left and—"

"It's OK, it's my fault—wait, *what*? What did your queue say?" I asked, noticing my hands were still pressed to his chest. I let them drop and imagined the water pushing through my fingertips, then felt my wings slowly receding. Max looked over his shoulder. The live patrols were walking toward the bar, and the Sweeper droid had just hovered down the first set of steps toward the main dining area.

"It's going to scan again," he said, taking my hand and leading us quickly back out the front door.

***

My head was spinning, and the sudden blast of cold air helped me regain my bearings a little. I didn't have time to process anything that had just happened between Max and me as a Sweeper droid hovered behind a curtain of snow on the curb across the street. Another was rotating a few blocks away to the left, and yet another a few blocks away to the right. There was no way we could go in any direction without one of them seeing us, and subsequently finding out I didn't belong on this side of the wall. Somewhere above, I heard the whining sound of a small motor, and when I searched the shadows of the building, cameras were panning over the sidewalks. Even if I flew straight into the air with Max, the Sweeper droids' lasers would cut us down.

"There's nowhere to go," he said, apparently observing the same thing. We moved back into the front of the restaurant where a crowd of people had gathered, all trying to get out the door.

"Where were all the patrols three months ago, huh?" Someone shouted. "Could have used you and your tin cans when we had a Feral ripping people in half in here! But no, you show up during the playoffs! Go guard the wall!"

"That wasn't a Feral," another person shouted, laughing and holding his glass up to the bartender.

"That was just Nick being a slave-driver. Drove the new kid over the edge!"

Everyone started laughing at this, and Max turned to me abruptly. "Halls, you said you could change into an eagle?" he asked, gripping my shoulders.

"Yes, but—"

"Do it. I have my chip, so they won't stop me. I'll keep looking for Eve, but you have to get out of here. They're extra paranoid about outsiders now that there's been a Feral attack behind the wall."

"But I don't think I can shift, at least not immediately," I said, my mind racing with everything around us and everything that had just happened a few minutes ago. "I've never done it before. The closest I came was..." I trailed off, remembering the beach and the ridges that rose in my arms. I didn't want Max to see me like that. "It just wouldn't work all the way last time."

"OK, well you have to try again. I'm going to get the attention of these droids. The cameras aren't equipped with lasers, so just go duck between these two buildings after you see the droids following me and change, all right? At least enough to get to the roof and out of sight."

"But the Sweepers *do* have lasers. *And* tasers. You saw them upload Jen's Miranda rights. I'm not letting you risk that."

"*Halsey,* damn it... That was in *The Grind*. I have a Citadel chip now, they won't do that to me here.

Please, go!" He darted through the crowd of people and started running toward the droid across the street before I could get out another word. "Help! There's a Feral in there!" he shouted, and as soon as the droid started to move toward him, he ran up the street. The Sweeper droid to the right followed him too, but he was fast and had already made it to the droid a few blocks up. All three of the droids surrounded him as he waved his hands in the air and ranted like a lunatic.

I darted between the buildings and just let the panic shoot through me without trying to route it or slow it down. I just let it come. My wings extended first, and then my arms began to ridge. Gold and brown feathers covered my hands, shoulders, and throat as my nose and lips began to tingle.

And then it all stopped.

"*Come on!*" I tried to yell, but it came out as a screech.

The prickling sensation that had moved over my legs had stopped, and I wondered if maybe I needed to be in motion. I flew to the rooftop, but still, the shift would go no further. I tried to yell out again, but again, it just came out as a deafening screech.

It wasn't working. I knelt on the cold, wet cement and watched the snowflakes melt on impact. I tried to call back the anger I felt when Leo left me at the edge of the tear, which made me feel like my blood was on fire. Even still, *nothing* else changed. I replayed Max's kiss in my mind, which I hadn't really stop replaying, so I was sure this would trigger the rest of my shift. Another wave of heat actually did rush through me again remembering the feeling of his hand in my hair, on my cheek, the look in his eyes right before his arm wrapped tightly around my waist. I was so distracted by my obsession with getting out of The Grind, with leaving everything about it behind, that I hadn't really understood what was happening with the one person who meant the most to me.

Even the crippling regret that washed over me wasn't enough to trigger the rest of my shift, nor was the building anger and frustration I felt as a result.

I closed my eyes and started to push the shift away, but stopped when I heard the police radio chatter in the distance. I'd heard it play a thousand times at home with my Aunt Alice, but now I could hear it from the live patrol radios and Sweeper units scattered all over The Citadel interior.

"Crisis Management code fourteen eleven, attention Sweeper units: we have a report of an incident at Ivy's Pub. Live patrols on site, precautionary medical transport en route."

Crisis Management? That meant Eve would be coming to Ivy's… Max did it! I ran to the edge of the roof, but he and the three Sweeper droids that were just hovering around him were gone. I touched my temple to queue him, but nothing would connect.

All the breath left my lungs at the idea the network could have gone down. The network inside The Citadel *never* went down. Shops would close. People would be locked out of their homes. Everything in their infrastructure except their front gate depended on it.

I tried to listen for more of the police chatter, but even that had fallen silent. People were now scattering through the street, piling into cars and driving away, but I still didn't see Max. *Had he been taken to the police station? Did the Sweeper droids just leave him there while they went back into Ivy's?*

I tried again to queue him, but again, the signal wouldn't connect. This had to be Bryce's handiwork. And that meant Leo and the others were here, behind the wall.

"Hey, kid!" a man called behind me. I turned and saw a dark-haired man with his arm in a sling and a blonde woman coming over the edge of the roof toward me. They only got a few steps off the ladder before they both stop in their tracks. "Whoa..." The man said when my wings extended again, and the light around him shifted from bright red to gray. He held out his hand to me and turned to the woman. "She didn't say anything about a flying kid. I'd have distinctly remembered the words *flying kid*."

"Halsey..." the woman said, a yellow-orange color flashing briefly in her eyes before it spread around her. She came into the light, and I recognized her from the news report at Ivy's.

"You're that CPC researcher on the feeds…" I said, getting to my feet. I touched my temple again to see if maybe those would load, but they didn't.

"That's right. My name is Frankie," she said, taking a step toward me with a hand extended to the man next to her. "This is Jack. Eve tracked your queue after you called, then had the network cut when we found you. We came to take you to her… Will you come with us?"

I nodded, and the man she called *Jack* shook his head as he muttered to himself and turned to go back to the fire escape. "This is terrifying with one arm by the way," he added. "Why do they come to the roof? We just got off a roof."

***

We didn't go back to Ivy's like I thought we would. Instead, Frankie drove us *away* from The Citadel.

"Wait, we're going back to The Grind?" I asked, worried that Max would still be stuck somewhere with the Sweeper droids.

"Technically," she said as we turned down the road that led to the docks, which was right in front of The Citadel.

Rusty barrels lined the entrance to the roped off pier, and I really hoped we weren't going anywhere near the water.

"So, I have this, like, condition with seawater…" I said, asking without *really* asking if this whole thing was about to go south for me.

"Boats float, kid. Calm your ti—" Jack started to say, but Frankie backhanded him in the chest before he could finish.

"What month is this? Is it August?" I asked. "And when the network will come back up? I'm worried about my friend," I added as we got out of the car and started walking toward one of the bigger boats in port.

"It's August. Eve will have to explain the snow," Jack answered, then held out a hand and angled his head toward the boat. "As for your friend…"

"Halsey!" Max shouted, slipping through the deckhouse door. I ran up the dock steps into his arms, nearly knocking him off his feet. "Eve was at the station when the droids brought me there."

"You did it," I whispered. "You found her."

"Yeah, well…" He laughed, then shrugged once he put me down. "Come on. She's waiting for you."

Chapter 33

Nobody was sitting on the narrow, tan couches or at the small table when we entered the deckhouse, and the wood paneling on the walls made everything feel a little claustrophobic.

I only had enough time to finish this observation when the door at the back of the room opened, and a Mediterranean woman with short, razor-edged hair approached us. A golden light lit her eyes for several seconds before it started to radiate all around her, and I exhaled in relief when I recognized her as Eve Adams. She was dressed in a tailored, but comfortable looking dark pantsuit, and I marveled for a second at how old she must be, though up close, she only looked around forty.

"Were you followed?" Eve asked Frankie and Jack, who were standing behind me.

"No, there were a lot of cars coming and going, but the road to the docks was empty," Frankie said, sitting carefully on one of the tan couches along the wall, wincing as she held her side.

Jack climbed another set of stairs behind us to the helm and started the engine. I must have looked alarmed because Eve smiled at me, her green eyes almost twinkling.

"Don't worry, we're going somewhere safe."

"OK, I have questions…" Max said abruptly as the engine leveled off and we started moving. "You're supposed to be *Eve*? The Garden of Eden *Eve*?"

She nodded slowly, her small smile widening just a little. "It's a fairly long story."

Max narrowed his eyes, then glanced at me. "So what about the name *Adams*?"

"I never did like to be called *Adam's* Eve," she said, raising a dark eyebrow. "And a surname became necessary after a dozen centuries or so."

"*Centuries*," Max repeated flatly with a nod. He and I exchanged incredulous looks, his suggesting he didn't believe a word she said, and mine no doubt conveying shock about how old she was.

"And I imagine you must also be wondering why I sought out Halsey after she was bitten, and why it's snowing now in August," Eve added as the yacht picked up speed on the open water. She shook her head as she took a seat on the other tan couch and gestured for us to do the same. "Another plague has been sent among humanity. You've likely heard it called—"

"Red Fever," I finished for her. "It killed a girl at our school—the one who bit me."

"I know," Eve's expression fell. "She came up on our grid...right before you did."

"What does that mean? What *grid*?" I asked warily.

"It's complicated, but just know that those who change like you do are trackable, Halsey. And it's dangerous if the wrong people find you."

"Why? Who are the wrong people?" Max asked, leaning forward in his seat.

"I don't know how much they told you at Eden's Bluff, but there's a supernatural presence at work to poison humanity, an Elemental queen who governs the viability of all life on earth."

"A *what* Queen?" Max squinted.

"I'm afraid that's another long story," Eve said. "I'll try to explain once we're safe."

"I thought a *drug* from Wu Fong Pharmaceuticals was causing Red Fever," I offered, careful not to seem like I was directly contradicting the several thousand-year-old alleged mother of humanity.

Frankie leaned toward me. "Why do you think that?" she asked, her brows darting together.

I explained about the man in the woods who had tried to give me the colored vials, then about seeing him again at school chatting up Lauren just before everything that happened to her—*and me*—afterward.

"I saw the same spontaneous human combustion happen on the island with Knox," Frankie said to Eve.

"Knox *Ryder*? He's dead?" I asked, feeling my heart pounding suddenly in my ears. *Had Uri found him*?

"No," Frankie corrected. "There were others infected on a prison island—it's also a...long story.

How do you know Knox Ryder?" she asked, her wide, blue eyes narrowing at me in suspicion.

I glanced at her, then at Eve. "I overheard Ghob and Uriel talking about how they wanted to find him so he could lift the veil and let the trapped Elementals through to this world."

"Hang on," Max interrupted, holding up his hands. "*Uriel*...is that Uri? From the Eden's Bluff promo? Who's Ghob? And *what* veil? Can somebody explain what's going on already!?"

Eve smiled. "Uriel is an angel. Ghob is the Elemental queen. And the veil separates our world from those beyond. We think Knox holds the key to lifting it, and somehow, Ghob also knows."

I turned to face Max. "Uri sent a group of others like me—I mean, but way stronger than me—who can fly and shift into other things—*to kill* Eve so they could get to him. Max, they're still coming."

***

Jack stopped the yacht engine, but there was nothing in sight except endless black sea when I looked out the window. It was still snowing, but not as much here.

"Where are we?" Max asked.

"Somewhere safe. We won't be heard here," Eve said as we glided to a stop. Above deck, we were surrounded by trees save for the end of a long inlet behind us, which was lit by intermittent lights on either side. We went down the stairs and were greeted by two older men and women. They were all dressed in richly colored clothes that looked hand-sewn with patches and beadwork.

One of the women was very tan with flowing dark hair, streaked with gray, while the other was very pale with long, silver hair. The older, also pale man, had white hair, while the last man was darker and had closely cropped black waves like an old time movie star. A flash of gold lit behind everyone's eyes and spread all around them, and I knew instinctively that they were going to help us.

"Welcome back," the tan woman closest to the water said to Eve.

"Thank you, Alma. How is our guest?" she asked, walking into the foliage. Max and I exchanged glances, and I turned to Frankie.

"Where are we going?"

"I don't think it's much farther."

She was right. Another twenty feet or so and the dense trees opened up to a large, circular pool holding several neon green, striped fish. Three kinds of seahorses also wove in and out of bushy green plants that reached toward the surface of the water, which was dotted by a scatter of white-flowering lily pads. The snow had stopped, and it felt at least forty degrees warmer—like it actually *was* August here.

"Wow," I gasped, transfixed.

Black, iron benches surrounded the white-stone pool, and vines with fuchsia flowers were climbing the arbors over each one. The lights in the stone path reflected dancing water patterns over the cottage, which I'd thought was just a stone wall until the white-haired man opened a slate door for us.

Inside, I audibly gasped to see the stretch of oak floors that led to a giant window overlooking a nearby waterfall. Small, white lights danced around the differently colored flowers that lined the pool at the base of the rock, where more water lilies floated on the surface.

We passed simple, clean-lined furniture as we walked through the open room and made our way down a very long, winding hallway that led behind the kitchen. After several minutes, the walls and ceiling opened to the outdoors. We walked out to find ourselves at the top of a wide cliff that overlooked the ocean, and the sky was masked in clouds and falling snow. But it was still *warm* up here.

"*Holy. Shit.*" Max whispered next to me.

"It's quite a view," Eve said, looking out on the moonlit horizon as she led us into a stone seating area carved right into the cliff with a recessed fire pit. Several poured glasses of what looked like tea, and trays of fruit, small sandwiches, and cut vegetables sat around the fire on top of the wide, stone ledge that doubled as a table.

"Are you kidding me?" Max marveled.

"How are you keeping these plants alive?" Frankie asked, scanning the ground. "Some of these species are tropical... They take years to get this big—and this is Portland, *Maine*," she added, turning to Eve.

"And why isn't it snowing here, but it is out there?" Max asked, nodding toward the edge of the cliffside.

Eve held up her hands like a teacher trying to settle a class. "I know you have many questions, and I apologize for not being able to give you any context yet," she said. "It was important to arrive here safely before sharing any other information about what we know. May I introduce you to Alma, Silo, Petra, and Tirius?" Eve extended her hand to the four older people who greeted us when we first arrived. "They are Elementals, and have been my friends for centuries. Alma is a Gnome, Silo is a Sylph, Petra is an Undine, and Tirius is a Salamander Elemental," she added. "They've created the microclimate that sustains the beautiful gardens all around you."

"That word again. What's an *Elemental*?" Max turned to me. I started to answer him, but was cut off.

"It's a pleasure to meet you all," Tirius, the darker-complected movie star man said, bowing slightly to us all.

"Especially you, Halsey," Petra, the fair, silver-haired woman said. "We've heard much about you."

"You *have*?" I asked, a little too abruptly. The four traded smiles with Eve.

"You must be hungry," Silo, the white-haired man said. "Please sit and make yourselves comfortable."

He passed each of us a small plate and a glass of tea, and invited us to start eating while Eve explained to everyone what I already knew about the tears in the veil, what the Elementals and the Elemental queens were, and about the fallout in Eden. But then she started talking about something I didn't know already.

"The snow is the result of the sun beginning to die," she started, which halted the breath in my lungs. "In the beginning, after our banishment, Ghob took the discarded forbidden fruit from Eden and from the Seeds of Knowledge, created a replica of the Tree of Life. But without Grace, the tree took life rather than gave it," she said, and I could barely breathe. "This was the tree responsible for Red Fever. When Knox killed the tree, a gate to Hell opened in its place." Eve took a slow, deep breath. "Paralda and Djin, two of the Elemental queens, were able to close the gate, but not before being dragged through it themselves. Soon thereafter, Ghob took Cora, the queen of the Undines to *protect* her, but this is not how her people see it."

"This is insane," Max said, scrubbing his hands over his face. "So how does this mean the sun is dying?" he asked, shaking his head.

"Without their queens, the people of the sun and the atmosphere are ungoverned. Natural disasters are already beginning in the East in protest. Fires, tornadoes, and when the Undines—the water Elementals—organize, I imagine there will be tsunamis and flooding."

"But they're Elementals," I said, gesturing to the men and women around us. "Can't they tell their people that it's Ghob's fault their queens are in Hell? Knox was just trying to stop what she's been doing; why punish humans?"

Eve sighed. "Silo and Tirius were not banned from The Garden with the rest of us," she glanced at Petra and Alma. "But they stayed with us anyway. For centuries, we have been working with pockets of Elemental allies to keep Ghob from inflicting mass genocide, but the majority are too distant now. They wouldn't listen."

"So if the tree was causing Red Fever..." Max started, "is that what Halsey has? What those people who are coming after her have? Being an Elemental is a *disease*?"

"The *First Bloods* are the ones who survived their exposure, like Halsey, Knox, and the others." Frankie nodded. "They're the ones who still had traces of original Elemental DNA, so in a way, yes, but the disease was only the catalyst that began their mutation."

Max glanced at me before returning his focus to Frankie. "And everyone else? They just become..."

"Feral," Jack said. "Mutated monsters trapped in their own evolution until their body just can't take it anymore. We're supposed to kill each other off until the only ones left alive are the Elementals—old, new, it doesn't matter. That's what Ghob wants."

"But it's not her true nature," Alma, the tanned, dark-haired woman spoke up. "We must repair the rift that lies between the Elementals and humanity, or this will never end."

Eve nodded to the group. "But we must stop Ghob's current destruction, and this is why I sought you out, Halsey. You and Knox Ryder are two of the new generation of First Bloods," she added, gesturing to Silo.

He rose, his white hair like a torch in the night air, and returned with a younger, athletic man whose angular features and haunted dark eyes sent a shiver through me even at a distance. I tried not to look startled, but it was suddenly as if even the air around him rushed in different directions just to get out of his way.

The man seemed restless, pushing a hand through his dark hair as he walked out of the shadows, and I flinched when I saw the flash of glowing red light silhouetting ghostly white fangs behind his lips. The deep red glow spread out around him with interspersed rays of golden light appearing and disappearing, until it all faded away.

He stopped walking and met my eyes. "It's all right," he said. "I know what you see, and I won't hurt you."

Chapter 34

"You're the one who can lift the veil…" I said with the last of a breath. Knox glanced at Eve.

"He's like you? Um…all of you?" Max asked me, then looked around at the other First Bloods.

"Sort of," Frankie said, answering for Knox before she turned to me. "Knox was injected with a drug produced by Wu Fong Pharmaceuticals too, but instead of it only activating some long-dormant Elemental DNA like it did for you, for others, it activated something...*else*," she trailed off, and a tense silence fell over the group as she crossed to Knox, interlacing her fingers with his.

"What's wrong?" I asked. "What else is he?"

Eve stood and moved to Knox's other side. "Ghob was not the only one put out by the creation of humans. Many of the angels rebelled, refusing to share anything with us."

A blinding flash of lightning lit the sky, followed by a crack that reverberated in my bones. A deep, echoing laugh filled the air and somehow even made it hard to breathe as a small, gray storm cloud began to gather. It grew into a black, churning mass of lightning and explosions that were only getting stronger.

"You mean *kneel* before you," a male voice boomed from every direction. Seconds later, an angel appeared from the center of the storm cloud wearing a black tunic that was on fire, but not burning. His black wings stretched the length of the entire storm cloud, and it was then that I realized the lightning and explosions were not originating in the cloud. They were coming from him.

Within seconds, Rhea appeared from behind the angel, her blonde hair covered by scaled body armor that matched the color of her long, red and gold wings. Half her face glowed from within, revealing the nostrils and the wide, golden eyes of a snake. Another bolt of lightning shot through the sky behind the angel, followed by an earth-splitting crack as Leo emerged, his black wings nearly as big as the angel's, and his horns long and twisted at the ends. Behind his eyes, though, a red glow illuminated the long, serrated snout on his right side along with jagged, dagger-like teeth and round, reptilian eyes.

"Leo..." I whispered in disbelief, then shouted up to him." Don't do this!"

He glanced at me, but quickly looked toward my left, where a huge, gray wolf and a red fox had just appeared...*Bryce and Alita*, I thought. My chest tightened as they bared their teeth at me, and Alec climbed over the cliff edge to our right, a white glow surrounding him. I gasped to see two ghostly top layers of needle-like teeth behind his grin and a spiny fin behind his ear.

"You *know* these freaks?" Jack shouted to me.

"You said we'd be safe here!" Max shouted to Eve, who looked confused.

"The tracker blockers worked, don't worry," Leo said just before blowing a stream of fire into the cliff edge, which then ricocheted flames in every direction. He smiled at me. "We followed Halsey the old fashioned way."

"*Samael…*" Eve stepped in front of me. "I should have known it was you helping Ghob all this time."

"Ah, the lovely handmaiden. You're on borrowed time," he said, giving her a long, slow grin." I would watch how I spoke to the *Angel of Death*, were I you."

Everyone froze, including my former friends. Alec stopped advancing and turned to the black–winged angel. "*Uri?*"

Another flash of lightning lit the sky, followed by a roar that shook the ground. When it passed, Alec took several steps back from the edge of the cliff he'd somehow just climbed, and Rhea dove to stand by his side. Even Leo landed not far from Bryce and Alita and stood staring at the angel in disbelief. No one except for Eve and me seemed to have been able to see him as the one she called *Samael* until now.

"What happened to Uri?" Rhea shouted into the sky.

Samael laughed, flames flickering in his dark eyes. "At this very moment, he's sulking on a bench in that ridiculous poisoned garden."

"No, he was just here with us!" Leo shouted, every muscle in his torso clenched with the effort. "What did you do to him?"

Samael reached out toward him, and without even touching him, lifted him into the air by his throat. Leo clutched at the invisible hand, but it wasn't any use.

"*I* was here with you." Samael growled, the sound registering low in his chest and echoing off the stone surfaces all around us. He threw Leo to the ground, and both Bryce and Alita rushed over to him. "My *brother* wants nothing more than camaraderie among our kind. It wasn't any harder to persuade him to orchestrate my masquerade than it was to persuade him to allow me into The Garden…just for a *glimpse*." He turned his gaze on Eve and gave her a lecherous smile.

"What's he talking about?" I asked.

Eve raised her chin defiantly at the dark angel, still hovering above in flames.

"A small group of angels became obsessed with Lilith, the first of womankind, who was made from the same earth as Adam," she began. "Samael was *fascinated* by her, and talked Uriel into allowing him to walk in The Garden to praise and tend Adam as God had instructed all angels and First Bloods to do," Eve went on, all the while Samael's fire grew, and the same disgusting grin spread across his face. "He persuaded Lilith to leave Adam. To run away with *him*, instead. And on the twenty-eighth day of his seduction, that's exactly what she did."

"Of course she did!" Samael roared. "Why would she stay bound to a mud-packed mortal when I wielded the very fire of life?" Samael raised his arms to his sides, and the flames grew all around him.

Leo met my eyes, his, tortured and pitiful. Clouded black and purple colors smeared all around him, somehow suffocating me even from several yards away.

"God was furious and commanded Lilith to return to Adam, but she refused to leave Samael." Eve raised her voice over the angel's boasts. "He then commanded that any children who left their cave in the desert would be put to death, and any who survived would be turned into the *Lilin*…the vampyr condemned to live in eternal darkness," she shouted, as if to torment Samael. But he shot right back at her.

"How many times did I overhear Adam telling you the story of his lost love?" Samael mused. "How many times did I hear him compare you to her, and like a mindless clay tub of entrails, you did *nothing*."

"*Samael* wanted revenge for the curse laid upon his children," Eve continued, unflinching. "So he *left* Lilith to be dragged to Hell by the very three angels who were charged to kill the children. Instead of helping her, he blackmailed Uriel to let him into The Garden again, where he then tried to lure *me* from Adam by charming Djin snakes—the most beautiful and revered of all animals at the time." Eve took a step toward Samael as he began to bear his teeth at her, seething. "He *tricked* the snakes into allowing him to perch on their backs and fly him around like the king of all he surveyed. Finally, he sneaked Lucifer into The Garden disguised as a Djin snake, claiming he spoke for God…" she trailed off, the light around her dimming.

"Still bitter after all these millennia?" Samael sighed. "*But* so is Lilith. That is, until I return to her the blood of our blood." He turned his gaze on Knox and pulled a flaming scythe from the storm cloud behind him, pointing it at Eve. "First, *you* will return to the dust."

"No!" Knox and I shouted at the same time and started running toward Eve, but we were cut off by Bryce's snarling wolf. Alita's fox jumped on Knox's chest and started snapping at him as he struggled to keep her at bay.

"Stop! Didn't you hear *anything*?" Leo called to them, but they ignored him even as he and Alec rushed to intervene. "They were just using us!"

Samael laughed so loudly it shook the ground again. "*Ignorant* half-bloods. Look at yourselves! I have no qualms about killing *all* of you." His voice echoed as he lifted Knox a few feet into the air with an invisible hand. "All except the one who will lift the veil, and then return with me *to Hell*."

Samael raised his scythe again over us all, a black bolt of lightning escaping. Time seemed to stop for only a second as Max met my eyes while he ran in front of Eve—a second to say everything we hadn't had a chance to say, or didn't know how in the years we'd been friends.

It must have only been a second, but it was enough time for me to decide I couldn't let his life end this way, here at the beginning of it all. He would go on to become Authorized, or maybe he would manage Mr. Burke's store. I knew it didn't matter because he would make life better for others in either place. My purpose was to make sure there was still a world left for him to make better.

I ran as fast as I could. I ran until I flew. And I flew until I soared into the black lightning, moving through it as it moved through me. I felt it burn every centimeter of my body from the inside out, starting in the deepest cavern of my heart, spreading through my chest, and finally searing over my skin in every direction. I wondered if this was what Lauren felt in her last few minutes on this earth. I would never know, but I did know that my last few minutes would be spent freeing Knox Ryder. It would be up to Eve to make sure he could save the world.

I saw the edges of the flames, my own flames, gathering in my peripheral vision and blocking out everything, every distraction until there was only Samael's dark, incendiary eyes staring directly at me.

I screamed and heard the eagle so clear and high it felt like it shattered my own eardrums, the piercing, eternal, and final declaration of who I was and what I was meant to do with my life.

The last thing I saw before the flames engulfed me was Samael's hands—his empty, cowardly hands as he rose them to brace against our inevitable collision —until only the fire remained.

****

The silence had returned. The same all-encompassing vacuum between the worlds that existed on the fringes of multiple realities. One in the woods near my house. One near the edge of the cliff in the most remote corner of the Bermuda Triangle, and hundreds if not thousands more in between.

I thought about how many there might be...how many I might have seen if I only had more time.

A sea of stars filled the sky beyond the snowflakes, but they quickly seemed to flare and burn away. I smiled at the idea of the very suns of the universe, the fires of countless worlds, all alight before my eyes. But soon there were fewer sparks, and then there were none at all. There were only red, shimmering wings streaked in gold and royal blue. They were massive, and I tried to look over my shoulder to see who could be carrying me, but I only saw what must have been hundreds of glowing blue and gold plumes behind me, the tips glowing with the last breaths of a fire. I watched the singed edges fade and the feathers swallow the smoke trails that remained. It was as if the smoke were becoming the plumes themselves. I looked over my other shoulder and saw only more of the same, but more importantly, I didn't see Samael.

I turned to the cliff edge and found Max standing with Eve, his face awash with awe and hers with something I could feel more than see...*certainty.*

Alma, Petra, Silo, and Tirius all approached the edge of the cliff and held their hands out, palms down toward the sea. In seconds, a pocket of daylight beamed down around me, and the ocean below calmed, becoming smooth as glass. In the reflection, the royal blue and gold plumes stretched farther than I could see, and the crimson, shimmering wings were wider than the entire expanse of the cliff itself. I'd never seen this kind of bird before with its long body and graceful neck, even more colorful and elegant than the birds of paradise at Eden's Bluff. I turned my head to see the side of its long, golden beak, and the bird's head also turned.

I expected to be startled, to feel the prickling sensation crawling up my arms, but instead, I only felt warmth radiating through me. The reflection started to glow a soft, golden hue like the rays of sunshine beaming down. I felt myself drifting closer to the rocks where everyone stood, drawn in by Eve's friends, the ancient First Bloods. They brought me close to them as Alma took off her orange, beaded shawl and draped it over my shoulders.

I wasn't completely sure what I'd just seen, but I felt such a sense of peace it was almost surreal.

Max moved close to me and touched my hair. "It's blue..." he whispered, marveling.

"The blue of the hottest fire," Tirius, the Salamander Elemental said. "In my thousands of years on this earth, I have experienced many things, but I have never witnessed the birth of a Phoenix... *until now.*"

Chapter 35

Eve and the First Bloods brought Bryce, Alita, and me the most beautifully woven clothes to wear since our shifts had destroyed the ones we'd been wearing. Once we were all dressed, several minutes of awkward silence filled the air, and I wasn't sure how to break it. As if they somehow knew, Alma and the other Elementals shepherded everyone except Eve, Max, and me back toward the campfire, and I exhaled in relief.

"Not to jinx it or anything," Jack said, backtracking with a hand raised toward Eve. "But did the kid just kill the *Angel of Death*, or...?"

Eve smiled. "Samael isn't dead, but he *has* been returned to Hell. For now. We are only in the beginning to gain ground against Ghob's plan to eradicate humanity, even if it means imprisoning her own sisters."

"We didn't know," Leo said from the shadows he'd wedged himself into with Rhea, Bryce, Alec, and Alita, all of them sitting in self-imposed exile. "We were all taught that the other Elemental queens let Ghob back in The Garden so she could take that discarded fruit and make a replica Garden...*Eden's Bluff,* not another Tree of Knowledge," he explained. "The other queen's apparently didn't know either, and Uriel was being blackmailed by Ghob *and* Samael to keep his mouth shut," he added, nodding to me.

I turned to Eve to corroborate. "I didn't know Samael was blackmailing Uriel either until he confessed that tonight, but I did hear Ghob say she would tell her sister that he's the one who let Lucifer into The Garden…which must mean by proxy because he'd let Samael in."

"They were just brainwashing us," Rhea said absently. "And they'll just start brainwashing others at Eden's Bluff now that we're gone."

Alec sighed, then put an arm around her.

"I just wanted to fit in," Alita added. "Everyone was just so sure it wasn't a big deal. But when we actually had to attack them, I just—" She met my eyes, hers brimming with tears as she pulled her red hair forward and tried to hide her face. "I'm so sorry. I never wanted to kill anyone," she added, turning then to Knox and Eve as tears streamed down her face. "I'm so, so sorry."

"I've put my faith in the wrong people before too," Eve said. "I forgive you. All of you, if you truly believe you can see a clearer path now that your eyes are opened."

I wasn't as gracious as Eve, nor did I think I ever could be. But I guess she did have thousands of years of experience. I decided I would try my best when everyone started coming forward, first to Eve, then to me, all of them with heartfelt apologies for leaving me in between the tears in the veil.

I stiffened when Bryce approached me because he had been so adamant about eradicating humanity, but that all dissipated when he couldn't even get any words out. He just broke down in sobs, and I let him hug me. We stood there for several seconds before he finally regrouped, and while I wasn't as angry anymore, I would be lying if I said I trusted them.

I watched as Alma and the others went to the new generation First Bloods of their line and spoke softly, offered comfort and guidance as Frankie, Jack, Knox, and Eve watched on, smiling. But in the deluge of emotion and newfound fellowship, Leo's arms were still wrapped tightly across his chest. He'd already discarded the shirt Tirius had given him and was standing there as he'd arrived in just his black school pants and sandals. He paced slowly, turning away from Tirius when he approached, making his way to the edge of the cliff instead. Max stood across from me, watching it all like I was. We traded looks, and though there was so much we needed to discuss, we both knew it would wait. He nodded to me, and I started to walk toward Leo.

He wouldn't look at me as I stood next to him staring out over the moonlit sea. I didn't know what to say—how to begin. I didn't know if I forgave him, so I couldn't even offer. I didn't even know if he wanted to apologize, or even if I would believe him if he did. I didn't know if anything he'd said to me was the truth. If anything between us at all had been real, or just the façade that the rest of the island had been.

"You'd already taught yourself how to fly that night," he finally said. "You just didn't believe you could do it, but I knew you could."

"Why do you think that?"

"I felt it when I kissed you," he said without hesitation. "I knew then that Midori was right. You weren't a Sylph at all…" Leo met my eyes just for a second, the muscles in his jaw tensed as he took a deep breath. "You were the brightest fire I'd ever seen."

He gripped his elbows tightly when a visible shiver gripped him. *A shiver*? I thought, as he stood next to me radiating heat as he always had. But before I could say another word, his wings shot out behind us, and he leapt from the cliff. He caught the cool breeze and soared under the moon, into the falling snow, and disappeared into the darkness.

I stood there for several minutes watching the place in the sky where he had been, wondering where he might have gone, or if he'd be back.

"It's hard to hate someone you can't ever leave," Knox said, walking up behind me with his arms crossed over his chest in the same way Leo's had been. "And that's the trick… You can't leave, so you have to find a way to stop hating."

I looked up at him, his dark eyes and heavy brows seeming to hold up the weight of the world. He couldn't have been thirty yet, but he seemed much older, and so tired.

"I don't know where he went, or if he'll be back," I said, turning my eyes to the stars again. "I didn't get to tell him that I forgave him for betraying me."

"Do you?"

I glanced at Knox quickly this time, surprised at the question. "I guess I don't know."

A smile pulled at the corner of his mouth. "Then that's the only answer you need to work out." I smiled at him as he gave my shoulder a squeeze. "And thanks, by the way…for going all supernova and saving the world from the Angel of Death—apparently, my primordial great, great…OK, I don't really know how many greats *grandfather*."

"Any time," I gave him a half smile, but his expression suddenly sobered.

"*Any* time?"

I looked at him, surprised again. "Uh, yeah, why?"

He heaved a long sigh, then drew in a deep breath. "I went ten rounds with Eve on this, but you know, you never win an argument with a normal-aged woman, let alone one who's thousands of years old," he added with a chuckle.

"What are you talking about?" I asked, feeling my voice thinning as my heartbeat began to echo in my ears.

Knox sighed. "Someone has to go after those queens in Hell, and as much as I want to be that one and only person, I'm out-voted." He studied my face, his, sympathetic and resolute all at the same time, and I held my breath for whatever he was about to say next. "Halsey... That someone has to be you."

Poisoned Garden is the first book in the YA Fantasy series, *Eden's Bluff Academy*, a spinoff from the Dystopian Sci-Fi/ Supernatural Thriller series, *First Bloods*, noted below.

***

First Bloods Companion Series:

ELEMENTAL WARS
- Book 1: *Nervous Water*

EDEN'S BLUFF ACADEMY
- Book 1: *Poisoned Garden*

~~~~~~

Want to grab a free copy of *Feral*, the prequel to the *First Bloods* series? Join my VIP Reader Group at www.subscribepage.com/tracykorn

FIRST BLOODS
- Prequel: *Feral*
- Book 1: *Bad Seed*
- Book 2: *Bitter Fruit* (TBA)
- Book 3: *Killing Frost* (TBA)
~~~~~~

About Tracy Korn

Tracy Korn is a sci-fi / fantasy author and all around science geek who may or may not have a"Lip Smackers"chapstick addiction.

When she's not inventing dystopian worlds (and subsequently saving them or wrecking them more), she reads about other people doing it, practices her newbie cinematographer skills, and dreams of someday meeting James Cameron.

To be the first to hear about new releases, giveaways, and if Tracy ever really does meet James Cameron, sign up for her VIP Readers list: **bit.ly/TracyKornNews**

And of course, stay in touch on Facebook, Twitter, Instagram, and other platforms found at **TracyKorn.com.**

Just want book release updates? Follow Tracy on the following platforms!

Amazon: **amazon.com/author/tracykorn**
Goodreads: **bit.ly/TracyKornGoodreads**
BookBub: **bit.ly/TracyKornBookBub**